MW01173041

HIBERNIA

David J. Devine

First published in 2024 by Blossom Spring Publishing
HIBERNIA Copyright © 2024 David J. Devine
ISBN 978-1-0687019-6-2
E: admin@blossomspringpublishing.com
W: www.blossomspringpublishing.com

I dedicate this book to my wife, Francess, whom I met when HIBERNIA was a nascent concept. In her, I found the character the story needed and the woman I needed. She encouraged me, particularly through the crapshoot post-writing process of publication.

Hibernia

Noun: from Latin, the Roman name for the large island west of Britannia, Ireland

Chapter 1

The Inkling

The technician's voice came over the speakers from another room.

"Those jeans have a lot of buttons. Could you drop your pants?"

He had told her about the jeans when she instructed him to empty his pockets. He shimmied the pants down to his knees, but left his boxer briefs, freshly washed, in place.

The machine instructed Sean McAuliffe. Breathe, breathe, and hold. He held his breath as the led analogue clog spun back to 12. The machine let out a loud whirr. He had to hold his breath for thirty seconds, but it felt like ten minutes. His mind raced through his inventory of ailments until the self-hypnosis techniques he collected from a Master Class kicked in.

He was too young to retire but too broken to work. A back that resembled a game of Jenga and failing eyesight had Social Security cashing out Sean's working days as of January 1, 2020. Were he to try and work, they would pull his check and more significantly his medical insurance. The doctors would fix his back. His eyes were another story – cataracts in both eyes, glaucoma in the right. Surgery made matters worse, ruining his depth perception and causing double vision. The lack of peripheral vision had Sean constantly bumping his head and running into poles and other obstacles. He had trouble parking a car, no wonder he had struggled operating a forklift. The arthritis made his joints ache at night. He was wary as to the results of his CT scan.

The technician gave the next instruction over the speakers.

"Now I am going to push the iodine. You should feel a warmth or burning sensation."

He did. It reminded him of his first drink. The burning emanated throughout his body from the IV in his right arm rather than from his gut like a shot of whiskey. Liquor no longer had that effect on him. He was not worried about developing a CT scan addiction as the iodine hit the $8,700 price tag seemed prohibitive.

The machine took the next image. Breathe, breathe, and hold. Whirr. Again, he heard her voice over the speakers.

"You can put your arms down and pull your pants up now."

As the technician was half his age, Sean bit his tongue as he thought, 'If I had a dollar for every time I heard that ...'

She returned to the imaging room, "We're done here. Your doctors should receive the results next week."

She exited before he finished straightening up – belt, keys, hoodie, and shoes. He did not move as fast as he used to. The UCSF Imaging Center was only a block from Irving Street and the N-Judah line. He would ride it west to the end of the line.

The streetcar dropped him literally at the front door to Java Beach Café owned by his friend Pat Maguire. They played soccer together in high school. Thanks to a foreign exchange student they won the City Championship. Over the years they had played with and against each other in every combination of adult age/level offered. He ordered an iced coffee and acknowledged the 'kid' stealing wi-fi in the corner. Patty, as everyone called him, was a twenty-something nephew of Pat's who had been busted for hacking into numerous government and corporate information systems. His 'career' started with altering school records and making traffic tickets disappear for his high school classmates. He hacked mostly for the sport of it. He was court-ordered to not own any internet-accessible devices. At 5'10" and 150 pounds with black wavy hair, Patty reminded him of his young geeky self. He had used Patty to trick out his phone with some shady software you could not get at the app store.

Reading the Chronicle at the café was a tradition he could not practice during his working days. When Sean was a kid, the sports section was printed on green newsprint hence it was known as the Sporting Green. The big Sunday paper's entertainment section was oriented magazine style with the week's TV listings. Printed on pink newsprint, it was called The Pink. He thought you could tell a lot about a person by how they read the paper at the coffee or donut shop. Sean had always been a Sports, Business, Front Page guy. Woe would be the day when he started with the Obituaries like his mother did with her crew at Simple Pleasures on Balboa.

The Sporting Green still had team reporters. The Giants were hard to follow now; the championships of the 2010s were in the rear-view mirror. The brain trust of Baer/Sabean/Bochy was gone. Only Crawford, the shortstop, remained on the roster. Sean grew up during the lean, windy years at Candlestick though, 'You don't change your team no matter what.' He texted his brother their father's mantra: *Wait 'til next year.* Looking forward, his brother replied: *Not sure the Niners have a QB.* The McAuliffes are a loyal breed.

Sean watched Patty's day-trading. He was monitoring

two stock exchanges and three options markets on the laptop. The business section still printed an extremely abridged stock table probably more for nostalgia than decision-making. Sean wondered if he could sell a Masterclass on how to score a baseball game with a follow-up course on box score reading.

The Chronicle, like most newspapers, was a shell of its former self. The onslaught of USA Today in the 1980s accelerated the demise of the daily newspaper. The tactility of newsprint slicked. The ink no longer transferred to your fingers. Newspapers merged or went out of business. Much of the content presented was culled from wire services.

He did not bother to read any story with an Associated Press credit. The one business story which caught his eye was the ante-mortem on Murphy Printing. Founded in 1921 by Irish immigrant Tom Murphy the company grew from a custom printing and engraving company to a commercial print house serving the entire Bay Area. The current management, Tom's grandsons, had run the company for 40 years. There was no next generation of Murphy to keep the business open. A skeleton staff is completing standing orders and preparing for liquidation. He winced. It had been his job to close failing retail outlets. Gallows humor had been his tool to get some form of production out of soon-to-be laid-off employees. Worse still had been his own bankruptcy. A victim of recession and shallow pockets, he had fallen on his own sword. He had been a small business owner with no mercy from his landlord, suppliers, the State, or the IRS. It took years to rebuild his ego and pay the back taxes.

A week-old copy of the Irish Times, a nationwide daily out of Dublin, lay on the counter.

"Mind if I take this, Pat?" Sean queried.

Pat retorted, "I sell coffee not papers."

Sean folded the Times in half and tucked it under his arm; he left his copy of the Chronicle for the next patron. Ocean Beach was nearly deserted that weekday morning. Being Spring there was no fog he could just make out the Farallon Islands, the seals were barking beneath the Cliff House. He counted three container ships waiting to enter the Golden Gate. He liked living near the ocean, the tide was rising. Whereas most people there were connecting spiritually with nature or getting in their exercise, Sean found himself caught in morbid self-reflection.

'How could a guy as smart as me have mucked things up so bad?'

He knew. Terrible women's choices. Each one since his first wife was a charity case. The last couple were headcases as well. The houses he owned had soared in value – after he sold them. He had always been impatient and short-sighted with the jobs he chose, the business he ran. His bank account suggested all he would leave his children were bills.

He thought of his ties to the City. His birthright. Irish-San Franciscans have a unique and strong cultural identity. The large expatriate community brought the Irish experience to the City. Sean had that connection even though he had never visited Ireland. He was second-generation American. His grandparents' brogues were so thick he could not understand their speech until he was six. Sean reveled in the stories of his father's and uncles' scofflaw adolescents as they committed peccadillos throughout the Mission and Avenues. His father worked the reference desk at the San Francisco Library evenings answering phone calls to settle bar bets decades before the internet. Still a teenager he had a set of master keys to the library which in those days were master keys for all City of San Francisco locks. His father and compatriots had free run to City buildings and venues. Uncle Kevin, future chemist, had constructed a still in the basement with discarded glassware from the Sacred Heart Chemistry Department. Uncle Gene was forever catching the ire of the nuns & brothers.

Depending on their success at navigating the parochial school system the career paths were well defined: Priesthood, Policeman, Professional, Blue Collar. Uncle John went to the seminary but became a cop after the Korean War. Sean's father became a banker spending his entire career at Hibernia Bank. He was a vice president of auto loans at the end. Uncle Gene was a telephone company lifer after Vietnam. If you needed a car, you went to Sean's father. If you were in a scrape, you saw Uncle John. If you needed tickets, a deal, or just about anything else, you saw Uncle Gene. The Irish-San Francisco underground was alive and well.

Sean had learned from the best of them. If there was a loophole, he found it. Last century, he found a loophole in the University of California system which ensured his acceptance. He timed his disability case to ensure Social Security would not suggest retraining. More than once he took advantage of no-down, preferential rate government-backed financing to purchase a home.

Nevertheless, it was a check-to-check, month-to-month existence. He had reviewed the regulations. Social Security would offer a brief back-to-work trial but would reduce benefits quickly. Any regularly compensated employment would likely cause the loss of his retirement and insurance. They allowed the publication of one book but that seemed like a longshot; he might as well play the lottery. He could receive passive income but that required ownership of rental property. There had to be an angle to play.

Sean had walked north toward the Cliff House then back south passing the Windmills at Golden Gate Park down to Noriega Street. Flanahan's Pub opened at noon. It was a classic San Francisco/Irish pub established in 1978. The décor of hardwoods, polished brass, and dark leather never changed. Framed team pictures, immigration documents, and special mementoes hung among San Francisco and Irish championship banners. They had the best-corned beef in the City. The regulars called out Sean's name when he walked in the door. Stephen, the bartender, gave him a nod. Stephen was tall and had a wingspan that could reach from one end of the bar to the other.

Francess Phillip brought warm Irish soda bread and Kerrygold Irish butter to his table. Everything about her spelt 'smitten' for Sean. She was an Irish national though she was born in Grenada. Her voice was a combination of brogue and Island dialect. She was clever, 5'8", deep brown eyes, age-appropriate, and fit. He had seen her dressed to the nines more than once. Each time with high heels. Striking.

"Well, Sean. How's the craic?"

"Divil a bit."

"Would you like the corned beef?"

"Please, corned beef on a roll, Colman's, and chips. Jameson rocks with a Harp back."

"Hmph." She uttered with a tone of disapproval.

Harp Lager was a nice Irish beer not heavy like Guinness. He tried to watch his day drinking; his family,

7

as many do, had some issues. Regardless, he thought the order appropriate as he was planning on spending the afternoon digesting the Times. The corned beef was hot, sliced thin and piled high. The sourdough roll was sublime through and through. Firm crust, lactobacillus San Francisco and candida milleri were a combination only capable in the environs of the City. Colman's mustard hand prepared from the tin just like his father used to do. The chips were hand-cut, rinsed and double-fried. Properly nourished, Sean ordered a second Jameson with another Harp. He would organize the Times similar to the Chronicle: Sports, Business, Front Page.

Pop, his grandfather, and Sean spent hours roaming Golden Gate Park. It was only a few blocks from Pop's home at 15th and Irving. The park was filled with wonders – the Bison, the Japanese Gardens, the Academy of Sciences, Kezar Stadium and Big Rec. Pop loved the Forty-Niners and Giants; Sean did too. They would listen to games in the basement; Sean still had Pop's radio. He introduced Sean to San Francisco's Gaelic Games played on Saturday and Sunday afternoons at Big Rec. They were fast and rough. Gaelic football played with what most would consider a soccer ball, combining aspects of soccer, rugby, and basketball. Hurling added a stick and used a ball similar to a baseball. Gaelic football players wore guile and wit for protection. Hurlers added a helmet and facemask as either the stick or ball could cause concussion or broken bones. The Gaelic Athletic Association, Ireland's equivalent of the NFL or MLB, is the essence of amateur athletics that calls to anyone who has ever worn a pair of cleats. Pop was a dairyman in San Francisco. He had been a fisherman in Ireland even though he could not swim. He said the water was so cold it did not matter if you could swim. Sean could not imagine him as a young man.

The Times Sports page coverage was thorough. He read about hurling, Gaelic football, rugby, and horse racing. The business of sport was present but not paramount. Sean had Stephen stream recent hurling matches on the television. He found it interesting that Kerry and Dublin dominated all-time in Gaelic football, and it was Kilkenny, Cork & Tipperary for hurling. Rumor suggested Stephen had played goalie for Dublin back in the day. This fascinated Sean, but he didn't want to pry into another man's glory days. Sean maintained grand notions that this was the premise for a blockbuster movie: Irish landscapes, an underdog county banding together to take down a giant, action–action–action, maybe an American walk-on, throw-in a romance. Of course, he had no script, backers, or experience in movie making.

He completed the Sudoku game. The crossword was difficult as he did not have enough cultural knowledge and he was not up on his Irish idioms. He had completed the word scramble in the Chronicle earlier.

The lead story in the Business section was BREXIT. The UK and Northern Ireland would be leaving the European Union within months. Gabriel Makhlouf a British citizen born in Egypt who had become the Governor of the Central Bank of Ireland just a year prior following a position with the New Zealand Treasury was interviewed on the impact to the Irish economy. His close ties to Britain and short stay in Ireland made him an unpopular figure to the general population. Comment was also sought from the President of Ireland, Michael Higgins. He was serving his second and final term; he had a long history with the Labour Party. His concern was for the ancillary impact to the Irish job market from a decline in the British economy.

The story that caught Sean's eye though was below the fold, 'Ireland 20 Years of EU a Review'. Although Ireland joined the EU in 1999, the euro became legal tender for transactions January 2002. By the end of that year, ninety per cent of Irish banknotes and coins had been retired. Bernard Sheridan, Director of Currency Central Bank was interviewed, "Every year since the changeover we exchange a dribble of punts and coins for euros. The Central Bank has provisions to exchange the remaining €224 million in banknotes and €123 million in coin. It's the law." By law, the exchange rate was fixed at €1.27 to IR£ 1.00. Sean read the article again.

"Francess." he called, "I believe I will do another round. I have some cogitating to do."

Francess brought the round over. "Ya plantin' roots here, Sean? What's caught your eye?"

"I'm not sure. I'm thinking about taking a trip to Ireland."

"Ooh. You'd like it there."

A thought kept running through his head. *'300 million 20-year-old Irish pounds worth 375 million euros, 400 million dollars are out there. How can I get a piece of that action?'*

Chapter 2

Research

It was midnight; his knees were barking. He was still awake after an hour of *Barney Miller* reruns. He would try an episode of First Run *Columbo*; he usually fell asleep before the killer's errors were revealed. Kismet thought Sean. It was the very last 1970s episode. The one where an Irish raconteur was on an American fundraising trip. Theoretically, on a humanitarian mission, he was actually acquiring weapons for the IRA.

He searched the internet from bed. The Central Bank of Ireland website and the rules for the exchange of old Irish banknotes ranked high in the results. Any transaction in excess of IR£ 700 required proof of ownership. There were some illustrations of Irish banknotes; he needed more details. He downloaded the organization chart for the Central Bank to identify the players.

The idea was still strong in his head the next morning. He knew where to go to further his research. His ears popped as the BART train descended through the Transbay Tunnel under Golden Gate Bay. It was an eastbound trip; the trains were full westbound with commuters in the morning. The Downtown Berkeley station is footsteps from the University of California, Berkeley. The library system housed one of the finest collections in the world, certainly the best at a public institution. Sean maintained stack access as a member of the Alumni Association. The stacks, most of which are subterranean, hold thousands upon thousands of books, annals, digests, and any other reference item of academic significance. He actually worked in the Map Room during college.

He checked the online catalogue. His first stop was Sublevel 1 to secure a copy of *A Flask of Fields*. The first coffee table book a young Sean, age 12, had purchased. It included anecdotes and photographs of W.C. Fields. Sean went to the study desks. He leafed through the pages reminiscing of Fields' physical comedy – juggling, golf, billiards, table tennis, and his persona – sot, underdog, child & animal hater. He initiated the passive radio frequency app which Patty had installed on his phone. He cloned the security identification tag from the Fields book.

His next stop: Sublevel 3, shelf position PL-510-642, ISBN: 978-0-9543457-2-3. The aisles were narrow, not wide enough to pass without turning sideways. The shelves started six inches off the ground with the top shelf reaching seven feet. It was temperature controlled at 65ºF to preserve the specimens. It had been years since Sean was in the stacks; it smelled the same – knowledge. He grinned when he recalled getting caught making out with Mariko in the stacks.

Paper Money of Ireland by Bob Blake and Jonathan Callaway is the definitive guide to the history of Irish banknotes. It included thorough descriptions and color illustrations of all series and issues. Sean needed a graduate degree; he had found the text for the entry-level course. This would be his starting point. He used his folding box cutter to remove the RFID sticker from the back cover of the tome; he did not want to be on record in the library system. The 744-page, 4-pound volume gave form and substance to his backpack.

He stopped at the self-check-out kiosk. He passed

Paper Money of Ireland over to the reader and had the app on his phone broadcast *A Flask of Fields*. The kiosk printed his reminder slip: Sean McAuliffe, *A Flask of Fields*, due in 21 days. He cleared the security gates and egressed the library without incident. He put a note on his calendar to return to the library in 18 days to "return" the book.

He could not leave Berkeley without a stop at Top Dog the hot dog dive that kept him alive for four years. It had been in continuous operation since 1966. He ordered two New Yorks, all-beef natural casing. The eight-inch dogs peeked out of each end of the seven-inch buns. A whole selection of dogs and sausages warmed on the side of the flat top. The clerk/cook places the ordered dogs over the hot portion of the flat top and toasts the buns alongside. The patron finishes the dogs with condiments, in this case diced onions, warm sauerkraut, and spicy mustard. His right eye twitched; he had it just right.

Satisfied with his find and lunch Sean returned to the BART station for his trip back under the Bay to his lair.

The Irish Free State had three series of currencies from 1928 until the adoption of the euro. Series A was issued by the Currency Commission from 1928-1977. The Central Bank of Ireland issued Series B & Series C from 1976-1993 and 1992-2000, respectively. As one would expect, the security features increased over time with metal security threads, latent images, optically variable ink, and micro-lettering. The primary security feature on Series A notes was the watermark. Sean looked further into the exchange of banknotes. At the end of 2001, there were €4,344 million worth of Irish banknotes in circulation. Eighty-five percent had been exchanged by the end of February 2002. The rate at which banknotes were exchanged reduced greatly after that but the provision remains. Although by percentage there were more IR£5's and IR£10's in circulation, Sean believed targeting late series A 100-pound notes was the ticket. Approximately 15% were still in circulation. The IR£ 100 was not issued in series B, and a metal security thread was never added to series A even in the 1970s.

Sean studied into the wee hours. It was a crash course, but he felt prepared to give a dissertation on the Irish banknote.

One thing was clear. He would need help. But he also knew that the larger the crew the greater the risk. He needed multi-talented close-mouthed comrades. It might just be possible to exchange sham Irish banknotes for euros. Some serious blarney would be required.

Chapter 3

Governors, Deputies & Directors

Bernard Sheridan had a system, fifteen white, 100% cotton, 15½" neck, 32/33 arm, button-down shirts. Five are for the current week, five for next week, and five at the cleaners for laundry & pressing. Medium starch gave the shirts an essence which he felt enhanced his presence as a banker. His ties were 100% silk – dark blues and dark greens. He had one red tie for Christmas. He preferred double Windsor knots. His suits were wool-appropriate year-round in Dublin. He continued to dress like a banker should at least a banker circa 1990.

Sheridan checked his watch. It had only been 7 minutes since the last time he checked. The meeting, a recently initiated weekly division meeting, would soon enter its second hour. The coffee had his bladder on high alert, and he really did not need to hear the mire of Human Resources or the setbacks of outsourced programming with Information Technology. He had the most tenure of any Central Bank employee, far more than the other Directors or any of the Deputy Governors.

Marcella Flood loved to hearken back to her start at the bottom as a programmer with the Bank of Ireland, although most of her career was spent in insurance. Three months ago, she was brought over by Makhlouf, the latest Governor, from Allianz to be the Chief Operating Officer for the Central Bank. No wonder the Bank had lost its heritage. Sheridan was frosted as he had groomed his entire career for the position and believed he was owed the title and accompanying retirement package.

Flood and the new Chief Enforcement & Money

Laundering Officer were bantering about strategy and direction. It was all Sheridan could do to keep his eyes from rolling like a teenage girl listening to a parent. His thoughts turned to dinosaurs. When did he become a dinosaur? B. Sheridaurus: old, white, male. Had he been named COO he would have stayed on another five years to complete 40 years of service. He could have retired with Deputy Governor level compensation and continued to serve on the Board. As it is, his retirement package is maxed out for a Director; his 35th anniversary with the Central Bank was six months away. He could make it. He would become the fourth Banker ever to earn the XXXV service badge.

Finally, after an hour and 18 minutes, she turned to Sheridan.

"Bernie," she started. Flood was the only person with the gall to be so colloquial. That bint. He hated it. 'Director', 'Sheridan', or for his friend, 'Bernard' were acceptable not even his wife was that casual.

"Bernie, I have been reviewing the statements. Can you explain why there appears to be a €350 million perpetual asset labeled exchange reserve on the balance sheet?"

"Yes, ma'am," using proper respect for the position although it felt like nails on a chalkboard.

"As you recall, Ireland joined the EU in 1999. The euro became legal tender in 2002. The Central Bank exchanged 90% of outstanding Irish banknotes and coinage that first year. By law, the Central Bank is required to maintain reserves for the exchange of all outstanding Irish banknotes and coinage. A small percentage of old notes we expect remain outstanding as keepsakes, some unintentionally destroyed, and much may be lost. The balance is likely buried in backyards, stuffed in mattresses, or squirreled away in safe deposit boxes waiting to be discovered."

"That's terrible. That money needs to be in circulation aiding the economy. You need to do something about that. Bring me a list of alternatives next week."

"Yes, ma'am. Do you have any questions or concerns as to the Facilities?"

In addition to Currency Management Sheridan was also responsible for Security and Facilities Management.

"No. Just bring me the list."

'Feckin' eejit' Sheridan ventriloquized with an inaudible murmur. A term he felt comfortable using towards men but had not directed at a woman before. She had the title. Why not give her all the accolades associated with it? Half the Directors and Deputy Governors were women. Times had changed. It wasn't the fact they were women that bothered him, even the men coming in these days seemed like twits. It was amazing he had lasted as long as he had.

He knew Irish law required the reserve. He knew the Bank would not spend money to drum-up exchange. He knew he would put together twenty minutes of poppycock to appease her.

"How was the meeting, Bernard?" Gertrude O'Shea, his secretary, queried cautiously as Sheridan stormed toward his office where he dropped his leather-bound folder performed an about-face and stormed out again.

"Two hours of life I will never get back again," he replied without missing a step.

The subway tile flooring felt 100 years old. The chrome fittings were polished so fine you could tell if you had cabbage stuck between your teeth. The porcelain fixtures were sturdy and substantial. He was seeking refuge at the urinal. He fumbled with the hook & bar, two buttons, and one zipper to unfasten his trousers; he nearly peed himself. However, he relieved himself like a college student who had three pints too many. What had things come to? He was hiding out in the jack.

His lifestyle and status were in for an undeserved comeuppance. Gone would be his position in the banking community. Gone would be his laundered shirts and wool suits. Gone would be his expense account and corporate perks. He had seen his peers struggle to adjust to life on pension. The light at the end of the tunnel was a train about to run over him.

'Taking lunch out. Keep messages. Text if crisis. See you tmrw morning,' he texted to his secretary.

'K. Understood,' was the reply.

The breeze was on his face as he walked along the River Liffey. Rowers in shells strained upriver against the wind. His wing tips were quality and broken in, so the twenty-minute walk was easy on his feet. The 55° weather kept him from breaking a sweat. He walked around the Custom House to The Celt, a locals pub. He took a short booth halfway between the door and the jacks. He did not want to be drawn into a bunch of blarney with the eejits.

The waitress, Lily, brought soda bread and butter.

"How's the craic, Sherry?"

There was something about this pub that disarmed Bernard. They could have called him Sam and he would not have cared.

"Divil a bit. How are the cockles and mussels today?"

"Fresh off the boat."

"Sounds good. I'll have them with a Jameson on the

rocks and a Harp back?"

"You got it, dote." She winked at Shery then turned towards the bartender and yelled.

"Liam, can I get a Molly Malone, Jimmy on the rocks with some music for Sherry 'ere!"

He tugged the knot on his tie freeing an inch to unbutton the top button, and pulled the tail out of the back of the knot to release the tie. After folding his tie and inserting it in the suit's breast pocket, he removed the suit jacket and carefully laid it between himself and the wall. He rolled his sleeves to three-quarters. Eating cockles and mussels was a sloppy task. He would not go back to the bank that afternoon.

The steamed shellfish was bathed in butter and garlic. Some chopped leafy green stuff was tossed on top for effect. The dish was served with plenty of soda bread and napkins. Sherry had a bucket for the shells and wiped the bowl clean sopping up the last of butter/garlic/brine with a sponge of soda bread. Lily came to check on him.

"Sherry, you devoured that. I'd ask you if you liked it but, what's the point? You're half undressed. Are you done for the day?"

"I'm done. Period. Just playing out the string."

"Would you like anything else?"

"Set me up again. Did I notice a copy of the Times on the bar?"

"Yes, milseán. Give it a go?"

"Le do thoil."

Lily brought him the round and the newspaper. Even though he had been a banker for three decades when he was out of the office, he started with the Sports section. He fancied himself quite the Gaelic football player back in the day. He was left-footed and played right midfield.

He had the knack; he could envision the shot or pass. Seeing the play before it happens was a gift. Sports developed the values on which he built his professional career: training, teamwork, courage, and execution. Dublin had won the championship five years running a New York Yankee-like streak, but underdog Donegal was victorious in the semi-finals (2-09, 0-12).

His article was below the fold on the front of the Business section, 'Ireland 20 Years of EU a Review'. He read about himself, *'Bernard Sheridan, Director of Currency Central Bank, 'Every year since the changeover we exchange a dribble of punts and coins for euros. The Central Bank has provisions to exchange the remaining €224 million in banknotes and €123 million in coin. It's the law.'* It's the law, he thought. The law indeed. How could he have been passed over for the Deputy Governorship by an insurance lady? That bint cost him €200,000 a year in pension; it was like he missed the lottery by one number.

A thought kept running through his head. *'Millions of useless 20-year-old Irish pounds are out there. And all those euros sit waiting. I deserve a piece of that action.'*

Chapter 4

Recruiting – Phase I

Sean McAuliffe was a certified member of the American Production & Inventory Control Society (APICS) circa 1985. A professional organization at the forefront of quality and standardization policies popular in the last decades of the twentieth century. He had programmed computer systems on IBM mainframes. Unlike most of the programmers though, he had a more thorough understanding of how computers worked writing job control language (JCL), assembling code for operation, and swapping magnetic storage tapes. Companies were continuously taking backups upon backups hoping to never need them. Once, he successfully duplicated an entire hospital system on a different mainframe, offsite. A failure would have done irreparable damage to the project. It was a Hail Mary that Sean pulled off from the bowels of UCSF Medical Center.

His history with personal computers goes back to high school when he wrote his first program using BASIC on a Commodore PET, which used an audio cassette tape for storage. His department, Industrial Engineering, had UC Berkeley's first network of personal computers with eight units featuring Intel 8086 processors. He was no stranger to formatting floppies, c:/ prompts, and dial-up modems. He even toted around a first-edition portable computer. The 25-pound Compaq 386 had a built-in 10" amber screen, a fold-out full-sized keyboard, and a shoulder strap. Today's web-based systems were Greek to him though. He could learn scripting in Java, HTML, SQL, or PYTHON but it would take years. This old dog did not have time for those new tricks.

He was not lost when it came to concept and project management. This would not be any different than in the past: project goal, human resources, physical resources, timeline, and execution. He did not have a client nor want to leave an evidence trail so the PERT (program evaluation and review technique) chart and critical path management would not be recorded or tracked formally. His mind raced; his heart palpitated.

Did he need a sales pitch or a recruiting pitch? Maybe a bit of both. Testicular cancer concerns be damned, did he have the cajónes to take the euro out of Ireland? Or would this just be another case of overrun grandiose fantasy?

Streetcars clanking on the rails and foghorns were the soundtrack of the Sunset. He was on the N-Judah again heading to Java Beach Café.

"Pat, can I get an iced coffee? Do you have a minute?" Sean parked at a table in the back near the kitchen. Most of the patrons used the sidewalk seating or balanced on bar stools at the picture window. Patty, Pat's nephew, was in his usual corner. He was day trading stocks on his uncle's laptop from his uncle's account.

"Here you go, Seany. What's up? Are you short this month? Did you hear about the scan?"

"Always short, but I get by. Still hurts when I pee. I try not to look. I had to get off MD-Web. My diagnosis had me dead in six months."

"Damn, Seany. I wish I could offer you something a little stiffer than an iced coffee. What can I do you for?"

"How's Patty?"

"My nephew?"

"Yes. How's he doing? Is he still on technology

probation?"

"Why? Have you heard something? Do I need to watch his back?"

"No, oh no. I might need someone with his skills, but I don't want to pull him into something that would be too much for him."

"Patty *works* for me here at the Café. His job title for probation is busboy. I set him up with a $10,000 trading account. He's quadrupled it for me while taking a small percentage of his pay. He wears an apron so he could spring into action should anyone official come by to check on him."

"He helped me trick out my phone. How good is he?"

"He's freckin' amazing."

"Can he keep a confidence?"

"He's a Maguire. You don't need to ask."

"Just making sure. Do you think he would be interested in a challenge that could hit strong?"

"No drugs or guns? Maguire's do not do drugs or guns."

"No drugs. No guns. No innocents getting hurt."

"Can you keep him under the radar? He's not really an out-front player."

"I'm looking for a systems man. OK if I pull him for lunch today?"

Pat winked, "I think we can get by without him."

Pat took Sean's iced coffee and refilled it. He also prepared a triple-shot espresso, Patty's order of choice. Sean sat across from Patty and placed both drinks on the table ensuring they would not create a spill hazard.

"Mind if I join you?"

"You already have." Patty deadpanned without looking up from the screen. "Is something wrong with your phone?"

"No. I wanted to talk with you about a project I'm considering. My skills are 20th Century, and this will require some 21st Century magic. You free for lunch today?"

"You buying?"

"Sure am. Do you know Flanahan's?"

"On Noriega? How about 1:30? The markets are closed then."

"Done."

* * * * * * * *

"You're right, Sean. This corned beef is incredible. And this Harp is smooth I've never tried one before. How's Janey? She doesn't live in the City anymore."

"She moved to the Peninsula with her *boyfriend* after graduating from Cal. He's a nice guy; I hate him. She jumps from company to company in Silicon Valley."

"How're your sambos, boys?" Francess timed her query so they each had a mouthful. Nodding heads and grunts indicated their approval.

"So, you're telling me there are millions of euros just waiting to be exchanged for old Irish banknotes even though it's been over twenty years."

"Exactly."

"Do you have any?"

"No. But I plan to."

"Why tell me? I'm not a printer."

"Not a printer, but you are a systems whiz. It's a component."

"How's that?"

"The bills are just one aspect of the exchange. The

24

story and the people have to come off just as authentic as the bills. And that, if you're interested, is where your skills are needed."

"I'm listening."

"We will need passports and driver's licenses that pass physical scrutiny and computer validation. Valid Social Security numbers, bank accounts and tax records which do not arouse suspicion. There may be sophisticated graphics software for banknote design and coloring."

"Humph. That's a lot of systems here and abroad. So, you want to forger all sorts of documents beyond the money?" In his head, Patty was already designing solutions.

"Not necessarily. The best fake ID is a real ID. What if we planted the individuals in the various systems and let the authorities provide us with authentic documents?"

"Brilliant. That makes so much sense. How much could we get?"

"Think of this like a three-legged stool: backstory, banknotes, players. Each leg is equally important. Whatever we take is a three-way split."

Patty was intrigued, "Why? Why would you take the risk?"

"A whole life's worth of circumstances has left me with a sharp mind and zeroes in the bank. I see an opportunity for me here. The risk isn't so great for me anymore and the reward could help Janey and Mary."

"Why me?"

"Your skills are being wasted. You've been dealt a rough hand being ostracized from your talent, your passion. You could stretch your skills and gain a little breathing room."

Duhh-da-da-Dun. It was Sean's phone.

"What was that?" Patty did not recognize the opening notes of the Dragnet theme.

"That's my text. Let me check. …. The results of a CT scan I took the other day are in. I have to see the Doc this afternoon."

"If you're one leg and I'm another, where's the third leg?"

"Are you in?" Sean was sealing the deal.

"I'm intrigued. Technically I'm already violating my probation. I might as well go big and have some fun doing it. Where and when?"

"Come to my house tonight around seven, 3400 block of Rivera. There's a '68 Cougar in front, Glacier Blue. Bring your appetite."

Chapter 5

Groundwork

"Hi, Gene," Sean yelled into the phone. His Uncle Gene was hard of hearing, and you never knew if he was wearing his aides.

Gene had heart issues, both knees had been replaced. He had a hard physical life climbing telephone poles from Viet Nam to Hunters Point. He had built cabins at Tahoe and rehabilitated a Victorian in the Castro.

"It's Sean. Your nephew. How's your knee? They just gave me a CT scan. There had been blood in my urine, and they were looking for the cause. Next is a scope up my willy. I know. Worse than a colonoscopy, and I'm due for one of those also." Gene laughed. A response that could only bring a smile to Sean's face.

"When I saw the Doc this afternoon, he came in the room late of course. Without looking up from the chart he said, *'Wow, there's a lot going on there!'* I don't know about you, but I do not want the doc thinking my scan is remarkable. Anyway, I've got three hernias, kidney stones, and some plaque on my arteries." Sean expected no pity from Gene; he was just reporting the facts.

"Deal with it." Gene responded.

"Niners camp opened today. I don't know if either of their quarterbacks has the heart of a champion. Montana had it. So did Young. Even an undersized Garcia had it. ...We'll see."

"Hard to think of them as the City's Niners with them playing in Goddamn San Jose."

Gene had been a season ticket holder for years. He gave up his seat when the team moved to Santa Clara in

2014. A move Sean had predicted twenty years ago when the practice facility moved south from Redwood City.

"Gene, did you see where Murphy Printing is shutting down? Didn't you do the wiring there when they moved to Bryant Street?" When Ma Bell was antitrust busted in 1984 Gene had stayed with AT&T. He had stopped climbing poles and riding cherry-pickers; he began running wires for communication and data throughout the businesses of the City.

"The article said there wasn't a Murphy left who wanted to keep it going." That was the comment that released the history lesson.

"You know, Sean. We completely rewired them. It was 40-year-old wiring and could barely hold a dial tone. It was just after the Ma Bell break-up. Bob was still running the company, but he was trying to get things straight before turning it over to his boys. They were a little older than you."

"Wasn't there a story about my dad and Uncle John there?"

"Yes. It was a couple of years before I redid their wiring. The print manager, Pete Durkin, was what they used to call a key employee; he really kept the place running even though he wasn't in the family. Durkin grew up in Boston; he came to the City in the 50s after the Korean War. His wife, Kitty, was from the Mission like your dad and Uncle John. Kitty went to Star of The Sea Academy with your mother. There were four Durkin kids."

"It really was a tight community. Everybody 'knows a guy' or 'knows a guy who knows a guy'" Sean interjected so Gene could catch a breath.

"So, one Friday this asshole steals $3,000 from petty

cash, empties the family account at Hibernia, and leaves his wife and kids in the lurch. He was on the run to Reno for a divorce. Kitty called your mother and auntie. Durkin wasn't going to be able to get to court or a bank 'til Monday. This did not sit well with your dad and Uncle John. They went to Reno and tracked his ass down. They persuaded him that Murphy's $3,000, the bank account balance, and another $1,000 he had would be better served in San Francisco. They also *negotiated*, read dictated, the alimony and child support agreement. They made clear the consequences of a missed payment. Between your dad's banking and John's police connections, they placed the fear of God in Durkin."

"I remember that weekend. Steve called me at CAL and relayed how the adults huddled in Mom & Dad's bedroom before Uncle John and my dad sped off. He was confused. I told him to mind his own business."

"We take care of our own Sean. Always have. Always will. Murph's boys were too young to have done what your dad and John did. Murph stepped up also. One of the Durkin boys was in college, and Murph paid for his fees and books. The girls weren't even in high school. The other boy was 16. Murph hired him to sweep the floors but paid him a working man's wage. He was literally learning the business from the ground up. Murph knew the money was going to Kitty. I hadn't thought about that kid in years. He was my wire boy for the two weeks I was there. Murph pulled him off the line. He was a good worker, not like those weed-addled slackers I see today."

"How's your mother? Sean? Do you go by and see her? Is she alright with not driving?"

"Best thing that happened to her in years. It simplified

her life. She has a network of neighbors and friends who help her about town, shop for her, give her rides to Simple Pleasures or the doctor. I should go by and see if she'll let go of some of the junk in the basement."

Gene laughed, "Good luck with that."

"Her emergency earthquake kit has cans of tuna that expired in 1996 and weepy batteries for the flashlight."

"That's Mary for you. She's a survivor, not a survivalist. ...I've got to run, Sean. Well, not run. Really, I have to hobble off to dinner. 'I've got to hobble.' just has no ring to it."

"What's for dinner?"

"I don't know, but it better involve red meat and a large glass of wine."

"Cardiologist special?"

"Sean, I don't want the autopsy report to say my last meal was steamed broccoli and prune juice."

"Amen to that, Gene. Go Niners."

"Go Niners."

Sean was a daily shopper. Not for lack of planning, but because he hated to see food go bad in the refrigerator. He did not understand people who let fresh produce liquify in the back of the vegetable bin. The clean-up was disgusting. As this would be a business meal, he purchased quality products from Andronico's on 15th Avenue. It had been a Park and Shop located just a few blocks from Pop's house. He folded the paper grocery bag and added it to the stack in the broom closet. It amused him that paper bags were back. He felt the question, 'Paper or plastic?' should refer to how you would pay not how you wanted to carry your groceries.

Candlestick lamb chops, roast baby potatoes, and quick spinach were on the menu. He loaded the charcoal chimney. The bottom was filled with a torn-up grocery bag and scrunched packing paper, newsprint would have sufficed also; the top two-thirds contained briquets. There was a light breeze off the ocean; it would help the briquets catch. It was always a good barbecue when he only had to light the charcoal once.

There is little to no clearance between houses in the Sunset. Most have garages with one-car doors which are referred to as basements. They run the length of the building and the back half of some run the width as well. A back door accesses the small backyard with five-foot weathered fences to enclose the postage stamp. Stairs run alongside the garage to reach the living level. Security gates are located at the base or top of the stairs. Visitors buzz their arrival to request entry.

'BZZZ. BZZZ. BZZZ.'

Sean held the release button just inside the front door until he heard the clank of the gate releasing from the lock. The 14 granite stairs were tread worn; the house was sturdy post-World War II construction. He had come to appreciate the durability and soundness of plaster and lath over drywall. Between his last job, forced unemployment to win his disability case, winning the case, and romantic entanglements he had moved six times in the last 10 years twice cross-country. He had learned the hard way not to trust home inspection reports. He checked that windows opened, whether interior doors were square, for water stains on the ceiling. He would drop a marble on the floor to check for level. He no longer had the resources for moving companies and without help from his at the time wife or stepson, the result was twins, right and left inguinal hernias. He was tired of moving but were he to move again he would not do the lifting.

"Nice place. Been here long?" Patty probed.

"About six months. It had been my Aunt's place. It went to my brother and me as she had no children. I worked out a deal with him. I keep up on the mortgage, taxes, utilities, et cetera, and when the day comes to sell, we split the proceeds. The mortgage is ridiculously low and the whole note will be paid off next year.

"How do you connect to the internet here? Do you use cable?" Cable was not a foregone conclusion in the City. It was the early 1970s when Sutro Tower, a huge tinker toy-like red and white antenna tower, was erected. It improved reception throughout the hilly city; for whatever reason cable infrastructure lagged.

"I've got Xenith for TV and the Internet. The cable modem and router are behind the television over there."

"Can I see your phone and laptop? Do you have a desktop or any tablets?"

"No desktops or tablets. My phone and laptop are on the kitchen table. You going to stealth us up?"

"Something like that. Are you familiar with VPNs – virtual networks that hide your IP address?"

"I get the concept, but I have not used one before. I did use incognito mode for last night's research."

Patty was not impressed. "Nursery school security. If we keep rotating the VPN, then we will have some misdirection should someone start to snoop on us. My top four reroutes are Roswell, New Mexico; Assawoman, Virginia; Truth or Consequences, New Mexico; and Massanutten, Virginia. What's for dinner?"

"Candlestick Lamb Chops, Itsy-Bitsy potatoes, and quick spinach."

"Huh?"

"Candlestick Lamb Chops. My father took us to a Giants night game; he brought the hibachi. I figured we would have hot dogs in the parking lot. He pulls out fresh loin lamb chops and a canister of garlic salt. He seasoned those babies up, and seared them on one side, then the other. Bone in hand, each one was gone in three or four bites. Cleaned the bones like sucking a lollipop. The best."

"Itsy-Bitsy's are oven-roasted creamers. I call them that as Mary could not say 'baby potatoes' when she was three. The potatoes are oiled and seasoned. About 35-40 minutes in a hot oven and they pop in your mouth. They do not even need butter or sour cream, but you can take it to that next level if you like."

"The quick spinach is just like it sounds. I like to heat some bacon grease in a wok. Add copious amounts of spinach. As soon as it's wilted it's done. Hit it with a little lemon juice. I can't stand it when people boil vegetables to mush."

Patty's mouth was watering, "Damn, that sounds good."

"Assawoman?"

"Yeah. It's a real place. Could you imagine going to Assawoman High? What if that was your last name, Jack Assawoman? These lamb chops are really good. You can cook."

"Thanks. Food is easy; it comes naturally. The trick will be if we can hit the zone with this project. Your uncle and I played soccer together."

"When was that?"

"Last century. Did you play? Or is your experience limited to video games?"

"You know my uncle. I played. We won the City

League and went to State my senior year. The team was lucky it didn't have to forfeit after I got busted."

"Do you know that feeling when you can see the shot before you take it or your pass threads the needle? You strike the ball on the sweet spot, and it rockets effortlessly?"

Patty's head was nodding, "I do."

"Well, so do I. And that's how this project has to feel. Effortless. What position did you play?"

"Fullback."

"Perfect. Defense. It was your job to thwart attacks on goal. That's just what we need you to do for us. It is your work that will backstop, mixed metaphor intended, our every move."

"You keep referring to 'us' and 'we'. I only see the two of us and neither is a printer. Seems like 'we' are missing a big piece. What are you going to do put a Gig Listing on Gregslist?"

"No, but I do plan to do a little fishing tomorrow. Have you ever noticed what the first section of the paper people your grandparents' age read at the café?"

"I don't know. The front page?"

"No. It's the Obituaries. They want to see if any of their friends have died. Some actually plan their social calendar around memorial services."

"That's sick."

"Maybe 50 years will change your perspective. Me, I start with the sports page cause I always have. Next, though, I turn to the business section to see what companies are closing, shuttering locations or downsizing. The job market is brutal, particularly for older workers."

"I thought you were retired."

"I am, but I'm not dead. I like to keep my eyes open to what's going on in the community. I Look to mine the confluence of inspiration and desperation."

"Huh."

"The same day I read about the old Irish punts the Chronicle had a story about a 100-year-old family printing company that is in the process of closing. Murphy Printing was opened by an Irish immigrant in the 1920s. Three generations have operated it, but there is no fourth generation to take over. The story said it is limping to the finish line with a skeleton crew."

"Heh, I forgot to ask. How'd it go with the doctor this afternoon?"

"Well, they didn't find what they were looking for, but they found a bunch of other stuff. I'm going to have surgery next week, and they will continue to run tests. They said it will be minor surgery. I'd say it was minor surgery if it were happening to my neighbor. Since it is happening to me, I'd say it is major. I should be on light duty for a couple of weeks."

"Damn. You're going to live to see this thing through, aren't you?"

"As long as I don't get hit by a car or fall off a building."

Patty was concerned about a case of 'hurry up and wait'.

"What should I do?"

"There's an online police seizure auction that closes tomorrow. Do a little secret shopping for your system needs. I'm assuming you are stealth at the café. Nothing fancy, just find one with the power you need to do the job. Give me the info and I'll bid anonymously."

"Anything else?"

"Look into, but don't alert the agencies where we will need to establish presence: Social Security, DMV, Department of State, Credit Bureaus. We'll have to arrange a bank also. I'll get word to you at Java Beach."

"What's next for you?"

"Think I will peruse property records after I wash the dishes and pay a visit to Murphy Printing in the morning."

Patty surprised Sean, "I can help with the dishes."

"Erin go bragh."

Chapter 6

Murphy's Law

Murphy Printing was three short blocks north of McCovey Cove and PacBell ballpark and three long blocks west of the Bay and Red's Java House, a true dive – beer & burger joint. The Giant's waterfront ballpark changed the neighborhood. Over 25 years this industrial pocket of the City had turned professional and culinary. The print shop was a holdout. The neighbors were now an architect and a Thai Massage College. A software developer had replaced Sal's Auto & Body, Murphy's backdoor neighbor for 40 years.

The glass doors were plastered with promotions and accolades. Sean pushed the door and banged his head and knee on it. It didn't give. His peripheral vision did not pick-up the small 'PULL' sign opposite the handle.

"First time here?" Kenny Durkin asked. "We're not accepting new orders."

"I read that. My name is Sean McAuliffe." Sean extended his right hand.

"Kenneth Durkin, General Manager." He held his hand up to show Sean the ink stains.

"That doesn't bother me." Sean shook his hand. They each had firm grips as taught by their fathers, 'just make sure you are not the wet fish'. Neither tried to break knuckles.

"Do you go by Kenneth?"

"I have been trying it and 'Ken'. 'Kenny' doesn't look right on a resume for a 50-year-old."

"You been here for a long time?"

"I started sweeping the floors in high school. Feels

like I've spent my whole life in this shop. Never thought I'd have to find another job."

"It's tough looking for work when you are older. I don't want to tell you how many times I aced the test, got the interview, and nailed it for nothing. They'll keep talking to you but are intimidated or uncomfortable with your age."

Kenny sounded dejected, "I never went through the process even when I was young. It's disconcerting."

Sean changed course, "You mind giving me the tour?"

"You looking to buy the place? You'd have to get in line. A lot of people want the property, but not the print shop."

"Nah, I don't have any money to speak of. It used to be my job to go into companies and see how they tick. A million years ago I was an Industrial Engineer. I think it started with Mr. Roger's segments and continued with the 'How It's Made' Canadian television show."

"Ok. Who knows if I'll ever give the tour again."

The front office was 21st Century with graphics software and 3-D printing technology. The majority of the current business was digital printing. Operational but gathering dust at the back of the shop were large offset, intaglio, and letterpress printers. All the equipment Sean had read was required to print actual currency. Forgers who only used digital and offset techniques lacked the tactility of real currency.

"The article in the Chronicle said you were still servicing some accounts."

"We do a lot of printing for the Church. There are weekly bulletins for the 88 churches in the diocese. We're also hooked up with Holy Cross Cemetery in Colma and Sullivan Funeral Home for the prayer cards. The

Murphys see it as a responsibility. They don't want to burn in hell by pissing off the Catholics."

"Who keeps the machines running? Do you have a maintenance mechanic?"

"Nah. I can take each and every machine in this place apart and reassemble it in the dark. I can also work on the electrical, the plumbing, and the shop truck."

The layout was tight as the parcel was 25' wide and 80' deep. Even though the printers were not running the smell of ink permeated the air. Sean walked with his elbows extended like antennae to keep from running into the machinery. A trick he had learned working retail in stores that kept rearranging the racks. He hadn't realized how bad his vision was when he developed the technique. Kenny was a couple of inches shorter than Sean and about 75 pounds heavier. His shape kept him centered through the shop floor.

"Upstairs has all the paper stock. Some of it goes back decades. Murph always said, 'You never know when you might need the special stuff.' Want to see it?"

"Sure. I've always found the most interesting things in the dark crannies."

A network of racks and rollers was used to store and access the reams and rolls of paper. A small freight elevator transported the stock between floors.

Sean was setting the hook, "Shh. Did you hear that?"

"What?"

"My stomach. It was growling. Does Red's still have the lunch special? Would you like to grab a bite?"

"Sure, if you are buying."

"I am."

"When was the last time you ate there?"

"Let's see. I came back from Hawaii after Mary was

born. Must be 30 years."

Kenny laughed. "Man, you are in for some sticker shock."

*   *   *   *   *   *   *   *

"What the hell! A double cheeseburger and a beer for $16.69. It used to be $4.75, $5.00 with tax. Are you kidding me?" Red's was a true dive the last time Sean was there. It was a 5-block walk from his office on Market Street thirty years ago. A few times a month he and a few cohorts would take the walk in their suits and sit on the dock with the blue collars. It was a hidden treasure.

Ruefully, Kenny concurred, "Everything changed with the ballpark. Even Red's."

"Let's sit on the dock. I can't believe I'm turning into my father. I drive around the City pointing out all the changes. Explain that the doggie head by the zoo was from Doggie Diner home of the foot-long. Proudly wear the Croix de Candlestick badges at the 'Stick. I remember when Harrington's had to close on St. Patrick's Day as the insurance company refused coverage."

"Damn, Sean. I do the same thing."

"The funniest though was crossing the Golden Gate Bridge when there were still tolltakers. My dad would always mention that Johnny Mathis' brother Clem was a toll-taker. You know Johnny was an athlete too. He once bested future Celtic great Bill Russell in the high jump at USF."

Kenny was curious, "What is it that you do that you can visit random failing concerns offering free meals?"

"I retired early via the disability route. I had severe

spinal spondylolisthesis at 14, 15. That means my back looked like a game of Jenga just before collapsing. After the Medicare kicked in, I had fusion surgery. It eliminated a lot of pain. But that didn't help my failing eyesight. My right eye has almost no peripheral vision, and what vision there is is out of focus. A Stanford butcher tried a Hail Mary surgery and made things worse. The focal length of my right eye was shortened. I've lost my depth perception and sense of balance. My lawyer had me wait until I was 55 years old to file as Social Security would be less likely to force me to retrain for restricted work. It was a long two years to go through the process; I could only work under the table."

"Sounds rough. How do you feel now?"

"My back is a lot better, but my eyes, both of which have had cataract surgery, are fading. They say my right eye is glaucomic and my left eye is on watch. Sometimes I will wear a patch to counteract the double vision, but that makes the peripheral vision and depth perception even worse."

Kenny, as did everyone, made a pirate joke, "Aargh, matey."

"Yeah. Yeah. That's why I rarely wear it around strangers. ...It was no accident that I came to Murphy's print shop today. I wanted to see what kind of machines you had. I also wanted to meet the non-Murphy who might be running the skeleton crew. I have this idea."

"Is it legal?"

"Maybe. ...Can I ask you a personal question?"

"You can ask. I may or may not answer."

"Fair enough. First, I was pleased you're the guy running the show. You know how our community is tight."

Kenny had seen it many times, "Yeah. I know a guy. Or I know a guy who knows a guy."

"Exactly. Well, my guys were that guy for you a couple of times and neither of us knew it."

"How so?"

"Our mothers went to Star of the Sea together. And my dad and Uncle John grew up at 101 Bosworth, St. John's was their parish. Same neighborhood as your mom."

"And?"

"I don't know how many of the details you know. And I only got them secondhand. It has to do with when your dad ran out on your family."

Kenny intimated, "It was bad. He messed us all up. Left the family in the lurch. My mom did not know what to do. My brother Michael was gone to college."

"Apparently, your mom reached out to my mom. It didn't sit well with my dad and Uncle John. My dad worked at Hibernia Bank and John was a San Francisco cop."

"Were they the ones that chased Dad down?"

"Yeah. I was at CAL then, but my brother called and relayed that something was going down. I hadn't thought about that call in years until I called my Uncle Gene, Gene Sullivan, the other day. I mentioned the Chronicle article about Murphy Printing shutting down. He gave me more details about the bounty hunting in Reno. He also told me about the 'wire boy' who was in his pocket for two weeks."

"Gene's your uncle? We ate lunch here at Red's a half dozen times in those two weeks. He'd get me a double cheeseburger and a beer even though I was only 18 years old. I haven't thought about Gene in years; he was a good man."

"Still is. His body is broken down in more ways than you can imagine but his mind is sharp as a tack. Funny thing, one side of my family breaks down physically with age and the other side loses their minds but not their bodies."

"So, Gene, your dad and John were brothers?"

"My dad was one year older than John and they looked like twins. Gene was my mom's *baby* brother. Not that I would call him that. Only Mom calls him that. She still has a tone."

Kenny was letting his guard down, "Clearly, the 'know a guy' theory is in play between us. Tell me about the idea."

"One more question. I checked the property records. I know Murphy owns the building; it's probably the only reason why the print shop is still here. Would he sell you the business?"

"We talked about it. He would love to see the print shop continue to serve its special community of clients. I would do it too. This is all I know. From me, he would accept a sweetheart deal: $400,000 in cash and a percentage of the profits over the next 20 years."

"Considering the value of the building and the cost of the machinery that really is a bargain."

"It might as well be for four thousand dollars. I have no equity worth mentioning."

"Would Murph give you six months to make the deal happen?"

"I'm sure he would if I asked."

"Are you free for dinner tonight at Flanahan's? Say 7 pm, I have a proposal for you."

"Do I need to bring anything?"

"Just your wits."

43

Chapter 7

The Squeeze

Bernard Sheridan normally arrives home before 5 pm. It was nearly 6:30 pm. Margaret was less concerned about his welfare and more concerned about her evening funds. She could text for them, but she knew he disliked arguing via text. Best not to raise his ire. Rather than go back to the bank for his car Sheridan walked the 4 kilometres from The Celt to his home, 14 Westmoreland Park. He needed to clear his head from the day and prepare it for the evening. Along the way he purchased a €75 shillelagh just cause he liked how it looked. in the window. The shillelagh, a yard in length, was made from a branch of blackthorn dark, strong, and polished. The resin knob was a manly swirl of admiral blue and juniper green, it felt comfortable in his palm. He used it to wrap on their front door.

"Bernard? I didn't hear the car. Why are you knocking? What are you holding?"

"I walked. I wanted to make an entrance. This is my new shillelagh."

"Where the divil have you been?" He knew that tone. Margaret Sheridan was irritated at having to wait for him. She was 15 years his junior but looked 20 years younger. And she knew it. Her figure, size 10, cast the same silhouette as the day they married. She had recently allowed herself to go grey, but the hip shoulder length cut read sexy mature.

"Your cell has been going directly to mail. Gertrude said you left at noon; it's half past six! Explain yourself."

"First, my dear, I do not have to explain myself. I am

far from a child."

"Bernard, are you ossified?"

"Most certainly. That bint Flood set me off today. She had the gall to request a white paper on the punt/euro exchange. I might as well teach a university course in bank history."

"You only have six months left. I've been checking the real estate market here in Ranelagh. I should think you could get at least €900,000 for the place. We could do a lot of traveling."

Sheridan bit his tongue and closed his eyelids so that Margaret could not see the eye roll. He could not get her to understand they were mortgaged to the hilt. They had taken a second so that their child, the barista, could complete a graduate degree in art history. Margaret's BMW was leased, and he would lose his company vehicle upon retirement. They had been a one income family for 25 years. Her idea of retirement was a fantasy. Why not? So was her idea of everyday life. He had been something of a cradle robber meeting her in the hallways of the University. She was completing her undergraduate degree; he was taking a continuing education course in Korean, Ireland had targeted Korea as a trade partner.

"Yes, dear."

"There are bangers and mash in the fridge. You better get to sleep early. You don't bounce back like you used to. I'm going to the club. The girls have a bridge game going tonight. Put a couple hundred euros on my account just in case."

He wanted to scream. His knuckles turned white as he strangled the shillelagh. He uttered a resigned, "Yes, dear. Did you get the laundry?"

"No, I did not have time today. Ciao." She kissed his

cheek and then headed for the door. "Don't wait up."

Sheridan went upstairs. He found a slot for the blue/green striped tie on the tie rack with the others. He slipped off the finely polished loafers just holding the toe of his right shoe against the left heel. About five years ago he had switched from wing tips as he would get lightheaded bending over to tie or untie his shoes. He laid the dark grey pinstriped jacket on the bed for a moment. He sucked in his gut to unlock the trousers – hook & bar, button, zipper, button. They fell about his ankles. He collected the trousers by the end of the pant legs, he matched the seams to preserve the creases. He had wooden suit hangers with a spring-loaded pole for careful storing of the trousers before laying the jacket over the shoulders curved to preserve shape.

'Ugh.' He thought as he looked in Margaret's full-length mirror. Men with paunches shouldn't wear singlets. Boxers replete with Batman logos and black socks completed the unsightly ensemble. He leaned his right buttock against the wall while his left foot searched for the khaki's pant leg. With the left pant leg shimmied about his ankle, he switched buttocks so that the process could be repeated on the right side. He threw on a jumper and slid his black socks into a pair of earth sandals. He no longer cared how socks and sandals looked. His feet swelled during the day and once shoes were off, they would not be worn again.

As Margaret failed to deal with the laundry, he gathered his bag of shirts and headed out to Giles Laundry and Dry Cleaning. It was just a five-minute walk down Ranelagh. He would pick up his laundered shirts and stop at The Taphouse on the way back. Margaret's bangers and mash could remain in the fridge, or he might toss them out; twenty-five years later and her mash was still as lumpy as a sack of rocks.

"Kayleigh, Mo Chara, would you mind hanging my shirts in the office?"

"Of course, Mr. Sheridan, would you like a table, or will the bar do?"

"The bar will do fine. I'm dining alone tonight. Mrs. Sheridan is off to the club for bridge."

"Uh-oh."

"Indeed."

The Taphouse opened not long after the Sheridans moved to Ranelagh. The décor mimicked pubs that had been open 75 years. The brass was polished, but not too polished. Much of the masonry used was reclaimed. The stools were four-legged, mahogany stained, 22" diameter padded black leather tops. He chose a stool towards the far end of the bar near the jacks and across from a television. He planned to watch the first half of the Gaelic Football semi-final, Kerry vs. Dublin, at the pub, he would walk home at halftime.

Killian, the bartender, wiped his way down to Sheridan.

"Mr. Sheridan, will you be eating tonight or just tossing a few back?"

"Eating. Can you bring me a Kilbeggan on the rocks and a Harp back. Menu also."

"Will Mrs. Sheridan be joining you?"

"No. Mrs. Sheridan has an important bridge engagement."

"Oof. I'm sorry. You know the Kerry/Dublin semifinal will be starting soon? You're a Kerry man, aren't you?".

"Kerry man born and raised. I thought I would catch the first half here."

"There's a rumor going round that you wore the jersey for Kerry."

"Centuries ago, Killian. Old news. The game was rougher then. It was long before the black card. It's just like anything else, the players are faster, and stronger. Strategy remains though – constant motion, ball movement, accuracy."

Bzzzz! Bzzzz! Bzzzz! The phone vibrated in his pocket. Margaret was texting. He knew what that meant. It had been years since she texted him just to put a little vibration in his hip pocket. *'Need another 150 euro. Now. No questions asked.'*

'Give me a minute. I have to check your account.'

She resented that he would check her account to see how the funds were used. He did not care. Her posture that 'her money is her money, and my money is her money' was not acceptable any longer. She could not put two euros together to save her life. Sure enough, she had online gambled away half of the deposit before she even got to the club. The banker's wife had a gambling addiction, what an embarrassment.

He had three choices. One, refuse and initiate World War III, a la the assassination of Archduke Ferdinand. Two, reason with her. This would lead to pitiful followed by vitriolic interchange ending with capitulation on his part. Three, send the money with shameful disgust and illusory threats. He was too tired to fight.

'It's done. No more. Don't ask. If you don't have petrol to get home, walk. You better do something about your ways. The money is going away in six months.'

'Thanks, love'

'Whatever'

                    *   *   *   *   *   *   *   *

Gertrude had noticed Sheridan's vehicle had spent the
night in the car park. The engine was cool to the touch.
He would be arriving on foot or hackney. She could only
remember this happening a handful of times and it never
was good. She placed two ISHKA's and a bottle of
aspirin on his desk. His morning calendar was light and
easily manipulated. She moved his in-person meetings to
the 1300-1500 window and set the conference call for
11:15.
    "Top of the morning, Trudy." He sounded chipper, not
what she expected.
    "Not really, Sir. I juggled your morning around. You
have a conference call in two hours and a few meetings
this afternoon. I wasn't sure if the morning would work."
    "Thank you. Did you see where my boys took The
Dubs last night?"
    "It was a tight one 2-08 to 0-12. I was on the edge of
my seat."
    "Atta girl. Place a data request with the analyst –
Punt/Euro conversions by denomination since 2000 in
five-year buckets; detail for the last five years; total
currency printed by series & denomination; and any
estimates as to outstanding currency by denomination."
    Flood would get her white paper. More importantly,
Sheridan was looking for the edge. He wanted 'feck you'
money. He wanted rid of the two bints.

Chapter 8

Say Cheese!

He preferred a briefcase, but no one else seemed to any longer. Once, they were as common as telephone booths or shoeshine stands. It was only a 15-minute walk north to Flanahan's. Sean switched the Kelly Green Chrome messenger bag between right shoulder hanging to his side and then to the left shoulder, across the chest, resting on his butt a dozen times. In college, he was the odd kid who was never comfortable carrying his backpack by a single strap.

"That's a pretty purse, Sean." Francess' eyes twinkled as her voice dripped with sarcasm.

"Why, thank you. But it is not a purse. This is a new laptop, and all the cool kids use messenger bags."

"Oh, so now you're a cool kid."

"Just cool in general. Is anyone using the back room tonight? I'd like to set up shop there for the evening if it's free."

"That should be fine, but I'll check. Can I get you anything?"

"Just a Harp. It could be a long evening."

Sean was sure Patty would be pleased with the unit he purchased at the police auction. It operated at 5.0 Gigahertz; the Terabyte of storage was equivalent to 745,000 of the 5¼" floppy disks Sean used to format with colon prompt commands last century. At under 7 pounds, the laptop was feather-light. The machine was a blank slate being stripped of all data and software. The police seized it from a modern-day fence that disbursed ill-gotten goods under the guise of an online pawn store. It was important to Sean that the machine had not been used for child pornography or exploitation, no bad mojo.

"The room is yours." Francess pointed with her head as she was carrying a tray of drinks. "I'll bring your Harp in a moment."

The 18'x30' room was generally reserved for banquets. Banquets being a very general term as Sean had attended everything from youth soccer parties to stripper-filled bachelor parties in the room. There was a 72" television hanging on the wall for sporting events or streaming. Square tables could be arranged in a variety of shapes depending on the event. Linens rented on request. When the lighting was up the chairs looked worn having already done duty in the pub.

"What are you up to, Sean McAuliffe?" Francess served his Harp and sat across from him.

"Were you sent here to give me the third degree or are you asking?"

"I'm on my break. Your spirit is up. I like it, but it's not normal. You've either won the lottery or come to peace with your humanity, everyone knows you've been to the doctor."

"Maybe a bit of both. When was the last time you were in Ireland? I'm thinking of going. I've never been."

"I came over 10 years ago when my daughter went to University. I've been back once when she graduated."

"Do you miss her?"

"Very much. She's a wonderful young woman. She has a good job but would love the chance to do her own thing. I'm only sorry I can't do more for her."

"I feel the same way about my kids. Would you like to be back in Ireland?"

"It's a special place, but my luck ran out there."

"Things better here?"

"It seems wherever I go, I am there. Grenada, Ireland, or here Francess needs to be ok with Francess."

"You're a philosopher."

"I'm a survivor. Just like you."

"Do you know Dublin?"

"Like the back of my hand. Dublin and The City are more similar than dissimilar. I think you would like it. Feel comfortable there."

'Screech!' The front door did not need a warning chime. It was swollen against the frame and mimicked fingernails on a chalkboard.

"I hear customers. I need to get back before Stephen passes a stone. I'll check on you when your mates arrive."

Sean closed his eyes and pondered the task ahead. Would Kenny buy in? Were Patty and Kenny the right men for the job? Did he have the cojones to be the frontman?

He checked his phone for the time. His phone was also his camera, calendar, address book, encyclopedia, and mailbox. It was 6:58. He smiled as he recalled the evolution of personal time management. There were people in the 1980s who made a living conducting seminars about how to properly use a day planner: Scheduling Meetings & Calls, Maintaining Contacts. Their obsolescence being doomed by Palm and the personal digital assistant. People would stumble with a stylus on the monochrome screen of a handheld device. They would carry a flip phone in one pocket and a PDA in another. He recalled working as a third-party logistics consultant at Handspring as they combined a cellular phone with a PDA, creating the first smartphone. He had always been a problem solver. We can do this.

"Patty! Right on time. I have something for you." Sean handed him the messenger bag.

"Kelly green Chrome bag. Man, you are with it. Let's look under the hood."

"It's stripped of all software and data."

"Perfect. I'd have to strip it down anyway. LINUX is my operating system of choice. How'd it go at Murphy Printing today."

"The general manager who will be out in the cold in six months is going to join us tonight. I laid a carrot out for him, but I still need to give him the details and get him signed on."

"Can you trust him?"

"Not surprisingly, my family and his have history; there's an inherent trust. Kind of like how my knowing your uncle helped with your vetting. He is the ideal candidate for us. He knows printing and he's in a pickle."

"How so?"

"He has worked at Murphy Printing for 35 years. He can do anything there, but there are no Murphys to run the business anymore. He has never had to look for work. Murph would sell it to him, but he doesn't have the money for it. Right now, he's running the place on his own."

Francess appeared at the door.

"There's a wayward soul at the bar asking for ya. Are collectors on your tail? What do you want me to tell Stephen?"

"Is he about 5'8", 5'9" and rotund?"

"Yes, he is."

"He's alright. Send him back. And could you bring a couple of menus?"

Kenny shook Sean's hand. Sean pulled a chair for Kenny across from Patty. Sean broke the ice.

"I was getting worried you weren't going to make it."

"Well, I weighed my offers. And your offer of a free meal and beer was enough to get me across town."

"Ken Durkin this is Pat Maguire. ... Just use Kenny and Patty, everybody else does."

"Patty Maguire? Is Pat from Java Beach your dad?"

"Uncle."

Francess was back with the menus. The limited food offerings were on the front and the extensive whiskey and beer offerings were on the back of the laminated, 8½"x11", light green, 12-point menus.

Kenny exclaimed, "I printed these. I remember the Shamrock and Harp logo. Have someone call me. I hate it when they handwrite new prices over the original. I'll reprint them for free as long as the artwork remains the same. Here's my card."

Kenny handed the card to Francess. Sean asked for one also. It was old school, embossed. Sean felt the weight of the card and ran his fingers over the letters.

"That's a nice card. My dad taught me how to feel the card before reading the title. So few people even use business cards today and most of those look homemade from a Microsoft template. No offense, Patty."

Patty looked up from the computer, "None taken."

"I'm a stickler for quality." Kenny felt his own card. "I'll have the leg'o'lamb dinner and a Guinness."

"And you, young man?" Francess wanted Patty's order.

"Patrick, but you can call me Patty."

"And you, Patty?"

"The corned beef sandwich was great, but I think I'll

try the lamb sandwich tonight. And a Harp."

"Sean, would you like a corned beef hash with another Harp? Or should I add a whiskey?"

"Am I that predictable? And just the Harp for now."

"I can read you like a paperback at the check stand." Francess liked to rib Sean.

"Ouch!"

"It shouldn't be too long, Lads. I'll go get your beers."

Pleasantries completed Sean walked around the table so that Kenny would be on his left and Patty on his right. He took the messenger bag from Patty and pulled out the Irish Times Business Section.

"Kenny, I'd like you to read this article."

From that seat, Sean could use his good eye to observe the reader. Would his pupils dilate, would his eyebrows raise and furrow with interest? Or, would he miss the significance, and shrug with a 'so what' attitude?

"Hmph! That's a lot of money just sitting there. Are you thinking..."

"Yes. I am. This is an opportunity to liberate funds that are not going anywhere. No one will miss a meal or lose a home. No one will be held at gunpoint. No lives will be ruined with drugs."

"Why us?"

"You and Patty are each very good at what you do. I believe that those skills properly applied could tap those funds. To fulfil the opportunity, we will need a plausible and verifiable plan. You need funds to buy the shop. Patty has been deprived of using his God given talent. This could be my only chance to retire well and leave something for my children."

"Counterfeiting money isn't easy. There are security features."

"True. But I propose that making old currency is easier than making current currency. The security features are less sophisticated, and there are less eyes watching for it. Patty, bring up the website for the Central Bank of Ireland. They have a page dedicated to old currency and instructions as to how to exchange it for euros."

Sean took *Paper Money of Ireland* from the messenger bag.

"Take this home. Study it. Tell me what you find."

"A library book?"

"Well, it is stolen. I suppose I am at risk of a hefty library fine. This is practically a how-to on Irish currency."

"Do you have an actual banknote? I'd like to see it, feel it."

"Working on that."

After they dined, Francess cleared the plates. "My God, these don't need to go through the dishwasher. I can just put them back on the shelf. Can I interest you in those whiskeys now?"

Sean ordered his with a raised eyebrow. He was pleased when Kenny chimed in, "I like mine neat."

When Patty requested his with cola. Sean and Kenny shook their heads and snickered. Sean changed the order, "Let's not waste the good stuff. How 'bout a Jack & Coke?"

Kenny concurred, "Stick with us kid. You've got a lot to learn."

Patty acquiesced, "OK, Pops. But I've got a few tricks up my sleeve also."

"I'm sure you do." Kenny threw Patty a wink.

Sean called to Kenny, "Help me set this up." Flanahan's still owned a portable movie screen. The type used at bachelor parties in the 70s & 80s. Erecting the built-in tripod and wing extensions was not for the uninitiated.

"What is that?" When Patty grew up schools no longer had A/V (audio/visual) departments. Monitors and computers were the norm.

Kenny informed, "That was the screen people would use for home movies and hardcore flicks at bachelor parties."

Sean explained, "Today, though, I thought you could use my phone to take some face shots which you could use later for licenses, passports, or wherever we need a photo ID. You can alter the background as needed, right?"

"Oh, hell yeah. Hand me your phone. Who's first? Kenny?"

Kenny stepped in front of the screen. Sean directed: one series with a quarter grin for the driver's license; another series expressionless for the passport. Kenny took Patty's photographs. They were almost finished with Sean when Francess returned.

"What the divil is going on here!?! I hope you are not being deviant. And don't expect me to fold that thing up!"

Patty turned as red as a boiled potato. Kenny shot a glance at Patty; they both were tongue-tied. Sean answered without missing a beat.

"Patty was telling us how he could digitally drop our images anywhere in the world – Hawaii, Grand Canyon, Blarney Castle. He also promised to make us personal avatars; not that I would know what to do with that. You want to play?"

Kenny picked up on the ruse, "Take a couple of shots. You'll look better around the world than our sorry mugs."

Francess gave Sean a bit of a side-eye as she lay down her empty tray and moved towards the screen. Sean became director.

"Big smile! Say cheese! Point to the right. Astonished look. Smirky look. Both hands up holding a beach ball. Pouty look." He lowered his tone, "Dour look."

"I'm not taking my clothes off."

"Of course not. We'll save that for another day."

"Sean McAuliffe! You're a cheeky one, you are."

Patty finally found an ad-lib, "I've got plenty of pics. Give me a couple of days to put them together."

Kenny and Sean disassembled the movie screen storing it carefully to ensure it could once again be revived from hibernation. Francess bussed the wreckage from the evening, the dishwasher wanted to go home.

Patty turned to Sean, "That was some quick thinking."

"Less thinking, more reading the play. If you stop and think, it doesn't feel natural. Being well-prepared allows one to react without thinking. We'll need that good preparation to make this thing play out."

Kenny added with a smile, "You're full of shit."

They all laughed.

Sean wanted to proceed, "Kenny what's your schedule look like? Do you think we could get together around noon tomorrow? Discuss your assessment of the project. Identify the slam dunks and the land mines."

"Sounds good."

"If you don't find a hard stop, could we have Patty join us later?"

"The skeleton crew will be done before 3."

"Patty, could I get word to you at Java Beach before 2pm?

Patty nodded, "Sure."

Sean had one more request, "Gentlemen, can you bring your birth certificates?"

Kenny nodded, "Sure. It's in my personal papers file at home."

Patty was puzzled, "Why?"

"I can see you are going to need a lot of explaining as we go along. That's alright. It's how you learn. There may be a time though when I'll say, 'Just because or 'do it!'. Can you live with that?"

"Yes."

"Good. Kenny tell him why."

Kenny knew. "A birth certificate is the type of document you need to open a bank account or use as a secondary form of identification when dealing with a government agency."

Patty was beginning to see his knowledge base wasn't as comprehensive as he thought. "I think my mom has it. I'll see if she can find it tomorrow morning."

Kenny spoke what Sean was thinking, "Oh my God, our future lies in Mrs. Maguire's basement."

Sean concluded the business meeting, "I'll settle up, boys. See you tomorrow."

The meal and bar tab was just under $60. Sean paid with his debit card. He gave Francess a crisp Jackson as a tip so that she would not have to wait for the plastic to settle nor run the risk of forced sharing.

"Thanks, Sean. That was generous and appreciated."

Francess shared an apartment just north of Moraga on the frontage road to the Upper Great Highway which ran parallel to Ocean Beach. It was prone to closures from sand build-up as the winds eroded the dunes.

"May I walk you home?" It was 10 minutes out of Sean's way, but he did not mind spending the time.

Francess quipped, "I have mace."

"Is that for your general security? Or are you warning me?

"Both. I have roommates you know."

"I am not harboring ill attentions. If I were, I would have driven and invited you to my place. A gentleman should not let a lady walk home alone in the middle of the night."

"Alright, you silver-tongued devil. You are nothing if not entertaining. Let me cash out my till and grab my coat. It will only be a few minutes."

'Screech!' Sean yanked the door open for her.

The walk to Francess's was one long block north on 45th Avenue and four short blocks west to Great Highway. Sean walked on Francess's right, the street side. The lighting was residential, muted. She could not notice but he raised his eyebrows like Groucho Marx to let in as much light as possible. He did not want to trip or stumble. When he was a boy his father had pointed out that you could tell if a person was from the city or country by the pace they walked. Sean's pace had slowed with time. He made an effort to comply with Francess's pace.

"You're such the gentleman, Sean."

"I don't see the problem with holding a door for a lady. Double-clicking the remote so the car door unlocks just does not seem very courteous."

Although the streets had been routinely maintained, the sidewalks were in disrepair. Some flags had settled leaving lips up to an inch. Others tilted towards the road or the home. Occasionally the city had placed a pylon or caution tape to mark an extreme hazard.

"How did you end up with Laurel & Hardy? Your

discussion seemed intense not like the normal pub dribble-drabble."

"Since I retired I am not allowed to work without risking my pension and insurance. I have an idea though. They have some skills I need, and they can benefit if it works. I have to keep things on the hush-hush though."

"Okay. Your secret, whatever it is, is safe with me."

"Thanks, Francess."

The pitch of the sidewalk made her sway into his shoulder. His foot missed the curb, and the four-inch drop sent a shudder up his sciatica. He did a two-step out of the gutter, hopped back onto the sidewalk, and clutched her elbow stabilizing the both of them.

"Oh my, Sean. I'm such a klutz. Lucky I wasn't carrying a tray of drinks."

"Trust me. I've had my share of pratfalls." He released her elbow and placed her hand in the crook of his arm. She drew closer. They were three short blocks from her door. Sean wished she had tripped earlier in the walk.

"Sean, are you alright?"

"That's a pretty broad question. I'm afraid you'll have to be more specific. Do you mean physically? In the head? Emotionally?"

"When you were in the jack I overheard Patty telling Kenny you were going to have surgery next week."

"Hmm. I need to talk to Patty about loose lips. I had a CT scan done last week; it was a fishing expedition. They didn't find what they were looking for, but they did find some other stuff to correct. First on the list is double hernia surgery."

"Ouch."

"Ouch is right. They say I'll get shaved where I've never shaved before. I should be in and out on the same day. Two weeks of light duty."

"I was a nursing assistant back home. My training and experience does not count here though. I've seen quite a bit in my day."

Sean found talking to Francess easy, "Do you like living near the beach?"

"Love it. I walk Ocean Beach every day fog or no fog. I find the Pacific evokes more idyllic thoughts than the Atlantic. I bet Hawaii is like Ireland with the heat turned on."

"I lived in Hawaii give or take for about seven years."

"Ooh. Did you enjoy it?"

"Unfortunately, it was right in the middle of my career. I was working like a dog. Everybody and their brother came to visit though, free room and tour guide."

"Would you go back?"

"In a heartbeat, but the housing is just as expensive as here."

Francess pondered, "Do you think there will ever be a time when we can relax and just enjoy life?"

"I have to. I don't need extravagance. I'd just like a comfortable existence, leave something to make my daughters' lives easier."

"Here's my door. I'd ask you up, but I have roommates who work days."

"Well, maybe you can walk me home some night."

Francess faced Sean and rested her hands over his shoulders behind his neck. He placed his hands on her hips. As they kissed their first kiss, Francess slipped her knee between Sean's legs. That was a pleasant surprise. His heart rate quickened. The darkness hid his blushing cheeks.

"Well, maybe I *will* walk you home some night."

Sean did the thirty-minute walk to his place in twenty minutes. He walked like a man half his age.

Chapter 9

Plausible

There was a loud knock at the door.

"We don't open 'til noon!" Stephen tried to chase away the nuisance.

"Stephen. It's Sean. Can I see you for a minute?"

Stephen opened the door. Like most pubs. Flanahan's lost its charm when the house lights shone bright.

"I'm setting up. You'll have to talk to me as I work. What are you doing here so early?"

"I've got a fish on the line, and you can help me reel him in."

"How so?"

"I got into an argument last night with Kenny that the embodiment of Irish femininity was actually a woman from Chicago. I saw him again this morning at Java Beach. He wouldn't let it go."

"Lady Lavery?"

"Exactly. She was born Hazel Martyn in Chicago. She became Lady Lavery when her second husband was knighted. He was commissioned to provide the portraits found on the original Irish Free State banknotes."

"Huh. I did not know she was an American. What's on the line?"

"Dollars to pounds. The larger the note I can produce and prove my point the more I get. If I were wrong, I would pay him double."

Stephen knew what he wanted, "And I've got an IR£100 Lady Lavery hanging behind the bar."

"Exactly."

"You've got the documentation on her background?"

"Printed it last night." Sean held up a manila folder.

"You'll get it back to me before the day is out."

"Absolutely."

Stephen shook his head, "I love a good bar bet. You mind if I use it in the future?"

"I'll leave you the background."

Stephen reached the framed banknote without a step stool. He handed it to Sean who carefully stowed it in his backpack.

"It's part of the background here. Can you get it back before anyone notices?"

"Will this evening work?"

Stephen nodded his approval and sent him on his way, "Now get out of here. I'm a working man."

Sean yanked the door shut on his way out.

*   *   *   *   *   *   *   *

Sean took the Muni downtown. The bus was full of Giants fans. With a day game he knew parking would be hard to find and the rates would be jacked up. This time he opened the door to Murphy Printing without fumbling.

Kenny suggested, "Sean, there's a taco truck about four blocks west that has really good burritos."

With a day game Red's was out of the question. Besides it was no longer a bargain. All throughout the City you could find Mission Burritos, a handheld meal wrapped in a giant steamed flour tortilla.

"All the meats and beans?"

"Yep."

"Let's go."

They were like salmon swimming upstream as the mass of foot traffic was heading towards the Ballpark.

Kenny took point parting the masses with Sean following like a tailback seeking the hole.

Sean was impressed with the offering, "You're right. It's rare when I see something I haven't eaten. You don't see goat or intestine every day."

"¿Qué puedo conseguirte?"

Kenny went first, "Super, Asada, and dos tacos."

The server dropped the pizza-sized tortilla in the steamer and hit the steam like he was pressing a pair of pants.

"¿Frijoles?" Queried the illegal assembling of the burritos.

"Refried."

The balance of the burrito was completed silently. The server held his hand over the queso; Kenny nodded in the affirmative. Kenny completed the order with hot sauce, guacamole, and sour cream. Total weight – 3 pounds.

The server raised an eyebrow as Sean ordered Cabeza (cheek) and black beans but was let down when he went with the mild sauce. Sean's third hernia was hiatal, and he was prone to acid reflux.

Kenny commented, "You were the real deal until you wimped on the salsa."

"My stomach is not what it used to be. There's a hernia on top of my stomach that the docs don't want to fix as long as I can manage it with eating Tums like Necco Wafers."

"Let's eat at the shop."

They rode the crowd heading to the ballpark like a wave at Ocean Beach. They were back at the shop in no time.

Kenny began, "You cost me a night's sleep."

"How so?"

"I could not put that book down. Reviewing the different series, the security features or lack thereof, and identifying the different print techniques. I was reverse engineering the process."

Kenny ate the first taco in three bites. He had his own bottle of Cholula Sauce that he dabbed before each bite of the burrito. You could not distinguish the food stains from the ink stains on his clothes. Sean allowed him a wide berth.

"Did you come up with a target?"

"I think the IR£100 series A notes are the ticket. I'd really like to get my hand on an authentic note though."

"Well, great minds think alike." Sean pulled the framed note from his backpack.

"Where did you get this?"

"I borrowed it from Flanahan's. It's part of the décor hanging over the register."

"Huh. I never noticed it."

"I fed Stephen some blarney about getting into a bet with you for $100. The woman on the portrait was actually born in Chicago. I contended the face of Ireland was American born and you contended I was full of shit."

"You won?"

"Yep. I figured you could make a passable digital copy and reframe it. I need to 'return' the note today. After you are done with it we will work a switch to replace the original."

"Devious."

"Thank you."

"What's to keep me from just printing notes myself and redeeming the euros?"

"Well, you are key for printing the notes, but without the backstory and proper digital footprint, you would be caught. Also, I'm not sure you are a good enough actor to actually walk into the bank and request the money."

"And you are?"

"I'm willing to try."

"Let's get it out of the frame and give it the once over."

A US Dollar measures 2.6 inches x 6.14 inches. The series 'A banknote' is huge by comparison, 4.5 inches x 8 inches. Kenny closed his eyes, holding the note in his left hand he rubbed his right thumb in small circles on the obverse with the index and middle fingers doing the same on the reverse. He turned the banknote over and repeated the process. He held it up to the light and inspected both sides. He placed it on a light table to expose the watermark.

"Damn. That's a big note. Close your eyes, Sean."

"What?"

"Close your eyes and hold out your hands." Once Sean's eyes were closed Kenny took a crisp dollar bill from his wallet. Kenny extended the IR£100 note to Sean's right hand and the dollar bill to his left.

"Now just pinch each and rub them a little to get a feel of what you're holding."

Sean complied. They felt similar. In fact, between his fingers he could not distinguish one from the other.

"I can't tell them apart."

"Neither could I. That's a good and a bad thing."

"How so?"

"It's good as I have a sense as to how the banknote is printed. Bad as the stock for printing is rare and controlled."

"Let's focus on 'First Things First'. Did Flanahan's give you the revised menu order?"

"Yes. I've already printed them."

"Good. Can you make a copy of the banknote that will pass when in the frame?"

"Certainly. I could just do a simple color copy, but I'd rather do an intense scan so we can analyze the layers later."

Kenny measured the bill dimensions with callipers and weighed it. He went upstairs in search of stock which would suffice for the copy. He chose a light, rag paper which they had used for insurance policies for the long defunct Fireman's Fund Insurance Company.

"The copy won't have the fine detail of printing but within a frame on a wall at 10 feet it should do. The revised menus are ready. Should we drop both off later?"

"Yes. Like to get that frame back on the wall before anyone notices. So, I'm sensing that you see your job as feasible."

"Well, it's a challenge right now. I'm intrigued. How much do you think we could get?"

"I'm thinking IR£3,000,000. Any more and the story would be hard to fathom. Any less and the risk wouldn't be worth the reward. If we pull that off each of us is looking at 1⅓ million dollars."

Kenny's eyebrows raised and a sly grin appeared.

"Do you think Patty can handle that kind of money?"

"I think Patty's going to learn a lot these next few months. I think we all will learn a lot these next few months."

"Let's get him down here and see what he can do."

*   *   *   *   *   *   *   *

Kenny had sent the skeleton crew home for the day and the storefront lights were out. He unlocked the door for Patty.

"You're late. We called you an hour a go."

"I know. I know. I had to go all the way up to 10th Street to find parking. Then the foot traffic heading from the waterfront was incredible."

"The Giants had a day game. Two vehicles can fit within my roll-up. I keep the shop van there. Next time honk when you are outside. I'll roll up the door so that you can park off the street. You won't run the risk of getting a ticket or towed."

He locked the door behind Patty. And they proceeded to his office where Sean was waiting.

"Sorry I'm late, Sean. The Giants game made me park all the way up at 10th Street. There must've been 100,000 people out there."

"45,000. That's capacity. The Giants won in 10 at least it was a happy mob. Did your mom find your birth certificate?"

"She did. I did some snooping. Creating these identities is a big job; there's quite a few places I'll have to access."

"Are you saying you can't do it?"

"No. I'll just need some direction when crafting the data."

"I can help with that. You will be creating Dan Reilly in my image."

"Who?"

"Dan Reilly – my alter ego who will be exchanging the pounds in Dublin. You and Kenny will only need strong enough covers for travel and bank accounts."

Sean retrieved a manila folder from the messenger

bag. He tossed it onto the desk; it landed with a thud. Patty started to leaf through the folder. No wants or warrants – San Mateo, County, California. No wants or warrants – Pierce County, Washington. No wants or warrants Oahu, Hawaii. The background check went back over twenty years. The FICO credit score was 686, Good; eight credit accounts opened, six closed or zero balance. Thankfully, the credit report was only seven years deep.

Patty was impressed and confused simultaneously, "What's this?"

"Those were my background check from the last time I was hired as a store manager and my credit report when I took over my aunt's mortgage. This is the level of detail Dan Reilly will require. I know I would run those checks if someone came to my door with three million pounds to exchange."

"There's a lot of detail here."

"I've moved more than the average person. We'll build a profile on the norms. The story will be manageable and creditable."

Patty was distracted. "Sean, I looked into something else."

"I know. What happens if we fail."

"Yeah."

"First, we're not going to fail. Second, none of us have any money to fine. Third, you and Kenny are accomplices likely to get probation or lighter sentences. Fourth, were I to get a major sentence it would likely mean life, so fifteen, twenty, or fifty is all the same to me."

"What's to keep Kenny and me from doing it ourselves, cutting you out?"

"You would fail. The two of you, talented in your

ways, lack the spontaneity and blarney factors required. Remember the other night when Francess caught us taking headshots? You turned red as a potato and Kenny paused."

"OK. I had to ask."

"I'm sure that one day your face game will catch up to your computer game. Give it time. We all can learn skills from each other."

Kenny realized Sean's assessment was accurate and this was his only shot to get the print shop. He put an end to the debate.

"If you're done with the 'come to Jesus' moment, can we get to work? Patty, I've printed the new menus for Flanahan's and Sean found me an IR£100 pound note that was actually under our nose the whole time. Did you put together those photos of Francess and the avatar?"

Patty nodded, "I did."

Sean handed his phone to Patty, "Can you load them directly onto my phone and change the origin data."

"Look at you, all crafty about the photo identity tags. You do have some game."

Patty used a USB phone-to-computer cable to directly transport the files to Sean's phone. He modified the creation data. He stored them in a folder named 'Francess'. He handed the phone back to Sean ready for his next task.

"What's next?"

"Let's start at the beginning. Birth Certificates. Here's your examples." Sean handed Patty the other originals.

"My God, yours looks like a copy of an old mimeograph. What's this?" Patty ran his fingers over the bottom right of the page.

Kenny knew, "That's an embossed seal to prove

authenticity. I can recreate the seal with our 3-D printer."

"Mine doesn't have it."

Sean explained, "Well, Patty, by your day the Bureau of Records had joined the 21st Century. Also, here's the names and parents I'm suggesting we use. Dan Reilly for me. Stanley Sullivan for Patty, and Oliver McGee for Kenny. I've been watching Gaelic Football at night to pick up names."

Kenny groaned, "Really, Stan and Ollie."

Patty did not get it, "What's wrong with that?"

"You've never heard of Laurel and Hardy?"

"I don't think so."

Sean defended himself, "Ideally, no one will put the two of you together."

Kenny sighed, "Patty, search for some black and white videos tonight."

Patty was back on task, "Kenny can you scan the two old certificates? I'll create a font based on the images so that I can alter the names as you want. I will alter the images and generate new TIFF files to store at the Bureau as well as add master records for any third-party search engines."

"I already scanned them. You can use my computer to do the altering, but you should probably use the laptop when you actually insert them at the Bureau."

Kenny relinquished his chair to Patty who could have used a restaurant booster seat. Kenny's chair was extra wide and well-worn. Patty fumbled with the lever underneath the seat to raise the height. Kenny rolled one of the guest seats around the desk.

"This will be easier. My seat is busted at Kenny mode. It works for me, and I don't mess with it anymore."

Patty had started processing the documents. He rose

out of the seat. His right-hand mousing, and his left-hand keying. Kenny slid his chair out from under Patty and slid the guest chair under his butt. He held it until cheeks landed lest the chair slide and Patty end up on the floor. Offering encouragement and celebration he talked to the computer like it was a teammate.

Sean and Kenny shook their heads and smiled sensing Patty was just the man they needed. But then he moved the inbox to the left side of the desk and slid the monitor to the right. He called for the laptop. No one moves Kenny's inbox. Sean sensing the faux pas put his hand on Kenny's shoulder and gave him a 'kid doesn't know what he's doing look.' It was enough to calm him down.

He even offered, "There's a plug behind the garbage can."

Sean kept the wheels greased, "I'll get it."

Patty grunted and continued to work both machines. Sean gave Kenny the head nod and they went to the production floor.

Kenny asked, "How long do you think that will take him?"

"He left the blocks like Usain Bolt. And he has that savant focus. He may be done before I finish taking a leak. Was Hibernia Bank one of your clients?"

"They were. Old Murph had all the Irish-based firms. We have a wall upstairs of all the obsolete paper stock. He was so emotionally involved with his clients he couldn't let them go."

"Can we check? I remember from when I was a kid my dad would bring home letters that felt ribbed."

They headed upstairs. Kenny started in the center of the wall. The old stock was not stored alphabetically or located by position. It was more of an archaeological dig.

"When did Hibernia go out of business?"

"Early '80s."

Kenny slid eight feet to his right. "Got it! Let's see. I've got plain bank letterhead and I've got Michael Tobin letterhead."

"Tobin? He was the top dog. He never said it, but I thought my dad was intimidated by him."

"You were right. The stationery has a column texture. You hardly see that anymore. Very '70s."

"This is good. We'll need this for the backstory. What are your biggest concerns about the print job?"

"The paper feel and the watermark. And the watermark more than the paper."

A voice boomed through the public address system, "Dan and Ollie to the office. Dan and Ollie to the office, please."

Kenny was dumbfounded, "What the hell. How did he..."

Sean stopped him, "He's good. Let's see what he's got."

Patty offered his report, "I could get used to that PA system. Check the printer for the Dan and Oliver birth certificates; they just need the embossing stamp which the 3-D printer should be creating now. I've inserted the three records in the Vital Records database and added your TIFF images to the digital documents file."

Kenny retrieved the certificates, trimmed them to size with a paper cutter, and embossed the stamp. He was impressed.

"These look good."

He handed them to Sean who concurred, "Nice work, Patty."

"I figured it would be best to order mine online, but I

need an address and a credit card or PayPal account."

"This is a great start. Let me work on the address and a way to pay."

"OK. What's next?" Patty was eager for the work, an uncommon trait for his generation.

"Tomorrow we'll talk social security cards and driver licenses."

"Cool. We need a name. It's like a mental folder for me."

Sean and Kenny looked at each other, shrugged and crooked their heads in a 'maybe the kid is onto something here' way.

Kenny suggested, "Punts-R-Us?"

Sean closed his eyes. Leaned back. Paused. Then uttered, "Team Hibernia."

Patty jumped on it, "I like it."

Kenny agreed, "That's better."

Patty shut down the laptop and reached to put the monitor and inbox to their original positions.

Kenny stopped him, "Don't worry about it, Kid. It looks like a pretty good setup. C'mon we'll give you a ride to your car."

After planning to meet again tomorrow and depositing Patty by his car, they proceeded out to Sunset and Flanahan's to clean up the rest of the day's business. It was 6:30, the after-work crowd had the pub at its peak for a weekday.

Stephen greeted them first. "Sean and Kenny, you're still talking?"

Kenny ignored the reference, "I have your new menus here."

"What do I owe you?"

"Nothing. Murph never minded keeping a customer

happy. That's the way I work also."

"Thank you, Kenny. Can I at least cover your tab tonight?"

"My arm can be twisted." Kenny never turned down a free meal.

"Good."

Sean asked, "Hey, what about me?"

"Do you have my IR£100 pound note?"

"Right here."

Stephen turned back to Kenny, "Did he really take you for $100 with Lady Lavery being American?"

Kenny sheepishly, "Yeah."

"Well then, Sean, you should be able to pay for your own meal. ...But seeing as you educated this Irishman about his own Lady and I'm likely to use that to my advantage, your tab is covered also."

"Thanks, mate." Sean tipped his Donegal tweed cap. The one he had been wearing for nearly forty years.

"Francess, could you set my friends here at a table? Their tab is on me tonight."

"You think that's wise, Stephen?"

"I know it's not but do it anyway."

Francess led them to a booth near the jacks where they would not be disturbed by the pub din.

Francess winked, "You wouldn't be interested in reviewing our new menus, would you boys?"

"I think we're familiar," Sean replied.

"Stephen said you're covered tonight. Will it be a meal?"

Kenny hankered. "I've been thinking about that leg of lamb and roast potatoes all day. A Jameson and Guinness sounds good too."

It was Sean's turn, "You can never go wrong with the

corned beef and cabbage. I'll also do a Jameson, but I'll back it with a Harp."

"Aren't you forgetting something?"

"What could that be?" Sean knew what she meant.

"The pictures. You promised me a trip around the world and an avatar."

"I have them. I just thought we could wait until it slowed down a little in here."

"You better not leave without showing me."

"No, ma'am."

"Alright, then I'll go get your drinks."

Over dinner, they discussed sports and family. They were both Giants and Niners fans. Sean recalled the Warriors championship of the 70s. Sean told Kenny about playing soccer with his uncle. Pat's game was just dirty enough that you loved him as a teammate and hated him as an opponent. Kenny gave up football when he was forced to work. He had been a linebacker starting Varsity his junior year. He told stories of working with Gene whose approach to work made an impression on Kenny that still guided him. Sean knew Gene to be a problem solver, get the job done, red tape be damned kind of guy. In Hawaii, you would have said Sean and Kenny were 'talking story'.

Francess cleared the plates and returned to the table.

"Slide over Sean. I'm on my break and I would like to see what your boy came up with."

Sean flipped through the photos Francess in St. Georges, Francess at the beach, Francess at the Pyramids of Giza, Francess kissing the Blarney Stone, Francess on the Golden Gate Bridge... Her avatar was svelte – jet black shoulder length hair, deep brown eyes, nice smile.

"If you give me your number, I can text the pics

to you."

"These are nice. I might use the one on Waikiki as my Christmas card. Do you think he could add a Santa hat?"

"I don't see a problem with that."

Francess and Sean began a little dance.

"Sean, is this just a ploy to get my phone number? You could have just asked."

"Why Francess, what kind of degenerate do you think I am?"

"I know the type of degenerate you are. That's why I mentioned it. Hand me your phone."

Francess added her number to his Contacts. She downloaded an MP3 with her favorite SOCA beat and set it as her personal ringtone on his phone. She sent herself an email with the entire contents of the Francess folder.

The meal and drinks were paid; Sean left another Jackson for the tip. Kenny said his goodbyes to head out lest he end up plastered and unable to drive.

With a disappointed tone, she asked, "Are you done already?"

"Well, Stephen picked up the tab. And, I have surgery tomorrow."

As she collected the tip Francess switched to a sly tone, "Oh, you spoil me, Sean. …Can a lady give a lad a ride home?"

Sean's eyebrows hit the ceiling, "That would be grand."

Chapter 10

Vicissitudes

"You can park in the driveway by the Cougar up there."

It was dark, Sean turned on the stairwell lights. "You go first. The treads are marble and not to code. I'll be your backstop in case you slip."

"Will you, now?"

He followed three steps behind her, his eyes at heinie level. Her stair climbing had a rhythm and bop that could serve as the bassline to an Earth, Wind & Fire classic. Distracted and failing to heed his own warning, his foot missed a step. He clutched both rails and righted himself.

"You ok back there?"

"Yes. My mind was somewhere else."

"I'll bet."

They talked about his double hernia procedure; he was too old for vanity. She recalled her days as a nursing assistant. He told her stories of The City. She shared how her family fled Grenada for Ireland when the Americans invaded. She talked of how different Dublin life was from Grenada. The conversation was comfortable and easy. She did not press him for information on the project. He showed her his grandparents' immigration papers from the 1920s. The hours were growing wee.

"Sean, you should get some rest."

"Oh, man. Déjà vu."

"How so?"

"Telling me to get some rest the night before surgery reminds me of my high school soccer coach."

"You had that rule here too."

"You know."

"Oh, yes. No sex the night before a big game. Of course, with your hernias, I don't know that you'd be in the starting line-up anyway."

"I'm sure I could think of something to do."

"Yes. Yes. I do believe that you would be entertaining."

He walked her to her car. They shared another embrace and kiss with her knee slipping between his legs. He really liked that move. As she drove away he closed the gate and climbed the stairs deliberately; he did not like the effect a single flight of stairs had on his pulse and breathing. He collected himself. Between the surgery the next day and Francess' visit he was far too wired to go to bed. He turned his attention to more research. '

He logged into the VPN which Patty had built and started typing his first query, *'Social Security Administration data storage warehouse'*.

*   *   *   *   *   *   *   *

Each nurse and assistant tooled around with a portable workstation. They would record vital statistics, allergies, drug & alcohol use, and religious beliefs, if any, that could impact care choices. Even though it was only an outpatient procedure, the registrar printed two pages of labels for charging out drugs, wraps, IV bags, and any other consumables they could possibly charge.

The waiting room was organized like the waiting area for a flight – two rows of back-to-back seating around the four-window reception booth. The locked access door to the pre-procedure preparation ward was near the corner so that the whole room could hear the call for next batter up. The wait had him half-dozed. He was traveling light per hospital instructions – no valuables, just identification and insurance cards. But, like all the other patients he had his cell phone. He also had his +3.0 readers.

"McAuliffe! McAuliffe!" called Azealia. Startled his phone flew off his lap; he batted it once, twice with his right hand and caught it in his left. The nurse/gatekeeper granted his access to processing.

"What's your name?"

"Sean McAuliffe."

"Birthdate?"

"July 18, 1962."

"I'm Azealia. I will be preparing you for surgery today. Do you know what they will be doing to you today?"

"Dr U, I have trouble pronouncing his name, will be repairing two groin hernias and tucking in the entwined bowels and intestines."

"Inguinal hernias, close enough. Pronounce the name slowly. Ooh-pa-die-ay. Like it's spelt, U-p-a-d-h-y-a-y."

He stood on the scale. Surprisingly, it was the same model that was used when he was a child. She measured his height to 5'10½". He had been 5'11¾" in high school, 6' even with his hair. She set the main counterweight at 150 and slid the smaller counterweight all the way out. The scale did not balance.

"Hmph." Azealia was speaking under her breath. "Let's try this again."

She slid the counterweight back to zero and moved the main counterweight to 175. As she slid the small counterweight the indicator started to budge from its upper limit. 179, 184, 189, 192! The indicator was floating level.

"Five-ten and 192, you could stand to lose a few

pounds. Your blood pressure is a bit elevated. Are you nervous?"

"A bit. I can control it if I take a moment to set myself."

"Don't worry, Sweetie. Dr. Ooh-pa-die-ay is a good one. ... I will give you a minute. Strip, and I mean everything, put on this gown, and get on the bed."

She left closing the curtain not quite all the way. He slid both socks in his right shoe. He would stow his phone and readers in his left shoe just before they wheeled him to the show. He struggled to tie the paper gown behind his back. He closed his eyes and pictured the knot he was tying. The bed angle and pillow position were not natural, it was the hospital he just waited uncomfortably.

Azealia returned with a service cart. She made some more entries and notes on her computer station and turned towards Sean.

"You naked under there? ...Good. Did you shower this morning?"

"Yes."

"Shave?"

"Yes."

"Not your face."

"Oh. No."

"Alright then. Sit up."

She untied the back straps he had struggled to secure in the first place.

"Were you a boy scout? That's quite the knot."

"Definitely not a boy scout."

"This is the part where I'm supposed to be professional, but I find it to be quite personal. Lay back, relax. Let me adjust that bed and pillow. Oh, my. I'll need the trimmer before the razor."

She made another entry on the computer. She cleaned him front and back with sterilizing wet cloths. The discards from the trimming were just as depressing as those of a haircut. So much grey. The bedpan water was hot and the shaving cream was generic. Azealia hummed as she lathered then scraped away at his nether regions.

"Alright, Sean McAuliffe. I am going to start an IV. And I will be done with you for now. The anesthesiologist will be next. From that point, we will have our way with you until you are waiting for your ride home."

"So long, Sean McAuliffe. I wish all the best for you."

$$* \quad * \quad * \quad * \quad * \quad * \quad * \quad *$$

Azealia brought Sean his going-home instructions and medications.

"Sean, Doc U says the surgery went well. Everything is back where it belongs. You may experience some discomfort. You have one medication for pain management and another for muscle relaxation. You can take one pain pill every six hours as needed for 5 days. The muscle relaxant is two pills every 4 hours as needed for a week. The instructions are on this sheet which I will put in your bag."

"When do I start? Now? As soon as I get home?"

"Whoa, Cowboy. I'm going to give you one last shot of the good stuff before I pull your IV. Start the clock when you get home. Remember – as needed. Now get your pants on I can't take you out in public like that."

Azealia tied his shoes and helped him onto the wheelchair. She wheeled him off the ward, to the elevators, and out to the street.

"Where's your ride? I can't just leave you here sitting on the bench. And you cannot keep my wheelchair."

"I called him a half hour ago."

Just then the roar of Pat Maguire's Shelby GT500 could be heard from three blocks away. The engine had a deep idle and he rarely used fifth gear. The green of Pat's car was as loud as the engine. He pulled up hot with no heed to the hospital zone sound or speed ordinances.

Azealia shook her head as she helped Sean into the passenger seat, "I should've known."

"Geez, Pat. You nearly gave the old ladies heart attacks. Anyway, thanks for picking me up."

"It's good for their circulation. You couldn't find another ride?"

"Well, most folk work a real job. And my kids aren't in The City."

"I know. I'm just busting your balls."

"Really, Pat. My balls. Today of all days."

"Sorry. It must be a sore subject."

"Argh. You're killing me."

"Alright. Alright. How's that thing working out with my nephew Patty? He seems way more focused than normal."

"Hard to say. It's early. I'm glad he's showing an interest though. A lot of young people are aimless."

"He says you are a fount of information."

"I'm old, well-read, and know how to ferret out answers. I also have a really good bullshit detector. Whether I'm being fed it or feeding it myself. Patty told me he has seven years left on probation. Is there any chance that could be reduced?"

"The lawyer said he could ask for a reduction as long

as he stays out of trouble, which he has, but it would cost about $200,000 in legal fees. His folks don't have it. I would have to take out another mortgage. He has resigned himself to stick it out."

"I'm over there by the Cougar."

Pat appreciated the classic, "Oh. That's sweet. Do the taillights bing, bing, bing?"

"They do."

"You know, Shelby carried that style over to this car. …Do you have a bad scar?"

"It was what they call a microsurgery. They went in from a couple of angles and robots did the work. It looks like I was in a knife fight. See." Sean pulled up his shirt and revealed the slits one above his belly button the others on either side of his abdomen.

"Go with the knife fight story Can you get up the stairs?"

Despite the surgery, Sean still had a sharp tongue, "Well, I don't plan to spend the night in the basement."

"Can I get you anything else? Would you like me to stay while you get settled?"

"No. I've got food in the fridge. I may fall asleep on the couch or in my bed; it doesn't matter."

Pat waited for Sean to get inside the gate. By the time Sean was halfway up the stairs, he was out of eyeshot. Sean forgot to turn on the stairway lights at the bottom of the stairs. The upstairs switch was inside the front door. He fumbled a bit trying to unlock the door in the dark.

He reviewed the meds they had prescribed, a muscle relaxer and a pain-relieving narcotic, oxycodone. They each carried the do not mix with alcohol warning. The relaxers were every four hours as needed for seven days. The oxycodone was four times a day as needed for five days. Sean was going to have to rely on his team to keep progress going this week. It was 4 pm when he popped his first set. He figured he could get one more oxy and maybe two more relaxers that night.

Patty had installed a secure messaging app on their phones. Sean messaged the team to come over. Despite coming from different parts of the city, Kenny and Patty arrived almost simultaneously. Kenny was walking up from 43rd as Patty was walking down from 41st. Each picked up their pace to reach the door first. Sean could see each coming from the panoramic front window. He buzzed the gate open.

"Patty, that app works better than the bat signal."

Patty didn't get it, "Huh."

Kenny exclaimed, "When the Commissioner shined the Bat Signal, Batman and Robin would race to the spot."

"Oh."

Kenny asked, "How'd you do today? How do you feel?"

Sean pulled up his shirt.

Patty gasped, "Looks like you've been in a knife fight."

Sean replied, "Yeah. That's a better story than I had micro-surgery."

Kenny knew what was next, "What kind of meds are you on? Are you whacked out?"

"A muscle relaxer and a pain-reliever. I can't lift hardly anything for two weeks. You two should keep an eye on my decision-making. I shouldn't drink on top of the pills. I've had surgeries in the past, I usually get off the pills before the prescription runs out."

That was good enough for Kenny, "OK. Mind if I raid

your fridge?"

"Go for it. I'm not cooking for you tonight."

"How 'bout a ham and cheese, Patty?"

"Sounds good."

"Mayo and what kind of mustard? Looks like he's got French's, Gulden's and some bougie French stuff."

"Mayo is fine."

"Patty, Patty, Patty. Live a little. The mustard will put hair on your chest. I'll set you up."

Kenny eyeballed the sliced sourdough round and the toaster; the slices were huge compared to the depth of the 4-slice machine. He would have to toast one side of the bread, flip, then toast the other. The resulting toast had a one-inch swath in the middle twice as dark as the rest. Kenny assembled the sandwiches and sliced them through the dark swatch. He served the sandwiches with Harps.

"You are consistent, Sean." Kenny tipped his Harp towards Sean.

"Mmm, this mmm is really good, mmm." Patty was commenting with a full mouth.

"Take a breath." Sean cautioned. "I don't want you choking before the job is done."

Patty took a swig, "OK, Boss. Good to go."

"Alright then. Here is a pre-paid debit card. Untraceable. Purchased with cash. You can order Stanley Sullivan's birth certificate with it. Use 3717 Clement St., 94121 as the address. My mother's maiden name was Sullivan. We will use that as the address for Stanley and Oliver McGee. Mom's mailbox drops in her basement. I generally bring it up for her. She doesn't throw anything away before I see it."

"Cool. I'll do that right now." Patty set up shop at the

kitchen table.

"We will need social security cards before driver licenses. I've done some research. It seems most scammers either try and steal someone's identity or recycle the number of someone they find in the obituaries."

"Eww."

"We are not going to do that. Patty, check the coffee table. I found an interesting report last night."

Patty read the title and started leafing through the pages, "Social Security Administration, Data Center Optimization Initiative, Strategic Plan. ...This is incredible, Sean. ...National Support Center, Maryland; Second Support Center, North Carolina; Electronic Vault, Colorado. All are listed as Federal Security Level 4."

"I also found a description of the security levels."

Patty was familiar with the federal security levels, "Oh, yeah. A four that would be Special-Sensitive/High Risk. It means financial/identity risk rather than weaponry or terroristic. It gets the interest of men in suits rather than uniforms."

"We're going to need you to add a work history as well as a master record for each of us. There are some guidelines you will need to follow."

Patty was curious, "Lay them on me, Daddio."

Sean was leafing through a stack of papers, but he could not distinguish the Social Security papers from the other documents. He surveyed the coffee table, then the kitchen table, even the entryway table.

Sean was in pain and exasperated, "I can't find my readers. Has anyone seen them?"

Patty looked at Kenny who threw a nod and an eye-roll back.

Patty used a tone reserved for seniors and toddlers, "Ahh. They are on your head, Boss."

Sean reached to his forehead and muttered, "Who put those there?"

He proceeded, "Historically, the first three digits of social security numbers are state-based, the next two are issued formulaically and the last four are random until the 9,999 are expired. I'm going to need you to get into the database and search around our actual numbers to find a hole. That will keep the new numbers consistent with our ages."

Patty's head was nodding, and his fingers were dancing on the keyboard.

"Uh-huh. Uh-huh. I can do that. What else?"

"Work history. Here's a copy of my actual Social Security Earnings Statement. It's a record not so much of where I worked but how much I earned and contributed to social security over the years. Try and find some statistics about the average number of jobs held by workers of various ages. We want our records to blend into the masses. Stanley is so young a handful of retail and food service jobs should suffice. Oliver and Dan will need to show more stable employment. We will tie their employment however to defunct companies. It's hard to trace references when there's no there anymore."

Kenny shook his head, "I just checked the dictionary. Your photo is shown for 'evil genius'."

"Before we request replacement social security cards, though. We'll need you to crack the DMV Security Operations Center in or near Sacramento. It's a unit designed to protect the integrity of DMV data. The driver's license and birth certificates are considered evidentiary proof of identity."

"OK. Birth Certificates, Driver Licenses, Social Security Cards. Anything else?"

"You will need our thumbprints for DMV. Check the desk. In the back of the drawer, you will find an inkpad that I used back in the day of rubber stamps."

Patty laughed, "You kill me, man."

"After we have the domestics established, then we go after the passports and establishing bank accounts."

"Aye. Aye, sir."

The first round of relaxers and pain relief was fading. Kenny could see it in Sean's face.

"Where does it hurt?"

"From my knees to my nipples. Kenny, how are things from your end?"

"My nipples are fine. But seriously, I've learned some things. Have some ideas. Why don't we table it until tomorrow though? You can take your next set of meds and chill. I'd prefer you well rested and sharp."

"Damn. Voice of reason. What time is it?"

"Almost 7."

"You are probably right. Surgery and evil masterminding tires a guy out. Check with me tomorrow?"

They nodded in concurrence.

Chapter 11

Make-Up

Margaret wanted a withdrawal from her personal ATM before he left for work.

"Bernard, I need you to put €250 in my account. The girls and I are playing bridge this afternoon. If the game is good, you will be home before I am done."

"What happened to the €100 I gave you Monday?"

"Oh, you know. Bread, milk, potatoes. This and that."

He knew what 'this and that' was – online gambling. He checked her account from his phone. Sure enough €175 in online gambling deposits all over the world: Hong Kong, Belize, Africa. She might as well light the money with a match. She spent five times a week on what he did including his expense report.

"I have to give a progress report on the Banknote/Euro exchange program today."

"My God, are you still doing that? Why don't you just give €10 to every man, woman, and child and call it even."

"If it were only that simple."

*   *   *   *   *   *   *   *

Louis Dennehy, a former J2 officer and Flood's pet pick for Chief Enforcement and Anti-Money Laundering Officer was in the Deputy Governor's ear twenty minutes before the weekly staff meeting. He was fanning the flames.

"Cella, you have to do something about Sheridan. Every time I float an initiative he comes up with examples from the past as to why it wouldn't work."

Flood was ruthless and calculating.

"I know. He only has six months left. It would cost me too much political capital to take him on. He knows where the skeletons are buried. Hell, he buried half of them himself."

"What about a pre-retirement vacation?"

"That's what he's scheduled to start in six months. He's one of those dinosaurs that banked over a year's vacation time."

Dennehy was impatient, "We've got to do something about him now. Everyone looks his way for approval."

"If he were five years younger, he'd probably be your boss instead of me. I will keep my eyes open for an opportunity to get him out of our hair."

Sheridan had learned from her first departmental meeting. No coffee and a trip to the jacks before sitting down. The remaining two of Flood's direct reports arrived as Sheridan was claiming his seat at the other end of the table from the Deputy Governor, the other seat of power in the room. Dennehy, the Chief Enforcement and Anti-Money Laundering Officer, and Molloy, the Chief People Officer suffered from title inflation – business cards more impressive than paychecks. Timoney, Director of Performance was caught in the middle. She was a good soldier for the bank and knew the bank, but was not a Flood choice. Her age would hurt her on the open market and retirement was far off.

Sheridan poked the bear, "Are we late?"

Dennehy bit, "No, Cella and I were just strategizing."

Sheridan grinned as the other Directors shot forward eyebrows peaked. Flood's face flushed as she tried to regain control, "Dennehy and I were discussing internal and external threats – domestic and international. Why don't we proceed with the Enforcement report?"

Dennehy described system weaknesses in electronic monitoring, cost overruns in oversight, and recent fraud attempts. Sheridan caught himself leaning back in his chair hands folded behind his head stretching to crack the vertebra in his back. He thought, 'What a shite show. Thank God we are not a commercial bank with thousands of transactions daily.'

The Chief People Officer was next. The title reminded Sheridan of his father who had been a loan officer with the Bank of Ireland. Every loan officer's title read Vice President. That bank must have had 30 vice presidents. Molloy, CPO nee Director of Human Relations, had few issues with banking personnel. His struggles were acquiring and keeping Information Technology personnel.

Finally, Flood turned to actual banking issues Timoney's report on Finance & Business Performance was quite technical. Position of reserves, foreign investments, the value of the Euro overall and its value within Ireland. These reports actually required a trained eye to evaluate the state of affairs. Of course, the financials included Flood's hot-button line item the €350 million reserve for old banknote exchange. Flood jumped.

"Bernie, what's the status on getting money out of that black hole?"

Sheridan responded calmly, "As you can see the rate of exchange has been flat for years. There was a blip however following the 20th Anniversary of Ireland's adoption of the euro. I believe that can be attributed to the press coverage of the Anniversary and the realization that punts could still be exchanged."

Flood was not satisfied, "What does that mean?"

"It means the easy money. The money in everybody's pockets was exchanged early. If you want any movement, I will make three suggestions. First, relax the documentation requirement to exchanges of IR£ 10,000 or more. Second, allow the foreign exchanges to be completed by wire transfer in the receiver's currency. And third, I believe a broader broadcast of the fund needs to be put out there: internet, print & media. The question is, 'Will you spend €100,000 in hopes of 100-fold return?'"

"Where would you conduct this campaign?"

Sheridan would propose what he considered a preposterous idea. One he would never approve if he were the Deputy Governor.

"Well, there are millions of Irish in the United States, Canada, and Australia. Ireland was wrung dry with the Anniversary. An internet campaign costs the same wherever you target. I propose a one-month tour around those countries bringing the fund to light on Morning Chat Shows and the like. A real PR campaign."

Timoney stifled her laughter. Molloy sat dumbfounded. Flood and Dennehy were caught off guard. Flood stalled.

"And you think this could be done for €100,000?"

"Maybe less. I always tend to be a bit conservative when estimating cost."

"And who would be the spokesperson?"

"Well, that's your call Deputy Governor. Who do you think best represents the Central Bank of Ireland in this matter?"

By this point, Dennehy would do anything to be rid of

Sheridan for a month. Without invitation he offered.

"Ma'am, I think Director Sheridan is the most knowledgeable and well-spoken on the topic. He would make an excellent presenter."

He feigned, "Media relations really is not my strength."

Flood also seized the opportunity.

"I can authorize a project up to €250,000 before going to the board. Write it up. I want to see the proposal before the close of business tomorrow. You could be in the air next week. Is your passport current?"

Sheridan now hoisted on his own petard was not sure if his passport was valid. He was not sure whether it was at the office or home. "Are we done? I have some action items here."

"I don't know, Bernie. A little pancake make-up and some Grecian Formula in those eyebrows. You could be a regular on The Late Late. Timoney, Molloy would you be able to cover Regulatory Services day to day were he gone for a month."

Sheridan trusted his troops and did not want others meddling, "My direct reports are well established and could easily stay the course."

The meeting closed with the normal kumbaya platitudes. Sheridan had four immediate action items: 1. Find Passport; 2. Write Proposal; 3. Find Web Nerd Reporter; 4. Convince Margaret she can't come along.

Not only did Gertrude have his passport she renewed it last year when she noticed it was within six months of expiring. He outlined the proposal letter to Gertrude. She had worked for him for so many years she was more than capable of filling in the details. Often he would not even read her final draft, though he would today.

"Gertrude, the proposal is perfect. Thank you. I think you might be the best candidate to replace me when I retire. You know the job in and out, up and down."

"Aww. Thank you, Bernie. But that's a pair of pants I wouldn't want to slip into."

"Gertrude, you divil!"

*　　*　　*　　*　　*　　*　　*　　*

Margaret's eyes were the size of saucers as Sheridan described his upcoming business junket.

"Bernard, a whole month of traveling. I can't wait."

"Margaret it's not a vacation. I'm working. Like a press campaign. The bank is stretching to send me."

"But Bernie, a whole month apart!?!"

He said the right thing, but he had no intention of babysitting her on an international junke

"Margaret it will be living out of a suitcase, hotel after hotel, many flights and layovers."

"Sounds wonderful."

"As always the house bills will pay directly. I have arranged a weekly stipend for you which will load Sunday evenings. I will not have access to move funds like I do here." That was not exactly true, but he did not want to deal with her addictions while he was out of town. She could really spin out of control.

"But why can't I come?"

"The bank will not pay for your travel, lodging, or board. It would cost us tens of thousands of euros. And there's no guarantee I could ensure we would travel together."

"Well, I don't like it."

"It's not like it was my idea. The bank is just screwing

with the short timer. You know that bint Flood is threatened by me, and her boy Dennehy is jealous of my knowledge."

Bernard packed five dress shirts; Gertrude had called the cleaner and changed his shirt order to folded from hanging. He would travel in his Donegal tweed sport coat and had a suit bag for the two dark grey pinstripe suits. Boxers, undershirts, and socks were added as well. He packed the make-up kit beside his ditty bag. He leaned his new shillelagh against the suitcase. He found it comforting, a throwback to yesteryear.

"Whose makeup is this?"

"Mine. I was told to get some foundation. My dome is going to be on television, zoom and the internet. I don't want to blind the viewers."

"What if something happens to me while you are gone?"

He paused. Pondered briefly. Then responded the only reasonable way.

"Nothing's going to happen to you. Besides we can video chat every night when you go to bed."

"Don't be disgusting."

"Time difference, Margaret. You'll be 5-8 hours ahead of me when I'm in the Americas. And nine hours behind when I'm Down Under."

"I don't like this one bit." She was getting a bit pouty.

"It's business. No one cares if we like it."

"Who is going with you?"

"It's just me and a web journalist who will document the trip and promote the cause."

"Himbo or bimbo?"

"We have not decided yet. Either way, they'll have their own room. We're not bunking up like a high school football club."

"Will you be *entertaining*?"

"I'm not selling automobiles. This trip is about spreading the word and trying to get some cash out of the reserve fund."

"I bet."

Bernard bit his tongue. He wanted to lash out at her habit. 'I bet' indeed. He was willing to bet her first plea for funds would come before he landed in New York.

Chapter 12

Watermarks and Details

It was Sunday and Murphy Printing no longer required weekend runs. The production for the week would not last through Wednesday. The remaining workers were laid off so that they could collect unemployment. Kenny was compensating them in cash for the few hours a week he needed them. It was an arrangement which worked well for the employees. Kenny was taking his needs from the proceeds of the weekly Diocese jobs. It reminded him of being an altar boy and skimming $20 from the collection basket. Kenny and Patty were working on their own.

"Kenny, is Sean coming in today?"

"I talked to him last night. He's almost off the drugs. He is still on restriction: can't lift anything, and has to watch his activity, watch his pee for blood and solids. He thought he might be able to come in tomorrow."

"Uh-Oh! That doesn't sound good."

"Everyone is prone to overreaction these days. Let's just stay on track. I had the banknote deep scanned. We have proprietary software for digital jobs and creating the printing plates."

"I see the software. Let me ferret around here for a minute to get a better feel for it. I did use it for the birth certificates the other day."

"So, if you look at a bill it is not printed in one fell swoop. For the series A, there are four steps. I need you to take that flat image and extract the four layers."

"Uh-huh."

"I will describe them from the last process to first, this

applies to front and back. So, the last layer is letterpress printing of the serial number, seal, and signatures. The second to last layer is the intricate engraved intaglio printing. The third layer down is the background – offset printed. And the first layer we will need is the watermark. It's actually embedded during paper production. No ink is used when the watermark is rolled."

"What's the difference?"

"Letterset printing is performed with raised images like typeset. Offset printing is an image transfer process like lithography if you know what that means. Intaglio printing is accomplished with a sunken or engraved image and engravers have historically been considered artists. The software and 3D printers allow us to circumvent much of the hand work."

"Is all that necessary? Today's printers are pretty damn good."

"Not good enough to not get caught. C'mon there is something I haven't got worked out quite yet."

On the production floor the printers were quiet Kenny had set up two folding tables. One had two sheet pans filled with an inch of water. The other had two more sheet pans sitting on hot plates which were also filled with an inch of water. Each pan contained two sheets of Fireman's Fund Stock Certificate printing sheets. Patty was intrigued and confused.

"What do we have going on here Bill Nye?"

"Bill Nye, The Science Guy, nice reference. Where did you find that?"

"My Uncle Pat is a nerd also. You should hear him talk about the science behind a good cup of coffee."

"Watermarks are normally impressed as part of the paper-making process. I'm trying to loosen the pulp just enough so that I can impregnate a watermark but not have the paper go completely to mush."

"Why two pans on each table?"

"The second pan on each table has baking soda added to raise the pH level. It is supposed to accelerate the loosening of the fibers."

"And the hot plates?"

"Same thing compresses the time and enhances the pliability. I can get two or three stock certificates out of each sheet. I figure six banknotes per sheet."

Patty was quick with arithmetic, "Three million pounds is thirty thousand notes. At six notes per sheet that would be five thousand sheets. Damn! That's going to take a while."

"I'm just trying to figure out the science, the mechanics right now. We can ramp up the production system once we know it can be done. If I don't figure this out we are dead in the water, so to speak."

"So, if you figure out how to make the paper pliable how will you implement the watermark?"

"I believe running the wet stock through the offset printer dry can imbed the watermark. By dry I mean without ink. You should be able to peel away the other layers on the scan and have the watermark image. It is supposed to be the 'Head of Erin' to the right and the letters 'LTN'."

"When I get back to the office I can lay out the individual components of the bill."

Kenny corrected, "You mean banknote."

"Right. Banknote. You can then tell me which machines we need to use to produce the plates/screens whatever for the different printers."

Patty returned to the office while Kenny continued to

experiment with the soaking rag paper. The room-temperature water trays did not offer any control over the process. It would take days to get to the proper state to accept the watermark. He believed the baking soda solution aided the process but wanted to try different temperatures to see if he could get a better result quicker.

Patty saw his job as three-fold at the moment: 1) Generate identification documents. 2) Support Kenny's technical needs for printing 'banknotes'. 3) Backfill histories should any of them get credit checked or investigated.

Patty reviewed his status. Birth certificates – check. Dan Reilly and Oliver McGee certificates printed. He needed Sean to check his mother's mail for the Stanley Sullivan certificate. He had tapped into the Social Security Administration Data Center and found Social Security numbers for each of them but was unsure how to coordinate the Social Security Cards and Driver Licenses.

"Kenny, did you understand what Sean was saying about coordinating the Social Security cards and Driver Licenses?"

"It was something about one driving the other particularly when asking for a replacement. I'm not sure though. Don't force it and mess things up. Why don't you just find your way into the databases? We can plant the data and request the replacements after we talk to Sean."

Patty pushed, "Do you think we can get to him today?"

"He's still on the drugs and probably pretty sore. We can check with him tomorrow. Let's go to Red's for a burger and a beer."

The Giants were on the road, so the foot traffic was not overwhelming. Patty was not used to walking around town.

"Why don't we use the electric scooters? They are everywhere."

"I'm not in the habit of paying $10 to save three minutes. It's the same reason I don't use the ride share services or worse yet the automated vehicles. Everyone is trying to get into your pocket or offer you a service to get your personal information. Now more than ever you need to be on your guard."

Patty nodded, "You got a point."

"Besides, I don't want to break my neck."

"Kenny, what are you going to do when we pull off Hibernia?"

"Just what I'm doing now. About half of my cut will go to buying the print shop. I'm too old to start at the bottom again. The rest I will just sit on. Patty, do you know the story of the greatest heist ever?"

"I don't know. Was it a bank, or jewels, or art?"

"Well, I don't know either. Because the greatest heist is the one that doesn't get solved. That doesn't get reported. That happens without anyone knowing."

"Wow. I hadn't thought of that before."

"The key is not tipping our hand. Living well but not extravagant. Not drawing attention to yourself. Not boasting about it."

"Damn. That's tough."

"Your probation doesn't allow you to even own a computer or smartphone right?"

"Yeah. I have another seven years if I don't screw it up. I can't even look for a job that interests me."

Kenny counseled Patty, "It's a discussion Sean and I have had. We know it will be tougher for you as you are younger. You may need to sit on your cut until you clear probation. Keep 'working' at Java Beach. When you are clear to relocate, the world may open up for you. Look, Sean and I will help. You just have to keep your cool. Any one of us gets too out of line and the whole jig is up."

"Hmm."

"Let's eat. We'll reach out to Sean tomorrow. ...The Giants are in second right now. They've finally gotten over the .500 hump. You think they can catch the Dodgers?"

Chapter 13

Purple Softballs

The pain had subsided to the point where Sean was determining whether he needed the pills or just liked the pills. He was glad the bottles were almost empty. He was under orders not to shower for a week. It was Sunday morning and the first time since the surgery where he wanted to put on his pants. He struggled with the buttons on his 501 jeans. He had hardly eaten since the surgery; it wasn't his belly.

Sean stepped out of his jeans and went to the bathroom where he turned on the light to check himself in the mirror. Horrors! His scrotum was a purple hairy softball. This could not be good. It was more uncomfortable than painful. Regardless, it was concerning. He had noticed they were redder and larger than normal yesterday. He was just hoping he would have more prodigious cajónes after the surgery. Doctor U's office was closed. He could ignore it, go to the Emergency Room, or call the nurse line.

It appeared to be getting darker by the moment. Now that he had seen it he could not stop checking it. What if it popped? Maybe something hadn't been sealed properly? His younger self would have been mortified to seek help for the purple, fuzzy softball. Now he just wanted his peach golf balls back. He opted to call the Emergency Room.

"I had double hernia surgery last week and something's not right. I think I need someone to look at this today."

"Are you in pain?"

"Not really."

"Is there blood in your urine?"

"A bit. That was worse right after the surgery."

"Then what seems to be the problem?"

"My balls have quintupled in size and they're dark purple."

"What color are they normally?"

"Pink."

"I'll check with the head nurse. Can you hold for a moment?"

"Do I have a choice?"

There was no hold music. As the minutes passed Sean wondered if he had been forgotten. He debated hanging up and calling back but figured he would just be put on hold again. He stuck it out.

"Are you still there? Sorry for the long wait."

"I'm here."

"The medical staff were baffled. They agreed you should come in right away."

"Alright. On my way."

Sean was commando under his basketball shorts. He drove himself to the Emergency Room each time he engaged the clutch there was a squeeze of the softball. He cautiously completed the quarter-mile walk from the parking lot. He had the same embarrassing discussion about his groin with the receptionist who was more interested in his insurance.

As he waited his thoughts turned to Hibernia. Had Kenny cracked the puzzle of printing the banknotes? Had Patty tapped the systems without raising any alarms? Was he going to be on the shelf for an extended period. He did not want the project to lose momentum. Apparently, his condition bumped him up on the priority list as his wait for an examination room was only 23 minutes.

"McAuliffe! Sean McAuliffe!"

Sean recognized the voice.

"Azealia? What are you doing here?"

"I like the overtime. And the emergency room is a change of pace from the vitals and shaving gig."

She ushered him and the computer cart into an examination bay, pulled the curtain not quite shut and took his vitals. Clickity-clack filled the air as her fingers flew over the keyboard. Without looking up she inquired.

"Are you in pain? Do you need more meds?"

"Not particularly."

"Are the wounds weeping? Did you get the staples wet?"

"No. I haven't showered."

"Well, what is it then? I know you didn't come here today cause you missed me."

"It's embarrassing. I'm swollen."

"Let me see. Drop your shorts. ..."

Azealia's air of professionalism disappeared. She gasped and blinked her eyes. The rubber gloves snapped as she wriggled her fingers into place. She came in for a closer look but didn't touch. Under her breath he heard.

"¡Ay Dios mío!"

Azealia collected herself and went in for another look. This time she gingerly poked at the softball.

"Does that hurt?"

"Not particularly."

"Don't worry, Sean McAuliffe. Let's have the doctor take a look at it. Just relax. It will be a few minutes before she can get here. You can pull your shorts up if you like. Or not if the air feels good."

Sean pondered her last comment for a few minutes

before pulling up his shorts. He needed to pee but was not sure where the lavatory was located. Also, he felt uncomfortable roaming the halls of the Emergency Room unauthorized. Azealia popped her head into the bay to let him know he was the penultimate patient. She laughed at his current consternation and pointed him towards relief.

The doctor finally entered. Wearing crocs, jeans, and a University of California t-shirt she looked more graduate student than doctor. She did not look thirty years old. Azealia however was whispering to her in a manner which suggested respect. The doctor was nodding her head as she was briefed on his situation.

"Well, Mr. McAuliffe you had some surgery earlier this week. And you are concerned about your recovery. Let's take a look. May I help you with those shorts?"

He thought, 'I'm not an invalid.' As he reached for his waistband the doctor dropped his pants. She was aghast at the site of the purple softball.

"Uh. Uh. Are you in pain?

"No."

She pulled a set of gloves from the wall.

"I'm going to have to inspect those."

She used her index finger to poke the purple pumpkin from all sides.

"Does that hurt?"

"No. I couldn't even feel it."

The doctor gave it a squeeze. It felt like a warm, heavy water balloon. She had not seen anything like this in her three years of practice. She tried to be comforting, but her advice was generic.

"I have never seen anything like this before. Take it easy the rest of today and see your surgeon in the morning. Let them know that you came to the Emergency

Room. I hesitate to drain it or prescribe anything. I don't know what would reduce the swelling. Whatever you do, don't fiddle with it. Any questions?"

"No. Apparently, I will live, and it does not seem to be falling off."

The doctor exited and left Azealia to discharge Sean.

"I've made an appointment for you with Dr. U at 9 tomorrow morning. Can you make it?"

"Yes. I'll reschedule any conflicts."

"Go home. Straight home. Try and stay off your feet. If you don't have food ready to eat, order something delivered. Are you done with your meds?"

"I'm at the end of the bottles."

"Take it if you need it. Flush 'em if you don't. No booze tonight. And do you remember what the doctor told you.?"

"Don't fiddle with it."

"Yes. And don't let anyone else fiddle with it either."

Sean requested the orderly wheel him all the way to his car. Normally, he enjoys driving the manual transmission Cougar around the City taking particular pride in managing the clutch on the many hills. Today, though, he was concentrating on the squeeze each shift put on the softball. He grabbed both handrails and pulled himself up the stairs inch by inch as though he were climbing the cable on the Golden Gate Bridge.

The cupboards were bare, and the refrigerator only had a half serving of his homemade chili left. There was no cheese to grate or onions to dice. He did not have or eat frozen meals. He had not had breakfast or lunch; his stomach was growling. Flanahan's did not normally deliver, but he would call and plead his case.

"Flanahan's. Stephen speaking."

"Stephen, it's Sean."

"Sean, you winker. How the hell are 'ya? When will you be able to get your arse in here?"

"Not sure. I spent the day in the Emergency Room."

"What happened? Did the wounds open?"

"No. This morning I was trying to put on my jeans, and my bollocks looked like a pair of dark purple sliotars."

"No shit! What can we do for you?"

"I was hoping I could order a meal for delivery. I know that's not normally your thing."

"No problem, Sean. What would you like?"

"I've been vacillating between a corned beef sandwich and a leg'o'lamb dinner."

"How 'bout a lamb sandwich with chips?"

"Of course. The doc told me no booze. Could you add a six-pack of Harp to the order?"

"Makes sense."

"Do you want my credit card number?"

"No, Sean. This one is on Flanahan's. You're still on Rivera, right?"

"Sure am. 3424 with the Cougar out front. Thanks, Mate."

Stephen wrote up the order with the note, 'Delivery, Gratis.' He hailed Francess to run the ticket to the kitchen. Her eyebrows shot up as she read it.

"Delivery? Free? What's gotten into you?"

"It's for a sick friend."

She turned the order over and read the address.

"3400 block of Rivera. That's Sean's house."

"How'd you know that?"

She lied, "He had a few too many one night. I rolled him home so he wouldn't hurt himself or get popped by the cops. …What's wrong? Didn't he have surgery last week?"

"Complications. He went to the Emergency Room. They couldn't really help him. He sees his surgeon in the morning."

"I'm almost off. I can make the delivery. You know I was a nursing assistant back home."

"Sounds good. If not you, I'd have to bribe one of the sots or lose my dishwasher for God knows how long."

Stephen pulled a chilled six-pack of Harp from the walk-in cooler as Francess packed the sandwich and chips in an aluminum pie tin. She scoffed at Stephen and returned the Harp to the cooler pulling a 2-liter bottle of cola instead.

In a maternal tone directed at Stephen and Sean in his absence she scolded, "I know that wasn't doctor's orders."

Sheepishly, Stephen explained, "Sean said the doctor advised no booze. He figured a few Harps was basically soda which is kind of the way I think about it too."

Francess was still shaking her head as she left Flanahan's for Rivera Street. It had been twenty minutes since Sean had placed the order. It would take her only five minutes to be at Sean's iron security gate.

Bzzzzz. Bzzzzz.

'That was fast,' thought Sean. It hadn't been half an hour since he spoke with Stephen. He had to ease his way off the couch. The button to release the gate was next to the front door only 18 feet away, but it could have been a quarter mile as fast as he was moving.

Bzzzzz. Bzzzzz.

"I'm coming. I'm coming. Hold your horses."

He released the gate and left the front door ajar. As he

shuffled back to the couch he could hear footsteps bouncing up the stairs. He called out to the delivery person.

"Door's open. Would you mind bringing it in the house?"

"No, Sean. I would not mind bringing it in the house."

"Francess!?!"

"Well, you haven't lost your powers of observation. Apparently, you've lost my phone number."

"Huh."

"You should have called me if you had problems. I told you I was a nursing assistant."

"It's embarrassing. And I was hoping you would be introduced to this area under better circumstances."

"I see. Trust me, Sean. I've seen it all."

"I don't know the Emergency Room staff was shocked. Heh, where's my Harp?"

"You're not cleared for Harp yet. Be thankful I brought you soda."

Francess popped the chips in the microwave for thirty seconds, placed the sandwich on a real plate, and poured two glasses of soda.

"Francess, you don't have to serve me here."

"Shut up! You could barely get the door open. What are you watching?"

"The Giants game. They are in town tonight."

"Slide over."

She settled in next to him dropping her head on his shoulder. He wanted to tell her all about Hibernia. How he would be set for the rest of his life, have something to leave for his children, how he was helping his cohorts. How he could take her away from the bar. Sean stopped and scolded himself in his mind, 'Focus, Sean. Focus.

You are thinking about doing just what you told the others not to do. Use your mind not your heart, Dummy.'

He would stay in the moment focusing on Francess rather than the project or his now almost black softball.

"I haven't showered in a week. I must be funky."

"We were all funky in the 70's. Are you asking me for a sponge bath?"

"Are you offering?"

"Maybe."

Sean cautioned, "It's shocking."

"You're just like the boys in Ireland. Scared when you get a little colorful and swollen."

"How'd you know? It's huge and purple."

"I'll be right back."

Francess disappeared on a scavenger hunt. Sean finished his sandwich and realized he had missed five innings. It was the 7th inning stretch and the score was tied 3-3. The remote was out of his reach so he was trapped by commercials full of side effects, charitable guilt, and order a second for a separate fee. The news tease caught his attention, "After the game tonight we preview Friday's feature on found money."

"Oh, my," was all Sean could utter when she emerged from the hallway. Francess had been in his closet and all she was wearing was his button-down periwinkle shirt. The contrast to her dark skin was striking. She was carrying a pot of hot water and two washcloths.

"Have you ever had a sponge bath before?"

"No."

"You are in for a treat. Let's get those clothes off."

She pulled his shirt over his head and removed his shorts in one fell swoop. Even at the swollen sight, she kept her cool.

"Well, I guess I'm safe tonight. What time is your appointment tomorrow?"

"Nine-thirty."

The sponge bath was far better than any lap dance he had ever had. She had cleaned him from tip to toe, front and back. She had just the right touch for his manhood – cleaning without fiddling. Oh, how he wished he was operating at 100%.

"Francess, this really isn't fair."

"I know. I'm pretty sure you are going to be alright. But just to be safe, I'm going to see that you get to your appointment on time. Is your game over? If it isn't, we can watch the rest in bed. I saw that you have a television in the bedroom."

"I don't know. I haven't been able to concentrate tonight. And it's not the drugs."

The game was in extra innings. They retired to the bedroom. He had changed from basketball shorts to soccer shorts the legs weren't as long and the material was silk-like. She was still wearing his dress shirt. He undid the top four buttons. She smiled. His spirits were surprisingly upbeat.

Brandon Crawford, the longest-tenured Giant, hit a walk-off homer in the bottom of the 11th to win the game. Chalk one up for the old guys. The post-game show was truncated as the game had extended past its time slot.

The news opened with the tease that caught his attention earlier.

"Next week, Mornings on Two will have Bernard Sheridan, Director of Currency Central Bank of Ireland in studio discussing how millions of euros are set aside just waiting to be exchanged for old Irish banknotes."

"Did you see that, Sean?"

"What?" Sean had definitely seen that but did not want to let Francess know he cared.

"That man from Ireland who will be in town next week played football against Stephen in the All-Ireland Football Final."

"You're kidding."

"No. Stephen played goalie for Dublin. And that guy was a forward for Kerry. Stephen said they hadn't crossed paths for years but left him a message at Channel 2. He invited him to Flanahan's for a whiskey and a pint."

Between Sheridan's upcoming visit and Francess' presence, he would not sleep a wink. She had fallen fast asleep. She did not snore. He snuggled up close and slid his hand inside his shirt the one Francess was wearing.

Chapter 14

Takes Steam to Make a Burrito

Sean's nostrils filled with the aroma of bacon. His periwinkle shirt was at the foot of the bed. Francess was no longer by his side. He wondered if she was cooking on the stovetop or in the oven. He liked to use the oven as the grease was better contained and the bacon stayed flat. It didn't matter he was not used to having someone cook for him.

He peeked under the covers; he could not tell. He turned on the overhead and the vanity lights in the bathroom for the self-examination. The softball had not become a shot put. The color was shocking though black through purple to indigo to a greenish-yellow ring. He eased his freak show into a loose-fitting pair of khakis and proceeded to the kitchen.

"What have we here?" It was breakfast obviously.

"I don't like to cook at my apartment. My roommates are animals. I thought I'd make you a breakfast sandwich. You don't have any sliced bread. I did find a loaf of sourdough. I had to slice it myself." She plunged down both sides of the 4-piece toaster.

"Oh, yeah. That's my bread. I've kept a sourdough starter going for four years now. I don't have any pets or plants. Just me and the sourdough starter."

"I poured you some pineapple-orange juice. On the counter over here. I could only find the coffee mugs." She used a fork to flip the bacon. He grabbed one of the mugs and took a gulp. There was no tang nor sweetness. The viscosity was wrong. He gagged.

"Nooo!" She screamed. "That was egg."

He swished juice to get the raw egg goo out of his mouth. Earlier she had whisked the eggs in another coffee mug ala Dustin Hoffman in *Kramer vs. Kramer*.

She freshly grated cheese just as he would have. The sandwich hit the spot.

"You know you don't have to take me to the appointment. I can drive myself."

"You could, but you won't. I didn't spend the night for you to bail on your appointment and go play with your friends. I have time before I go to work. Now ease your bones on down the stairs."

"Yes, Francess."

* * * * * * * *

The doctor took one look at him and laughed. He said it was normal and apologized for not warning him. Although the incisions seemed insignificant, the hernia repairs with mesh were serious surgery. There was a significant amount of bleeding during the surgery, and it was settling at the lowest point. The swelling would subside in seven to ten days. The color show would go on for weeks.

Francess wanted the diagnosis, "What did the doctor say, Sean?"

"It happens. The blood from the surgery is settling in my spheres. The swelling will go down in about 10 days. The kaleidoscope will keep turning for weeks. Eventually, this will all be history."

"Did he give you any instructions?"

"Absolutely no lifting. No strenuous walking. The painkillers are done. I can finish out the regimen of muscle relaxers. Other than that, I can ease myself back to daily activities. Can you drop me off downtown?"

"No. I'm taking you to your place. And FYI I took your car keys while you were asleep. I'll give them back to you when your softball resembles a baseball."

"How will you know?"

She winked. "Examination."

"I see."

"No. I will see."

Sean put his cell phone into secure mode and prepared a text for Kenny and Patty. '*OK, boys. Off the drugs. Not cleared to come in and work a full day. Come to my house at noon. Bring hot food, cold Harp, and updates.*'

Duhh-da-da-Dun. Duhh-da-da-Dun.

"That's quite the ringtone. Who is texting you right now?"

"That was the theme from Dragnet. It was the people I owe money to. They want to make sure I'll live to pay them off." He was not in debt to anyone.

"My alarm tone is the theme of *Mission Impossible*. Can't wait for you to hear it."

"Well, maybe when you can fiddle again I will hear it. Now get your arse upstairs, I need to get to work."

*　*　*　*　*　*　*　*

Much to Sean's surprise, Patty arrived first. He pulled three Mission-style burritos from the Chrome messenger bag, then the complimentary bag of chips with three personal containers of medium salsa. Finally, he withdrew the team's computer. Sean inspected it for salsa and bean juice.

"You could have gotten a bag for the food."

"They want fifty cents for the bag!"

"You're starting to sound like Kenny and me. I'll put the burritos in the oven to keep them warm. Patty, I think this is the first time you have arrived anywhere first and early to boot."

"I had enough of Kenny giving me grief about being unprofessional and calling me a slacker. Worse, every time I showed up late he would make me empty trash or sweep floors before I could get to real work."

Sean did not see it as punishment, "We need to keep the print shop in good order for Hibernia. Anyway, it's not like we can contract for janitorial services. Keep up on the punctuality else next time he might assign you to clean the toilets."

"Aggh!"

"How are you getting along with Kenny?"

"Did you know he's a mechanical genius over and above a master printer? He maintains all the machines at the print shop on his own. He comes off as blue collar but he's sharp."

"He is intelligent, street smart, and well-read. He has a lifetime of experience."

"Yeah. I am appreciating you guys and my Uncle Pat more and more."

"Patty, I talked to your uncle on the way back from the hospital. I'd like to pay for your legal fees to get you off probation if we pull this off."

Patty's stake was growing, "Sean, I thought about doing that, but I didn't want to tip our hand, draw attention to us."

"I'll set it up with the lawyer as an anonymous trust, untraceable."

"I don't know what to say."

"Say, you'll get to work. Now, are you having any

difficulties? We need to get moving so that the passports have time to arrive."

"I'm in all the data banks but I'm still confused about the order in which I need to order the documents without raising red flags. It seems like you can't legitimately get these at the same time."

"First, there's nothing legitimate about this. Second, you are correct. It is confusing. Let me draw it out on a piece of paper, old school."

Sean rummaged through his desk drawers until he found the transparent green plastic template. It was the template with which he drew flowcharts before personal computers and project management software. He had drafting (drafted) triangles and a French curve for straight and non-linear lines. Everything started with the birth certificate. Next was the social security numbers (which Patty had identified). With the birth certificate, a social security number, and mail they could get driver's licenses. The driver's licenses could then be used, with birth certificates, to order replacement social security cards. Finally, the birth certificate, driver's license and social security cards would allow duplicate passports to be issued.

Patty looked at the chart, turned his head to one side then the other, and tilted the paper as if that would help. Sean dove back into the drawer for a set of colored pencils. Patty was mesmerized as Sean sharpened the dull red, blue, and orange pencils with an electric sharpener. Sean took the paper back and colored the connections in order of operation.

"Here, let me color code the relationships. I am going to sequence the operation in the spectrum of light, Roy G. Biv."

"Roy G. Biv?"

"It's a mnemonic."

"What's a mnemonic?"

"It's like using shorthand to remember something. Roy G. Biv: red, orange, yellow, green, blue, indigo, violet. The spectrum of light, the colors of the rainbow. Just organize the work based on that order of colors."

"I can do that."

Sean could sense a change in Patty. The work had become more manageable, and Sean's support increased his resolve.

"Sean are you going to be alright?"

"Most people lament the functions they've lost. I can't do anything about turning the clock back. Physically, I'm just trying to hold my own. Intellectually, planning and executing this project is a Godsend."

Bzzz. Bzzz.

"That's Kenny. Let's keep my offer to pay for the attorney between us. Can you hit the release by the front door?"

Kenny barreled in with a six-pack of Harp in each hand.

"Sorry, I'm late. I had to repair the digital printer and complete the Church Bulletins for the Marin churches. The greater Bay Area gets dispatched on Monday, Tuesday, and the City on Wednesday. I was on my way over when I remembered the Harp. You're done with the pain meds right?"

"Yes. At the end of the muscle relaxers too. A Harp or two just sounded so damn good. Patty, could you get the burritos out of the oven."

Patty divvied up the burritos: lengua, black beans, and mild sauce for Sean; ground beef, refried beans, and hot sauce for Kenny; carnitas, no beans, verde sauce for himself. Sean removed all the foil and laid out paper towels for the drips. Kenny had a bottle of Cholula sauce in his jacket. Patty inhaled the burrito; he had to pick some of the foil out of his teeth. Sean tried to steer the conversation to sports, but Kenny was not having that.

"You don't seem to be on your deathbed. What happened?"

"An unexpected side effect for me that the doc said was not uncommon."

"Side effects like diarrhoea, nausea, dizziness, constipation, and drowsiness don't send you to the ER. What happened?"

"Alright. Alright. Clearly, you won't let this go. And believe me, I don't want you holding onto it. My ball sack swelled to the size of a slow-pitch softball and turned deep purple."

Patty gagged. Burrito was caught in his windpipe. He gasped for air. Kenny's blows on his back freed the burrito. Kenny handed him a beer to calm down.

Kenny blurted out what was on his and Patty's minds, "Damn, Sean. Are you kidding me? Let's see."

"Hell no! My testicles are reserved for medical professionals, myself, and ladies who mean business."

"Speaking of ladies who mean business, you and Francess seem to be hitting it off."

"I like her. She has not been read in on Hibernia. She knows Ireland. She helped us with the real banknote. I trust her but would not bring anyone into the program without you two knowing about it. A time may come when we need help. We are not there yet."

"Kenny, Patty got here early today. He's picking up some good habits from you. We reviewed his progress, and I gave him some insight to help with the documents. Did you catch the news after the game last night?"

"No."

"Well, the Currency Director for the Central Bank is on a promotional tour. He is due to visit San Francisco later this week. Francess overheard Stephen saying he invited him to Flanahan's. Apparently, they were Gaelic football foes back in the day."

"No shit. We better get the real IR£ 100 banknote back to Flanahan's." Kenny did not want the color copy discovered.

"No. No. I'd rather us put one of our Hibernia notes in the frame. It will be our first chance to test our product at very little risk. Also, I'd like to bug Flanahan's so that we can listen in on the conversation."

Patty could not speak as he had just shoved the end of the burrito in his mouth. He grunted and swung his arms to garner attention.

Kenny calmed him, "Relax man. Relax. Finish your bite."

"I can set up a dynamic listening studio there. I can plant software on anyone within range of Flanahan's free Wi-Fi – Stephen, Francess, rest of staff, customers. I can build in a self-destruct timer so that the app disappears. We can capture sound even if the subject moves about the room."

"Perfect. Kenny, can we have a Hibernia note in time?"

He gave an honest appraisal, "I don't know. I'm having a problem with the watermark. I need to loosen the fibers of the stock so that I can roll in the watermark. I need a process that I can control. I've tried cold soaks, hot soaks each with and without a baking soda solution.

The hot soak with soda has gotten me closer but I need to push it over the top."

Sean feared they would trip at step one.

"Look if we can't secure the watermark, we have nothing to build upon."

"I know. I know."

Patty, fearing he was out of his league, offered almost inaudibly, "You know they use big steamers to soften the tortillas when they make burritos."

Kenny had the death stare for Patty. There was silence for twenty seconds. The death stare was broken with a grin.

"You may be on to something there, son. Our blanks are larger than a super-size tortilla though. I need something bigger. A pants press would be long enough, but the width is too narrow."

Sean watched as Patty and Kenny brainstormed. He had seen this phenomenon before. The individual members of the project were acting to the common goal. The barriers of responsibility faded. There was no '*That's not my job*' attitude. Sean let them exhaust their imaginations – tortilla steamer, pants press, city steam pipes, bamboo steamer, sauna. When the brainstorming lost steam, Sean joined the conversation.

"I remember when we moved back from Hawaii in the 1990s. We bought a house in San Carlos with God-awful wallpaper. My wife at the time said we could take that down, remove the panelling and paint no big deal. It was a big deal, but I did learn how to remove wallpaper. We rented a steamer designed to loosen the glue in big sections. You quickly followed behind the steam hit with a scraper. The wallpaper came right off. The unit consisted of a tank of water, a burner to generate the steam, a hose, and a plate to deliver the steam. You'll probably find the biggest ones at a tool rental store. Check it out."

Kenny shook his head and rolled his eyes, "Why didn't you tell us that story in the first place?"

Sean smiled, "I enjoyed the process. It brought me back to another time."

While Kenny and Sean gave each other grief, Patty had researched wallpaper steamers.

"Here. Look. They are just like he described. The old ones could be large enough."

Kenny peered over his shoulder. Sure enough. They were both right.

"Damn. That might do the trick. Patty, do you still have money on the pre-paid card? Can you rent one of those on your way back to Murphy's? You are going back today aren't you?"

"That's the plan. There is money, I will pick one up. I better get going."

As Patty took his leave he shook hands with Kenny and Sean. He no longer fist-bumped or peaced-out. He was starting to act like a man.

"Kenny, what do you think of our boy?"

"He's come a long way. He's actually helping me at the print shop. I'll need an assistant for the production run. He's the leading candidate right now. You are a distant second although you may be our gofer. You know go for this, go for that."

"That's my read also. My intel says Sheridan, that's the Currency Director, will be at Flanahan's Friday afternoon, evening. If you can print the Hibernia note, we can make the switch Thursday. If you can't, then we'll have to swap the original back."

Kenny nodded, "I should know by tonight."

"I helped Patty sort out the order to go about creating our documentation. Expect the passports in 8-10 weeks. Can you meet that schedule?"

"If I could just get the watermark down, the rest of the steps are already set. The banknote production should not be a problem. We will still have to create the phony bank documents to back your story."

"Kenny, how are things with Old Man Murphy? Is he still being patient with you? Do you still have the six months?"

"I do. I love that shop. I just want to breathe life back into it and find someone I could groom for twenty years."

Sean acknowledged his goal, "Noble. Is the price still $400,000?"

"Yeah. Almost half my share."

"I don't think it's fair that you have to use that much for the shop. I'd like to make a $200,000 donation to the Durkin-Murphy fund at the conclusion of Hibernia."

"Sean, are you kidding me? I don't believe it."

"I'm serious. That will cut your investment in half. Give you more breathing room. Let you buy new equipment or improve the building."

"I don't know what to say."

"Say, '*Sean, please excuse me but I have three million pounds to print.*'"

"Sean, please excuse me but I have three million pounds to print."

Sean emphasized the criticality, "All this is moot if we can't nail this watermark. I mean the whole exercise will be a big jerk off."

Kenny sighed, "I know. I know. No print shop. Patty will be stuck at the coffee shop. An you... I don't know what will become of you."

Chapter 15

Step Into My Office

The clickety-clack of female heels could not be misinterpreted. The clerk seated in the jack went silent. He finished his business and egressed without washing his hands. The security guard at the urinal nearly missed. Flood and Dennehy took it all in the marble countertops, the chrome fixtures, and the aged subway tile. They counted the urinals and stalls.

Although it had nothing to do with his position, Dennehy shared the revised plans he had ordered for the Executive Floor. It included new facilities for women, equating the square footage and flush count to that of the men, and a facility for non-binary employees outfitted in grand splendor. The non-binary facility would be located in what was currently Bernard Sheridan's office. It was two weeks before Sheridan's return.

"Cella, I hired an office design firm. After analysis of our project and their construction resources, they could start at the drop of a hat. The project would take four weeks. It would start with the demolition of Sheridan's office."

She laughed, "That should take the crease out of his pants."

They exited the men's lieu and paced the floor taking note of new soft walls needed and cubicles shuffled. Sheridan's charges would be moved away from the windows and shoehorned near the elevator and stairs. His smaller new office would be a combination of the current broom closet and copy room. Their conversation was hushed but imprudent.

"Louis, not having that dinosaur around has really let me put my stamp on things. He knows too much and does not give me my proper dues. Given that we are EU and on the euro I don't know why we even need him."

Dennehy was intimidated by Sheridan, "He has no respect for my position. He constantly scoffs at my programs. Let me open up a dossier on him. I could force him into early retirement. If I plant a scandal he could lose his pension."

"He's connected in the building it wouldn't be easy."

*　　*　　*　　*　　*　　*　　*　　*

Gertrude had caught wind of the proposed construction plans and was aghast at the disregard for Director Sheridan's authority. She had refrained from contacting him unduly until she saw them come from the men's loo and survey the floor. She was wary that Dennehy would be monitoring her communications, so she used her personal email to contact Sheridan's contracted assistant.

"Sir, sir."

"Just a minute, Ginny. I'm completing a transfer."

Sheridan completed the €200 transfer for his wife. He was two weeks into the four-week trip, and it was her fifth request for funds. The shopping and gambling were out of control. She had no concept that the faucet would run dry with retirement.

Ginny, Virginia O'Connor his tech aide, was concerned he might shoot the messenger, "Sir, I just received a rather disturbing email from Gertrude from her private email address. It did not say *'for your eyes only'*. Here it is."

She watched his knuckles turn white as his face turned

red. She was concerned he was going to pop a gasket. He closed his eyes to compose himself.

"Sir. Sir. Are you alright?"

"I'm fine."

He was not fine. People are never fine. They are good, bad, and sometimes indifferent. Fine is a conversation diverter. The Deputy Governor and her hired gun were ruining the end of his career. His lauded career was coming to a shite end. Between the new blood at the bank and the old blood at home, he was at wit's end. He took the blood pressure wrist cuff from his briefcase and affixed the device to his right wrist. He held his hand over his heart as the strap constricted. It seemed to take an inordinate amount of time to release the systolic reading. He turned the machine off and restarted it as he could not believe the first measurement. The second measurement 182/118 confirmed his stress level was off the chart. Not following prescribed usage, he popped two blood pressure pills and a shot of Jameson's.

"What time is our flight to San Francisco?"

"8 p.m. We have a car ordered for 4:30."

"Here's $300 from our travel petty cash. Why don't you get some things you could only get in New York?"

"Really. Thank you."

He was already tired of the junket. He knew it would not really generate much more exchange. The tour still had a week in San Francisco and a week in Australia. At least while he was in San Francisco he could trade some old war stories with his foe from last century Stephen O'Kane. It had been ages since he had seen an old football chum. He was tired of his job; he was tired of his marriage.

A thought kept running through his head. *'Millions*

of useless 20-year-old Irish pounds are out there and all those euros sit waiting. I deserve a piece of that action.'

Chapter 16

Punts for Pints

Kenny had furloughed the remaining crew with a month's wages in cash allowing the print floor to be configured for Hibernia without any prying eyes. Clotheslines were strung along the back of the shipping bay. Eighteen sheets of rag paper each bearing six of the elusive watermarks were drying. They had been there for 24 hours.

Kenny backed the Murphy Printing panel truck into the shipping bay. He had done this thousands of times. He centered the truck between the parking meter and the Brisbane Box tree. He eased it back until the bumper kissed the rubber blocks on the loading dock. Sean still being on hernia repair restriction felt a tad guilty as Patty struggled with the appliance dolly. They had *borrowed* Sean's mother's tumble dryer, a 1990s Kenmore. He had to make sure the dryer would be returned unharmed.

"Make sure the strap is tight then swing that lever over. It will add tension and marry the dolly to the dryer. Get the dolly handles as high up as you can reach. Pick your back foot up and lay all your weight back like you were popping a wheelie."

The dryer started to lift.

"That's it! Keep pulling. You're almost there."

The weight began to rest on the axle. Patty caught and balanced the load.

"I got it."

"Patty, Kenny wants the dryer on the other side of the letterpress printer beyond the sheet-cutting machine." He nodded his head to the far end of the print floor.

Sean took one of the sheets down. It was still moist.

He held it up toward the floodlight. The watermark was visible. The 'Head of Erin' from the statue Hibernia. He put on his readers and held the sheet close. The image was almost spot-on. Kenny read Sean's expression.

"What's wrong? I know it is still moist. First, I could not get it soft enough. Now, I need to speed up the drying."

"That's not it."

"What then? Is it the image?"

"Yes and no. Where's the real banknote?"

"It's in the office. Bring that sheet with you."

The office had a fluorescent light table for inspecting proofs. Kenny flipped the table on and laid the sheet down with the bill next to it. He saw it immediately.

"Shit!"

Erin was facing left on their print stock rather than right as on the bill. The image was flipped.

Sean was not angry, "I know. Details. It took so much to even be able to place the watermark and then the image is reversed. Got to watch the simple things. I have an idea what to do about the drying problem also. Let me make a phone call."

Kenny was concerned, "I'm going to need that fast. We only have three days to produce a Hibernia note or we'll have to give up the real deal."

"Get Patty back in here. Let him know we need to start over. Also, we need to know how he's doing about getting the bug together for Flanahan's."

Sean made the phone call as Kenny paged for Patty. The youngest member of Hibernia was champing at the bit.

"What's up guys?"

The light table was still lit and Sean wanted to test

Patty's powers of observation, "How's it look?"

"I've got the firmware update ready to load onto the wireless Wi-Fi router. Once it is installed I can control the microphones on any device which is connected. I only need a minute or two with the router. Do you know where it is at Flanahan's?"

"I believe it is in the banquet room where we took the pictures that first night. I will need you Wednesday or Thursday morning O'dark-thirty."

"Aye. Aye. Captain."

"Take a look at the light table."

"Huh?"

Kenny with a touch of exasperation, "Look at the light table."

Patty studied the rag sheet with the six watermarks. He got close looking for differences in the images. He spent a good three minutes certain he would find something. Why else would he have been directed to the table? He was experiencing the block that follows a closed mind. Sean was afraid they would be there a half-hour waiting for him to find it.

"Patty, look at the bill also."

He finally saw it, "Oh, man. She's looking the wrong way."

"No harm. No foul. We proved we could place a watermark. It's a good reminder to pay attention to the details. The little, simple things are the easiest to overlook."

Kenny groused, "If I can't get these sheets dry, we'll never get any banknotes this week and we certainly cannot go into production."

Sean grinned, "Oh ye of little faith. Go to 2010 Cesar Chavez Street. It's a supply house in the Produce District about 10 minutes away. Go to the loading dock in the back. Ask for Petey. Tell him Sean sent you. Bring straps."

*   *   *   *   *   *   *   *

Sean still could not do any work; he was able to bring the breakfast burritos – orange juice, no Harps. Kenny was used to working at 7am. Sean and Patty were not. The print shop floor was now configured for Hibernia. The folding tables had been replaced with stainless steel tables. Two wallpaper removal steamers sat ready with a baking soda solution. The batch oven Sean had acquisitioned was placed across from the letterpress printer. The oven, normally used for baking bread or pizza, was set with thirty racks for drying the watermarked sheets. The tumble dryer at the far end of the shop would be used to randomize the bills when restacked.

The goal for the day was a complete batch of thirty sheets, one hundred eighty IR£ 100 notes. They had eschewed the soaking trays for a full-blast six-minute steam. Patty was at the steam station working two sheets side by side simultaneously. He fed the pulpy blanks to Kenny who ran them through the letterpress printer dry, no ink, with the 'Head of Erin' image. Once through the letterpress printer, the sheets were placed in the oven. They 'baked' for 20 minutes at 315°.

Unbeknownst to Kenny and Patty, Sean conducted a time and motion study to evaluate the process as to the critical path. The 180 notes took roughly 40 minutes from steam to serial number.

Kenny stacked the sheets and fed them through the

three printers. First, the offset printer was used for the background on the front and back. Second, the intaglio printer, with olive ink, for the engraved portions. And finally, the letterpress printer for the seal, signature, and serial number. With only 180 notes they would not need to use the dryer to randomize the serial numbers.

The Hibernians retired to the office. Each held a half-dozen notes. Kenny also had the authentic note. Sean used a magnifying glass with his good eye. The note felt right to his touch. Patty was impressed with their work. Kenny took a jeweler's loupe for his review. He laid his six notes on the light table framing the real note.

"Umm-humph. Umm-humph. Umm-humph. They're damn good."

Sean took three Styrofoam cups from beside the coffee pot. He pulled three green airplane bottles from the front pocket of his hoodie. It was 9:45 in the morning and a celebratory toast was in order. Sean poured the three shots of Jameson. Patty had never been included in the hard drinking. He gave Sean a look.

"Gentlemen, pardon the glassware, but let me congratulate you on the production of such a fine note. I believe we are ready to test the waters. There's a good chance that Central Bank man will see our masterpiece. If it passes muster, we go into full production. So lift your glass. To Hibernia! Cheers!"

Kenny and Patty toasted, "To Hibernia! Cheers!"

*   *   *   *   *   *   *   *

In the parlance of burglars, Sean had 'cased' the joint. He really just paid attention. He had not needed to pump Stephen or Francess for information. Flanahan's was as much local watering hole as an Irish pub. There was no alarm on the door and no security cameras in or outside the building. They banked at the Wells Fargo up the street; there was no safe to rob.

It was approaching O'dark-thirty. A shadowy figure lurked at the gate. He pressed the button with the secret code. Bzzz-B-B-Bzzz-Bzzz. Sean gave the release button the reply code, Bz-Bz. Sean snickered a bit as he grabbed his 50-cent Andronico's paper bag. Even though he found the secret code inessential, he took his inspiration from *Get Smart* when he designed it, 'Shave and a Haircut – Two Bits'. The marble steps were wet with the early morning fog; Sean slipped. When his heel handed a jolt was sent through his back.

Sean raised his eyebrows as he looked over his accomplice: black referee shoes, black skinny jeans, black turtleneck, black beanie, black gloves, and black grease paint on his cheeks.

"Why are you dressed like that?"

"We're breaking and entering. This is my ninja outfit."

"First, we are not breaking anything. We are entering. That outfit is my pass as normal in the Haight or the Tenderloin. Here in the Avenues that look is going to draw attention."

"Sorry, Sean."

"What's on your face?"

"Black grease paint."

"Wipe it off. That could get you a beat down if the wrong person sees you. I've got some wipes in the car. And, please, no more skinny jeans. They make you look like a girl, and you cannot pick something up off the floor or run from the cops."

"Ok, Sean. Ok. You are starting to sound like my

Uncle."

Sean parked four short blocks west of Flanahan's at Ocean Beach.

"Why are we parked so far away?"

"I don't want my car to be seen in the neighborhood. Today's the day you can take a scooter. Use the prepaid card."

Sean unlocked the fixie bicycle he had staged earlier. He knew he no longer had the balance to ride an electric scooter.

Patty was impressed, "You ride a fixie? Shocking."

Sean held the paper bag in his right so that he could operate the left brake lever. Noriega had recently been paved so potholes were not an issue. They were able to use the center of the lane in the early hours. Sean set the pace. It took but a few minutes to be at Flanahan's back door.

The City never was quiet, but at this hour it was as close to silent as it could be. The streetcars did not run on Noriega; it was too far south to hear the foghorns. The Sunset did not have the 24-hour craziness of other districts which were overrun with drug use, prostitution, homelessness, and mental health sufferers.

"Patty, shine the light on the deadbolt."

Patty pulled a headlamp from his messenger bag, placed it over the beanie, switched it on and crouched in close to shine the light on the deadbolt.

"What are you doing?"

"You said shine some light on the deadbolt."

"I meant hold a flashlight on it not peer over my shoulder with garlic breath."

In one motion, Sean rapped Patty on the back of the head and pulled the lamp off his head. He handed Patty the $4.99 LED flashlight he had purchased at Safeway.

"Keep the light on my hands and the deadbolt."

Sean pulled what appeared to be a leather-clad grooming kit from his paper bag. It contained what appeared to be flattened allen wrenches and multiple dental probes.

"Are you going to pick the lock?"

"We're not going to break a window to get in. Now quiet. I need to concentrate. It's been a while since I've done this."

Sean took one of the flattened allens and used it to put some tension on the cylinder of the lock. He would rock one of the dental probes to push the tumbler pins one by one until they cleared the edge of the cylinder. He could feel the cylinder freeing a bit with each lined-up tumbler.

A siren screamed closer and closer. They froze. Patty panicked.

"What's that!?! We need to abort."

"Quiet!"

Sean listened. The siren passed. He felt the vibrations from the weight of the vehicle and roar of the engine.

"It was a fire truck. Calm down. Hold the light steady. I have to start over."

Sean reset the tension wrench and started to work the pins. He was solving the puzzle with his ears and touch. As the final pin slipped into place the cylinder turned. Sean exhaled. Patty shook his head.

"How did you learn that?"

"We're not that different. Where you hacked the high school information system to alter grades, I was picking the lock to the office and doctoring transcripts. Used to get into concerts and ballgames when we could find an unmonitored lock to pick."

Patty flipped the light switch just inside the back door.

"Noo!" whispered Sean, "No lights. Use the flashlight."

"Sorry."

"Take care of the router in the Banquet Room. I'm going to switch the banknote out."

Sean groped his way down the back hallway. He knocked over a crate of empty long necks. Thankfully the thick bottles clanked a racket but did not break. He reached the bar rail and followed it to the cash register. He stooped to pass under the bar counter.

Clank! His head hit the rail. The reverberation rang through the empty pub. Patty rushed out.

"Are you alright?"

"I hit my head on the rail. Get back to work."

Sean replaced the color copy of the IR£ 100 note with a Hibernia note. He grabbed a bar towel to see if he was bleeding. He was not, but a ping-pong sized knot was throbbing where his hairline used to be. With the frame returned to the wall, Sean went to check on his accomplice.

As Sean shone his flashlight across the room he saw butt crack. Patty was trying to read the IP address printed on the back of the router. The router was under a table which was holding cases of Old Bushmill, Jameson, and Smirnoff vodka. There was not enough cable to safely pull the router from the wall. The circulation was cut off to Patty's lower extremities.

"Hurry up. We need to get out of here."

"I'm trying to read the label on the back of the router. It's a tight squeeze down here."

"It's tight cause of those damn jeans you're wearing. Get out let me try."

Patty reverse crawled to extricate himself from under the liquor-laden table. Kenny took his place and approached with the flashlight in his mouth and cell phone in hand. Despite being thirty-plus years older than his technical advisor, Sean crawled towards the table. Bang! Jingle, jingle, jingle. He hit his head again. He saw stars for a moment.

"Damn!" he said under his breath.

"Sean, are you ok?"

"Shut up."

Sean collected himself. He rotated the router so that he could get his cell phone camera in position. He snapped a series of shots to ensure he would not have to get his ass under the table again. He backed out and handed the phone to Patty. With the IP address, he completed the firmware update and restarted the router. Finding the IP address took 15 minutes. Updating the router took 3 minutes.

"That was clever. Taking the picture."

"If I tried to read it from the sticker, we would be here all day. Let's go before the sun comes up."

*   *   *   *   *   *   *   *

Patty brought Kenny a large black coffee – no flavor, no cream, no sugar. He brought a triple shot espresso for himself. They were at Patty's regular table in the back of the café. Patty inserted a pair of earbuds and handed the other pair to Kenny.

"These are two-person Bluetooth earbuds. Sean should be at Flanahan's any time now."

Kenny struggled as the earbuds kept falling out. He generally had problems getting these sorts of things to stick to his ear comfortably.

"Damnit. They don't fit."

"You're putting them in the wrong ears. The one in your right-hand goes in your left ear."

The eavesdropping app looked like a mixing board. A selection of phones appeared some identified by owner others by phone number. Each had a volume slider ranging from one to ten. He slid Stephen O'Kane and Francess Phillip to ten.

'STEPHEN, I NEED A JIMMY, A JACK, AND A SHIRLEY TEMPLE'

'JIMMY, JACK, AND SHIRLEY COMING UP.'

Kenny sprang back spilling his coffee, yanked out the earbuds. Patty shook his head like he was recovering from a punch. The microphones were more sensitive than he had anticipated. He slid the volume controls back to six.

"Sorry, Kenny."

"What? I can't hear you."

"SORRY, KENNY!"

"It was too loud."

"I know. I turned it down. Try the buds again."

"What?"

"TRY THE BUDS AGAIN."

"Try the spuds with skin?"

Patty took the buds from the table and mimed putting them back in his ears. Kenny acknowledged and inserted the buds.

"I hope you adjusted the volume."

Patty nodded that he had.

'Stephen, I need two Buds, a Coors, and a Virgin Mary.'

'Francess, I have a favor to ask.'

'Yeesss?'

'I have a friend coming in from the Old Country tomorrow. I haven't seen him in years. Would you mind tending the bar tomorrow night?'

'Planning on tossing a few back as you lay the blarney thick are ya?'

'Something like that.'

'Sure. I'd be happy to. You'll owe me one.'

'Screech!' The microphones were sensitive enough to pick up the door opening.

'Sean!' The regulars were glad to see him. It had been almost two weeks. Sean made his way to the end of the bar where Stephen processed the server orders. He would be able to have a running conversation with Stephen and Francess there.

"Kenny, can you hear now?"

"Yes. Shh."

'Sean! Your pants fit. What's with the golf ball on your noggin?' Francess gave him a more than friendly hug.

'My jeans fit again. I hit my head on a shelf...twice.'

Stephen pried, *'So, what happened to the purple cantaloupe?'*

'First it was a softball not a cantaloupe. This is a legend I don't need to grow with time. Second, they're back to jumbo olives. The deep purple is now a crimson red.'

"Kenny, did you hear that?"

"Yeah. Don't ask him about it."

Francess was wiring down the details, *'What time do you need me tomorrow?'*

'Five to Close. Friday night – midnight or 1am.'

'Not here on a Friday? What's up?' Sean asked although he already knew the answer.

'An old mate from my playing days is in town. He's been on a dog & pony show for his work. I think he could just use a pint or two, a familiar dish, and a friendly chat. He's had enough white tablecloth meals.'

Francess translated, *'I think you two just want to relive your glory days. Will I be getting bartender wages?'*

Stephen laid out the specifics, *'Yes and I imagine double my tips. I'll help you get set-up. He's scheduled to be here around 6. He has a spot to do with channel 7 on their afternoon news.'*

Sean editorialized, *'The local news is a sham these days. It's all recycled video and advertising for their website.'*

'Sherry works for the Irish equivalent of the Federal Reserve. He's promoting something to do with Ireland being in the EU for twenty years.'

Sean appreciated, *'Stephen, I wanted to thank you for the meal the other day. I really didn't expect you to pick up the tab.'*

'We take care of our own.'

Francess turned her attention to Sean, *'What can I get you today? Will you be around tomorrow night?'*

'I've got a hankering for a lamb sandwich with chips and a Harp.'

'Are you off the pain pills?'

'What? Me mix alcohol and medication. Never.' Sarcasm pervaded the conversation.

'Alright, alright already.'

'As for tomorrow, I might catch up with you late. Janey and her beau are coming over for dinner.'

Kenny got the jump on Patty, "I call beau. You can be Janey."

Chapter 17

Insights & Invites

A dollop of shortening had melted in the large stainless-steel pot, the one used for pasta and mashed potatoes. Sean dropped three kernels in the pot and put the glass lid askew on the pot. When he heard three pops he would add enough kernels to just cover the base of the pot. He knew when fully popped the corn would come just to the lid. Once the popping sounded like automatic gunfire he shook the pot so the popcorn on the bottom would not burn. The shaking continued until the popping fell to a sputter. He emptied the popped corn into a Safeway paper bag. In his smallest saucepan was a cube of butter divided into thirds; he set the burner low to melt but not burn the butter. He poured the melted butter upon the popped corn being careful not to soak the paper. He closed the top of the bag and shook it vigorously. He added salt and shook it again. He tasted the popcorn and repeated the process until the butter/salt mix was just right.

"Damn, Sean. You know you could just buy a bag at the store or use the microwave." Sometimes Patty still did not get it.

"First, I don't cook in a microwave. Second, taste it. Third, wipe your buttery fingers before you work the keyboard."

Patty stuffed a fistful in his mouth. His eyebrows shot up. Inaudibly with a full mouth, he mumbled.

"Hmm. Mmm. I get mmm it now."

Patty put on headphones to monitor Stephen's and Francess' phones. He would rout the audio to Bluetooth speakers once Bernard Sheridan arrived.

Kenny endorsed Patty's work, "After he blew out my eardrum yesterday the quality of his snooping was top-notch. Do you think Sheridan will look at our note?"

"If I know human nature, they will start by rehashing and boasting about the old days, talk family a bit, then work. The whole nature of his trip is around punts to euros. It's only natural to pull the commemorative banknote off the wall."

"Are you going to go down there tonight?"

"I don't know. If I do it would be after Sheridan is gone, remember I told them Janey was over for dinner. Whatever I do, I can't let on that I have any knowledge of what happened there tonight."

Patty flailed his arms and routed the audio to the speakers. It was as if they were sitting in the next booth listening to the conversation.

Sheridan fired the first shot, *'Stephen O'Kane, you are still as ugly as a mangy mutt at the scrap heap. How's the craic?'*

'Still trolling with the bottom feeders feasting on scraps are ya.'

The old foes hugged. Stephen had Francess draw two pints of Guinness. They settled at a booth, and each laid their cell phone on the table.

Patty enthused, "His phone is on the table. This is great."

In the mid-80's Kerry and Dublin met back-to-back years in the All-Ireland Finals. Dublin won the first, Kerry the second. The two regaled each other with stories from the games, the sidelines, and the girls. Stephen had the kitchen serve them family-style – roast lamb, corned beef, colcannon (mashed potatoes with cabbage and leeks), fresh sourdough, and Kerrygold Irish butter. They had a second round of Guinness with the meal.

Kenny was impatient. "They're just going to bullshit about the old days,"

Sean steadied, "Eat your popcorn. I think the plot is about to thicken."

'Stephen, I can't believe how good that bread is. This was the best meal I've had since I left. Where's your cook from?'

'The Philippines.'

'No shit? He cooks like a Devine.'

'I know. What say we have an after-dinner whiskey?'

'What's your best?'

'Francess, bring me the 18-year Jameson and two glasses.'

'Stephen, I was sorry to hear about your wife's passing. She was young.'

'Thanks. Your daughter must be what about 20-years old now?'

'23. Has a graduate degree in Art History and works as a barista.'

Stephen commiserated, *'I'm sorry. How's the wife?'*

'Bad. She's a gambler and a shopper. I had to turn my phone off before dinner as I didn't want to deal with her hitting me up for a deposit. I don't think she'll survive my retirement.'

'Ouch. I heard you were up for the Deputy Governorship.'

Sheridan winced, *'I was. They went with an insurance company outsider. She's filling the other Directorships with outsiders. Banking isn't what it used to be. They are really trying to get rid of me before my time. The bints. I hear they are redesigning the executive layout. My office is now the non-binary Jack. Can you believe it a non-*

binary jack?'

Sherry inquired as to Stephen's ownership stake in Flanahan's. The founder had been offering Stephen 5% a year for about five years. Unfortunately, his track to bar ownership would coincide with his reaching retirement age.

'You were all over the telly today Channel 2 this morning, Channel 7 this afternoon. Something about there still being millions of Irish pounds not redeemed for euros.'

'I'm afraid that'll be all I'm remembered for. The banker who couldn't drum up the pounds.'

'We have a 100-pound note hanging over the register. The Consul General came here the night we opened. He ordered a round for the house and challenged Soden that he could not call it an Irish pub if he would not accept it.'

Sean was on the edge of his seat, "Here we go boys. He's going to get the note."

'Hah! I've heard of Consul Generals pulling stunts like that before, but this is the first real confirmation of such a trick. Could I see the note?'

Stephen stepped to the register and hopped the bar. With his ape-like arms, he could reach the frame without a step ladder. He handed the frame to Sheridan.

'It's a funny thing. That note had been hanging there since 1978 and this is the second time it's been off the wall this month.'

Sheridan's interest piqued, *'Really?'*

Patty's foot was tapping the beat of 'Flight of the Bumblebee'. Kenny was wringing his hands as if he was working an imaginary rosary.

'Yeah. We have a regular here, a kind of jack-of-all-trades sort, who had a bar bet and he needed the note to

get his payoff.'

'What was the wager?'

'That the Princess of all Irish currency was an American.'

'Lady Lavery. He's right. Mind if I take it out of the frame?'

He felt the note between his fingers. Snapped it to feel its strength. Held it to the light to check the watermark. He checked the background and the engraved portions.

Sheridan admired the banknote, *'You know. I haven't seen one of these in months. It's a beautiful banknote. There's millions of pounds out there just waiting to be exchanged. I'd love to get my hands on some and stick it to the bints.'*

Kenny, Patty, and Sean were dumbfounded. This guy, albeit an insider, saw the same opportunity.

Sheridan ran the note under his nose like a fine cigar.

Kenny exclaimed, "What's he doing?"

Sean knew, "He's smelling it!"

'I always like to smell the note even though it's not an accepted method to detect counterfeits. This smells a little inky, but I suppose if it was new and encased for forty years it may have retained the scent. Want to exchange it?'

Stephen did not, *'No. It's the pub's good luck charm.'*

'I understand. I played every All-Ireland match in the same drawers.'

'When do you leave for Australia?'

'Sunday.'

Stephen invited him to a round of golf, *'You want to play 18 tomorrow?'*

'I don't have my sticks.'

'You can rent some. I'll give you a stroke for the

foreign clubs.'

'One on the front and one on the back and you're on.'
'Done.'

'Do you think the bloke who won the bet would like to play? I'd like to meet the man who knows so much about my pounds.'

Kenny and Patty are out of their seats waving like they are calling an incomplete pass. Sean is giving them the calm down hands out patting motion.

'He's getting over hernia surgery. He's Irish American and his bollocks turned near black and swelled to the size of a cantaloupe. He did make it in here yesterday afternoon. Said he's back to jumbo olives although they are crimson red.'

'That must've been a sight. Maybe he could join us after the round.'

'Let me give him a call.'

Kenny and Patty were panicking.

Kenny pleaded, "Don't take the call. Let it go to voicemail. Buy yourself some time."

Patty offered, "I could kill his phone from here. Fry the motherboard. Just say the word. It'll only take a second."

Again, Sean was calm, "No. No. Nothing out of the normal. Don't kill his phone. And he knows I take all my calls."

Sean's phone rang with the theme from the Rockford Files. Patty rolled his eyes.

Kenny scolded, "You just don't understand how cool a ringtone that is. But forget that now."

Sean eyeballed them both and answered.

"Hello."

"Sean, this is Stephen."

"Stephen, aren't you entertaining your foe from yesteryear?"

"I have been. There's a plate of lamb, corned beef, and colcannon if you come by later."

"Well, I appreciate that. Is that why you called? Did Francess put you up to it?"

"No. No. I was telling Sherry, Bernard Sheridan, about your Lady Lavery bet and he said he wants to meet the bloke who knows so much about his beloved Irish punt."

Sean feigned interest, "Really, now."

"He's offering the finest meal in the City on the Central Bank of Ireland."

"How can I pass that up?"

Chapter 18

Hash, Brash & Cash

Stephen would not let Sheridan take a taxi or ride share to his hotel even though it was downtown. The traffic was light in the Sunset, heavy through the bar, entertainment, and show districts. Like most nights, the financial district was a ghost town except for the panhandlers and homeless. Stephen explained their tolerated status and how although there was much mental illness and drug abuse there was also a portion for whom it was a lifestyle choice. When asked to come in for a 'final, final,' Stephen declined as his career depended on his not getting a Driving Under the Influence charge. He also knew more drinking tonight would impact his golf game in the morning.

Sheridan stepped into the glass elevator which overlooked the atrium. He was staying at the Hyatt Regency on the 18th floor. He looked down; he was already a bit tipsy. He backed away from the glass and clutched the railing. It was cool, but he broke into a sweat. He was struck with a feeling of déjà vu; he thought he was being watched. The escape of the evening was fleeting. His notification tone went off. It was morning in Dublin and his wife was out of funds again. She wanted €500. He knew she would be at the club begging for fronts if he didn't concede. She did not care that it would be considered unacceptable behavior for the spouse of a Director of the Central Bank.

He wanted to check his email before retiring; he too needed a good night's rest were he to liberate some change from O'Kane in the morning. His inbox was missing the Operations Division standard daily email outlining the key performance indicators used to monitor the health of the Irish economy as influenced by the Central Bank. He had designed the daily email format when the Central Bank introduced data mining software in the 1990s. The source systems had changed over the years, but his key indicators had stayed the course of time. He scrolled back through his inbox. He had not received the daily email all week. He called Gertrude on her personal mobile from his personal mobile.

"Trudy it's Bernard."

"It must be the middle of the night there. Are you alright?"

"It's late. I was just looking to catch up on my emails and I cannot find the Dailies."

"She didn't tell you?"

"Tell me what?"

"Flood spoke with each Director about ceasing the Dailies wanting each to focus on their own department only. She feels they do not need to be concerned with the overall Bank performance."

"Poppycock. What else has she done?"

Gertrude could not wait to spill the tea, "The floor's a mess. Your office is gone. They've turned it into a loo. Her boy, Dennehy, went through your files before they were sent off to storage. He wouldn't tell me what he was looking for. You know he's started wearing one of those earpieces that the Secret Service wears. He's even talking into his sleeve. What a tool."

"I can't do anything from here which is why they jumped at this ridiculous idea. Appreciate you staying out of their way and keeping your eyes open. Keep sending me business issues through the normal channels. Don't send any observations or opinions though. I imagine they are monitoring our accounts."

"My thoughts exactly."

He peaked out the window which faced the atrium. He rebooted his phone and computer hoping the restart would disable any foreign apps. He swept the room for bugs even though he did not know how to spot one. He turned on the telly to distract his mind. Mel Brooks' *High Anxiety* was on the free HBO.

*   *   *   *   *   *   *   *

Francess sat on a stool watching Sean prepare a late-night meal for her.

"Sean, you really don't have to go to all this trouble for me. A can of soup would be fine."

"Nonsense. You've been on your feet working all night."

"My dogs are barking."

"Well, after I feed you perhaps I could return the favor and give you a foot rub."

"My back aches also."

Sean cut the leftover corned beef and boiled potatoes into ¾ inch cubes.

"You see, Francess, the key to a good corned beef hash is in cutting the product into chunks. Too many restaurants and that canned crap make it look like baby food. Disgusting."

The cast iron was hot. He melted a tablespoon of bacon fat to coat the pan. The potatoes went in first followed by diced onion. The aroma filled the kitchen.

"Smells great, Sean. I'm starving."

He added the corned beef. The leftovers became hash

as he scraped the brown goodness of the cast iron with a steel spatula. He finished the hash with dried parsley and a pinch of dried mint. They ate on the couch washing the hash down with cold Harps.

"Sean, what are you up to? I see you running around with the printer and that kid all the time. Others haven't noticed but I have. You're not printing money, are you?"

"That's illegal. I can honestly say we are not printing legal tender. You're right though. We are working on a project that could be life-changing. Would you like a different life?"

"Being a bar wench in a neighborhood pub was always a dream of mine." She added sarcastically.

"Let me clear your plate. I'll be right back."

He disappeared to the kitchen. She kicked her shoes off and lounged across the couch. She brought up YouTube to stream some 70's music. She took in his search history: Gaelic Football, David Letterman, History of Irish Currency, sourdough, intaglio printing, Lady Lavery. There was no horror, no true crime, no vulgar humor. Her thought, 'He is a complicated, interesting individual'.

Sean appeared from the hallway. He was wearing the periwinkle shirt unbuttoned, sleeves rolled to three-quarters. He was wearing an undershirt formerly known as a wife-beater and light blue boxer briefs. He had a Costco-sized pump bottle of Vaseline Intensive Care lotion. He started with her feet.

"Ooh. Sean, yes. Yes. That feels good. Don't stop."

Sean was in no rush. He enjoyed the territory; he undressed her working up from her feet In an example of necessity being the mother of invention, he had learned there was more than one way to please a woman.

Francess squirmed from the attention to detail.

"Sean, where did that come from?"

"I played the trumpet for 15 years. Staccato was always my strength."

"Indeed."

She snuggled back to his front, grabbed his arm, and draped it over her side so he was cupping her breast.

"Sean?"

"Yes."

"Can you show me that again in the morning?"

"The corned beef."

"That too."

*　　*　　*　　*　　*　　*　　*　　*

Stephen and Bernard were full of excuses. Stephen strained his back lifting cases of Old Bushmills. Bernard was using loaner clubs. Stephen's tweaky knee from his playing days was acting up. Bernard was still suffering from the time difference. When they were done sandbagging they decided to play straight up. To make things interesting the wager was Flanahan's 100-pound banknote against $500 US.

The starter at Harding Park had paired them with a pair of twenty-something bitcoin brokers – arrogant, cocky, loud and four cheap beers in already. They were mock stretching, swinging at imaginary balls, and roughhousing like frat boys. The short one approached the old friends.

"Heh, Pops. You guys aren't from around here. How'd you get on the course? I thought you had to have a City Play card."

O'Kane fielded the inquiry. "First, I've lived in the

157

City longer than you've been alive. Second, I've never seen you out here before. Where are you from? And third, who you calling Pops?"

"Sorry. Sorry. We were just wondering if you two would like to make the game interesting."

Sheridan picked up the conversation, "What do you have in mind?"

"How about $10 a hole, team lowball?"

"That's hardly gambling. How about a 1-2-3 Nassau?"

"1-2-3 Nassau?"

"Team lowball. $100 front nine, $200 back nine, $300 game. Like you said, let's make it interesting. Unless that's too rich for your britches."

"Ok, Pops. Age before beauty, your tee."

Bernard opened a sleeve of Titleist 1's. He rotated the balls in his right ungloved hand. Put one in his pocket. He tossed one to his mouthy opponent.

"I won't be needing this today."

His grip was light, swing was supple and controlled. He drove the ball 235 yards down the fairway three paces left of center. Bernard threw Stephen a head nod and wink.

Mouthy, a 26-year-old crypto-currency broker named Cameron who took 5 years to get a 4-year degree, took the tee. He wore two gloves and squeezed the club like he was wringing out a hand towel. His stance was wide; he resembled a fire hydrant in his yellow togs. He swayed right in his backswing losing the axis of his set-up. His violent swing produced yardage but not direction. His ball sliced into the ninth fairway.

Stephen had 8 yards on Bernard, but the positioning was right of center leaving a less desirable line. Cameron's companion was in the first cut off the fairway to the left. Bernard parred the first hole while Stephen and Lyle bogeyed. Cameron picked up his ball.

The Irish were steady over the next seven holes -- two pars, four bogeys, and a birdie. The Millennials were mercuric -- no pars, two birdies, two bogeys, and a double bogey. The twosomes were even at plus 3 teeing off at the par 5 ninth.

Mouthy, not knowing to whom he was talking, had to bring out his business pitch.

"Pop, are you diversified into cryptocurrency? People are seeing their net worth grow exponentially. You probably don't have many earning years left."

Sheridan could not believe his approach, "You have a terrible sales pitch. Don't ruin the golf game."

Lyle had been carrying the Millennials posting his score on seven of the eight holes played so far. The par 5 ninth was statistically the second easiest hole on the course. It would take a 12-foot par putt by Lyle to match the Irishmen's pars. Lyle also sold crypto currency but was not as annoying as Cameron.

At the turn Cameron loaded three tall Budweiser's in his bag and another three in Lyle's. Stephen shot a glance to Bernard. When Cameron and Lyle came to the 10th tee, the annoyance continued.

"Really, Pop, you can do so much with the crypto these days. The value is through the roof."

Stephen took up the cause, "Can you use it at Safeway?"

"Well, no."

"Can you use it at my bar? …No, you can't"

"But all the new apps and online markets take it."

Bernard stepped in again, "Do you remember pogs?"

"Huh? Pogs?"

"Look it up. When you were a whippersnapper a market popped up overnight for milk bottle caps, pogs as they are known. And poof, the market crashed just as fast. There was no there, there. And there's no there, here."

Sheridan knew the score and was ready to press the youngsters. "Stephen, what's the score? Who won the front nine?"

"Looks like we're even at plus 3."

"Well, Cameron. That just puts that $100 on the back nine as well."

Cameron was adding through his beer-addled mind, "That would be ...uh 100, 200, 300. That would be $600 on the back nine!"

"Yes. Yes, it would. $600 is such an in between number though. Are you boys men or still pompous college kids?"

"Huh?"

"You wanted to make it interesting. Let's make it interesting. Make it $1,000 on the back nine, team lowball. And I'm talking US currency not that crypto bullshit. Do you boys have that kind of money?"

Cameron and Lyle conferred. They pulled their wallets out to check funds. Stephen and Bernard smiled; they knew the fish had swallowed the bait.

"Ok. You're on Pops. My man Lyle is away."

Lyle shanked his tee shot, a 50-yard dribbler to the left. The Millennials were pressing. Stephen and Bernard striped their tee shots, their longest drives of the day. The Irish birdied and the Millennials bogeyed, the Irish had two strokes after the ninth. After the 12th hole, the Irish lead had grown to four strokes. The Millennials were playing so tight it would take a prybar to get their drawers out of their arse. The Irish did not miss a fairway and they were putting for the dough. The aches and pains of age and the excuses before the round began were long forgotten. The lead was nine strokes at the 16th tee. The Millennials were silent. The Irishmen were laying the blarney on thick.

"You know, Stephen, the only reason you were a goalie was your knees knocked too loud when you ran. You could not sneak up on the defense."

"I know you were the definition of cherry picker. I don't think you made an honest tackle in five years of Cup play."

Stephen dropped the final birdie putt on 18. The Irishmen had taken the Millennials to school on the back nine. They laughed. It felt good to get one over on their brash opponents. Stephen directed the closing of the transaction.

"Boys, do you know Flanahan's on Noriega? It's about 14 blocks north in the heart of the Sunset. I'm buying and you're paying off your debt."

Mouthy was not used to this level of trust, "How do you know we'll show?"

"We know where you work. Do you really want me coming to your office on Monday saying you welched on a bet? That a couple of senior citizens kicked your collective arse."

Chapter 19

Greet & Meet

Sheridan and O'Kane were counting their winnings. Each sported a tan Guinness moustache. You could not work the bar at Flanahan's if you could not pull a perfect draught of Guinness with the centimeter head topping the pint – no more, no less.

Sheridan's restrained demeanor was back at the Hyatt with his suits and pressed shirts, "What a pleasure it was to put those two eejits in their place."

O'Kane was riding the same high, "We really got on a roll on the back nine."

"I think the little one wet his pants when I pressed him to a thousand."

"Like taking candy from a baby. What happened to the time difference and the borrowed clubs."

"Adrenaline. What about your balky knee?"

"Everything loosened up when those kids started talking. …Heh, I forgot about our wager."

"Me too. It was much more fun liberating their cash. Why don't we just call our wager a push?"

"Works for me."

"I did like seeing the old 100 punt note on your wall. Do you think your friend would mind coming down here for the meal I promised? I know I offered a real treat, but after last night and today's round it'd be a lot easier if he just joined us here."

"Well, Sean is pretty easy to please. As long as you don't go Dutch, I'm sure he would appreciate the meal. Let me call him."

Stephen called Sean and explained the situation: late

night, eighteen holes, taking a grand from the eejits, age. Sean was surprised they had anything left in tank. He offered to take a rain check, even though it was Bernard's last night in the City.

"Sherry, Sean offered to take a rain check."

"No. I'd like to meet him. He has to be more interesting than the pair we took on today. Anyway, this is my last night here."

Stephen returned to the phone. Sean had already heard the conversation. Still, he listened to Stephen's explanation and offer. He agreed to come over in about a half hour. Stephen dialed up the RTÉ 2 replay of the All-Ireland Championship. The two traded war stories while they waited for Sean.

Sean texted Patty through the secure app:

'Change of plans. Meeting Sheridan at Flanahan's in a half hour. Can you operate the bug from there.'

'Yes. And I can patch in Kenny.'

'Great. You two can listen in to see how it goes. Do me a favor and activate the remaining burner phone.'

'10-4. Over and out.'

* * * * * * * *

Patty texted Kenny on the secure app, *'We're live. Are you getting the feed?'*

'I am. I hope Sean knows what he's doing.'

'Me too.'

"Bernard Sheridan meet Sean McAuliffe. …Sean, Bernard."

Bernard extended his hand, "Sean, what's the craic?"

"All good." Sean met his hand with the firm shake his father had taught him. "I understand you two made a little change this afternoon."

"It wasn't so much the change but the joy of liberating it from the two young eejits."

Stephen had the kitchen set a table in the banquet room, "Boys why don't we move to the back room we can relax and let our hair down, wait you two don't have any hair."

Sherry took up the defense, "Oh, so it's going to be like that. I still have the scorecard and an eraser. I'm sure I had you on our side bet."

Sean played along, "Relax, Bernard. It's a good thing Stephen's not a butcher; he'd always have his thumb on the scale. As it is he only pours short shots to strangers. The rest of us have been around him too long to fall for it."

Stephen had to deflect the target, "Sean, are your bollocks still purple?"

Bernard heard the story the day before, "You're the bloke who had a volleyball, black and blue sack!"

"First, it was side effects of hernia surgery. Second, it was never bigger than a softball. And third, the boys are back and better than ever. Thank you very much."

"Sounds scary. What do you do for a living?"

Francess brought Guinness for Stephen and Bernard and a Harp for Sean. She also brought a platter of potato skins ala 1983. Complete with melted cheddar cheese and chives.

"I retired early my back was broken and my eyes are failing. They were able to fix my back, but my eyes are what they are. My right eye is particularly bad. I thought I could golf again after the back surgery, but I couldn't see the ball. I can't judge distance in the fairway or on the green."

"Damn, that sounds frustrating."

"If I try and work, I lose the retirement. It's a tight spot."

Bernard's phone rang. "Damnit. It's my wife."

'Hello, dear. ...I played 18 with an old football friend. My phone was off. ...I gave you €500 last night. You couldn't have blown it that fast. ...Alright, alright. ...Just stay home for a night.'

Sheridan was shaking his head and mumbling under his breath as he transferred another €500 to her account. He was beside himself. "Never marry, or stay married, to a woman with no sense of money and a gambling problem. She will not survive my retirement."

Francess came in to clear the appetizer plates and take dinner orders.

Sheridan continued with Sean, "Are you a married man?"

"Not now. I have a special friend though. She seems good with money." Sean's eyes caught Francess' eyes over Sheridan's shoulder.

Francess interjected, "Tonight we have a special, McAuliffe's Corned Beef Hash. The chef recreated a dish I was served last night. Corned beef hash like you've never had it before – hearty, crispy yet unctuous."

Bernard and Stephen ordered the special. Sean went with the leg'o'lamb dinner.

Stephen ribbed Sean, "You don't want to try the special?"

"I think I've already had it."

As Sean ate his lamb dinner he mentally critiqued the corned beef hash. The potatoes had been deep fried. The assembly looked as though big batches were held in hotel pans. It did not appear to have touched cast iron. It did, however, look better than any restaurant hash he had seen before.

"So, Sean, Stephen tells me you turned my useless IR£ note into $100. Genius. How'd you do it?"

"I'm not a numismatist nor a notaphilist. I am an observer. I saw your article in the Irish Times on 20 years with the EU. The old punts outstanding caught my eye. I went down the internet rabbit hole and came across the story of Lady Lavery. I knew Stephen had one on the wall. I also knew that I had many friends who held strong opinions on limited information. The result is a classic bar bet."

"Impressive. Stephen mind if we look at the note."

Stephen retrieved the note and brought it to Bernard.

"Are you familiar with the back of the bill?"

"Each series A note has a design representing a river on the back. I believe it's the River Erne on the 100-pound note."

"You are correct. And the watermark?"

"The head of Erin from the statue Hibernia."

"Sean, you are amazing. You know more about the note than the feckin' Deputy Governor they put in charge. Damn insurance bint."

"You sound frustrated."

"I am. The job I trained my whole life for was open. I was poised to take it, work another five years, and retire with Deputy Governor's compensation. As it is they brought in an outsider, she resents my knowledge and respect within the organization. Now, I'm being forced out in six months. Faster if they could find cause."

"Who is 'they'?"

"Marcella Flood, the insurance eejit they made Deputy Governor, and Louis Dennehy, her hitman in charge of

Enforcement, a former J2 officer. They are trying to strip my departments away from me. What do you expect? The whole Bank is being run by a Brit now. It's unbelievable that a third of the Board is non-Celtic."

"I saw you on the news. Do you really think the dog & pony will generate exchanges?"

"It's been so stable for years I doubt it. I suggested the tour as a joke. I didn't realize how bad they wanted me out of the picture. I received reports they are redesigning the executive floor. My office is now the non-binary restroom. They are moving so fast they don't know what they are doing."

"No shit."

Francess cleared the plates and took dessert orders. The offerings were basic ice cream, apple pie, and crème brulée, As he was in America, Sheridan ordered apple pie a la mode. Stephen went for ice cream and Sean crème brulée. Stephen requested three 18-year Jameson's.

Sean begged off to the jack before dessert. He went directly to Francess in the kitchen.

"Francess, was Bernie wearing a coat when he came in?"

"Yes. It's in the office. Donegal tweed with the gold lining. It's a nice jacket."

"Thanks, Babe." Sean gave Francess a quick kiss.

Sean made a beeline to the office and slipped the burner phone into the right flap pocket. The phone was slim and light; he would likely put the jacket on without even noticing it. Sean was drawn to the shillelagh. It was the first authentic one he had ever held – balanced, unique, handsome. He quickly peed before returning to the banquet room.

"Trouble peeing?" Stephen asked.

"Nowadays it's a victory if the stream is strong enough to pass my feet. Oh, for the days when I could pee like a racehorse."

Bernie agreed, "Amen, Brother."

Sean needed to know Sheridan's schedule, "Sherry, When do you fly out tomorrow?"

"It's an evening flight. Direct and all night to Sydney."

"That would be hell on my joints."

"I know. I'm not looking forward to it."

"What are you doing tomorrow, sleeping?"

"No plans. I may take a walk along the waterfront."

"Have you ever watched a baseball game? The Giants play at noon tomorrow. The ballpark is about a half hour walk down the waterfront from the Hyatt. I could leave you a pair of tickets at will call."

"I couldn't ask you to do that, Sean."

"Listen, it would be a dark day in the City when a McAuliffe couldn't come up with a couple of tickets to the ballgame."

"That sounds a little sketchy. I like it. You and Stephen seem to have this city in the palm of your hands. Reminds me of running about before I joined the Bank."

"The will call window is on the front of the stadium by the Willie Mays Statue. The line won't be bad, it's not like the old days. Today most people use their phone or print their tickets at home. You'll just need your identification."

"Will I see you there?"

"If I make it, I will certainly stop by and see you. Leave yourself at least a half hour before first pitch. The ballpark has a good selection of local fare. I hate being late for a game."

"It's like starting a match with only 14 players. Poor

form. I look forward to it. I saw where your team is still in contention. I will probably offer the other ticket to my assistant. She's put in yeoman's duty."

They ate their desserts and ordered one for the road.

Bernard liked him, "Sean, I feel for your challenges, bad eyes and being hamstrung about work. Not to mention putting up with Stephen."

"Well, we all have crosses to bare."

Stephen retorted, "Feck off the both of you. I have to go check the evening's receipts."

"Stephen's a good man. He could play back in the day. But you didn't hear that from me."

"Agreed. He's more family than barkeep. ...It sounds as if you have had an interesting career that's coming to an unfortunate demise and your home life is no dream either."

"I have crosses also. But enough of the doom and gloom. I have to say throughout this whole trip you have been the most informed person I have met. You are a breath of fresh air. I hope our paths cross again."

"You know ever since I read your article a thought has been running through my head. *'300 million 20-year-old Irish pounds worth 400 million dollars is out there. How can I get a piece of that action?'*"

Bernard reflexively raised an eyebrow and nodded his head. Under his breath and from the back of his throat he murmured, "Um-hmm."

Chapter 20

Mush-a Ring Dumb-a Do

Bernard said his goodbyes to Stephen who was reconciling credit receipts to the register. He would take a taxi tonight. Being an international traveler, he did not want to bother with a ride-share app; it was easier to have Francess call him a cab. The 65° degree evening weather was refreshing to the Dubliner. He was still basking in the day's events as he reached for the creaky door. Bernard forgot his jacket; Sean felt helpless. He could not call attention to it.

He breathed a sigh of relief when Francess stopped Sheridan at the door, "Bernard. Bernard! Your jacket and shillelagh. Don't forget them."

She ran to the office and brought out the jacket and shillelagh. He took the jacket by the collar and let it fold in half lengthwise down the back. He laid the jacket across his left forearm. Suit wearers have a way of managing a jacket and pants to minimize wrinkles. He twirled the shillelagh in his right hand and gave the bar a ceremonial wave.

"Thanks, Love. Cheerio, Gents!" Bernard was off to the Hyatt to pack for the final phase of his junket.

The glass elevator had five riders today. As the others gazed back at the atrium, Sheridan's eyes were focused on the lighted floor numbers above the door as one would normally ride in an elevator. He was not gripped with fear. He laid the tweed jacket over the leather executive chair in his hotel room; he planned to wear the jacket during the flight. He was relieved that his phone at the hotel had no missed messages from his wife. Apparently, even inveterate gamblers have to sleep. He texted Ginny that he was back at the Hyatt. He knew she would respond. She constantly maintained multiple text conversations.

Ginny had developed a portal that was accessed from the Central Bank website to facilitate out of Ireland exchange of punts for euros in quantities under IR£ 10,000, under the tax reporting requirement. Three weeks into the fiasco and the web traffic was encouraging, but funds registered was only IR£ 2,645. A total significant compared to the previous year's exchanges, not surprising to Sheridan, but fodder to Flood and Dennehy.

"Ginny, have you checked in for our flight yet?"

"We leave SFO at 8:20 in the evening. It's a 15 plus hour direct flight. We arrive in Sydney at 6:20 Tuesday morning. We lose a day. I have our seat assignments, but we still have to go through customs and security."

"Sean, the bloke who knew about Lady Lavery, offered me tickets to the baseball game tomorrow. Would you like to attend? Do you like sports?"

"You really don't know anything about me, do you? I was a mid for Cork in the Camogie championships during the 2010s."

"Really. That's awesome. Centuries ago, I played football for Kerry in the All-Ireland finals. Stephen O'Kane was Dublin's goalie. Sean said we should get to the park early for concessions and get our bearings. What say we meet in the lobby at 10:45. It is supposed to be about a half hour walk along the waterfront."

*   *   *   *   *   *   *   *

Kenny and Patty unloaded the second batch oven and additional steamers from the van. Sean was ready to work. He and Patty would operate dual steaming stations allowing the watermarks to be placed twice as fast. The second batch oven would keep blanks feeding to the printers which were nowhere near close to capacity.

Sean laid out the numbers, "The original run of 180 notes took about 40 minutes. Therefore, the 3 million pounds would be 30,000 100-pound notes. With four steamers and two batch ovens we will produce 360 notes every 40 minutes. We are looking at 55 production hours, 2-3 weeks."

"Damn." Patty was not used to that level of work.

Kenny was not fazed, "It will be good to put the printers through their paces again. With the new steamers and additional batch oven we could make more notes. I have more than enough stock. ...Patty, we can play this two ways. One, you could work all four steamers feeding me at the offset printer. Or two, and I'm only suggesting because of what you've shown me, I could work two steamers and you could work two steamers. You would run your blanks through the offset printer."

"Ok, boss." Patty was humbled that he would be considered to operate a press, "However you want to play it."

Sean was a bit shocked Kenny hadn't included him on the production team, "You know I'm cleared for duty."

Kenny was not a poker player as he could not hide his exasperation, "I know you are cleared to figure out how you are going to manage that Central Bank man, Sheridan. He's seen your face. I've come too far to not get the shop now."

"He may end up being our greatest ally. He's got

problems at home and work. I've already started planting seeds. Kenny, how do you feel about producing 5 million notes? That would be over 90 production hours, 4-5 weeks."

Kenny could handle the order, "We'll start today. Please, come up with a plan for Sheridan."

"Can you do without Patty for a day. I have a special assignment for him."

"Sure." Kenny was used to working alone.

"Do you think you could knock out a batch of 360 notes today?"

"Shouldn't be a problem."

"We are going to set up some online banking accounts and redeem IR£ 28,000 via the portal on the Central Bank website designed for *overseas* transaction. That should give us the operating funds we need for travel and get all of our personal bills paid. We don't want to run afoul of the law cause we're deadbeats."

Patty was curious, "What's on my plate boss? Do you need me to plant some data? Hack the Central Bank website?"

"No. You are coming to the Giants game with me today."

Kenny and Patty both exclaimed, "What!?!"

"I need you to run interference with Sheridan's assistant while I work on him. She's a technical wizard like you. It would be best if you let her talk systems to you, and you baseball to her. She doesn't need to know about your past or our future. You game?"

"A people job instead of a computer job. Thanks, Sean. I won't let you down."

"Today I need you to be Stanley Sullivan. Swap out all your identification. We cannot have her meet Patty

Maguire. And, you don't know me. You got the ticket from a friend of a friend and you could not pass up a Giants/Dodgers game."

Kenny was confused, "I'm less worried about Patty and more concerned with what you plan to do about Sheridan."

"Well first, with our added capacity I want to print *FIVE million* pounds. Now as to Sheridan, he's an unhappy man at the end of his rope. I see it playing out one of three ways. Two will be fine for us, particularly with the extra pounds. The third, not so good; he remains loyal to the bank that has turned on him and I get exposed. We will maintain a firewall between Sheridan and the two of you."

Patty smirked, "Firewall!?! I'm rubbing off on you."

"Patty, I want to send a text to the burner I planted in Sheridan's coat. Can you make the phone ring instead of sounding the notification? I need to ensure he finds the phone. And I want the message to delete itself after it's read."

"Not a problem. Is there a particular ring you want me to play?"

"Take the chorus from the Irish ditty *Whiskey in the Jar* by the Irish Rovers."

Patty found it quickly. He played the full song and then clipped out the chorus.

"Are you sure you want me to loop that?"

"Yes. It's from Kerry. The story of a highwayman whose wife betrayed him. I think the irony will strike him."

Sean scratched out the verbiage for the text and handed it to Patty like he was sending a telegram in a black and white movie.

*   *   *   *   *   *   *   *

... Mush-a ring dumb-a do dumb-a da
Wack fall the daddy-o, wack fall the daddy-o
There's whiskey in the jar ...

Sheridan's eyes were bleary, and his tongue needed a shave. He had not ordered a wake-up call. The alarm clock on the nightstand was unplugged. He recognized the song, *Whiskey in the Jar.*
... Mush-a ring dumb-a do dumb-a da
Wack fall the daddy-o, wack fall the daddy-o
There's whiskey in the jar ...

He poured himself out of bed and stumbled about the room. The sight in the mirror, wifebeater, pot belly, boxers, black socks, was not flattering.
... Mush-a ring dumb-a do dumb-a da
Wack fall the daddy-o, wack fall the daddy-o
There's whiskey in the jar ...

The song was coming from his jacket. It was a phone. He had no idea how it got there.
... Mush-a ring dumb-a do dumb-a da
Wack fall the daddy-o, wack fall the daddy-o
There's whiskey in the jar ...

He was alone but took the phone into the bathroom anyway. He read the text message.

'You have been robbed of your destiny, your legacy. I can help. Keep this phone. It is not GPS enabled. Currently, it only receives calls/messages. You will be

175

contacted. Listen for the code word, "Hibernia". Your response if interested, "Erin Go Bragh". ...This text will autodelete in 30 seconds.'

Chapter 21

Play Ball!

"This is a crazy city, Ginny. Eight miles across town it's shrouded in fog and 5° cooler."

"I was reading up on it last night. They call them microclimates. They say the old ballpark was in a terrible part of town for wind and cold nights. A real boondoggle in its day. This ballpark was built on waterfront property that was industrial and underutilized."

"I noticed as we flew in the Oakland waterfront was all containers. I could see where the geography here does not lend itself to be a 21st-century cargo port."

"Sir, do you always talk business."

"It is what most people ask me about when they hear my profession. But, no, Ginny. I don't always talk business. Seeing as we are going to a ballgame why don't you call me Bernard or Sherry or whatever feels natural? Who knows we might even talk about our playing days. I'm sure my tales have grown larger and falser than yours. It has been many more years."

He grabbed his shillelagh and they started the 1.5 mile trek along the Embarcadero. The foot traffic increased the closer they got to the ballpark. They noticed groups of people sitting on the dock with sausages and burgers. They were early.

"Ginny, what say we get a sausage here? Red's Java House – quite the name."

"I think they call them hot dogs."

They queued. The eating menu was rudimentary: hot dogs, burgers, fries. The beverage list was heavy on bottled beers and Irish Coffee. Ginny ordered first –

double burger with cheese, onion, pickle, mustard, no ketchup & a Bud Light. Bernard followed – double dog with onion, sauerkraut, mustard & a Budweiser. They ate on the back patio. There was a channel between them and a waterfront warehouse across the Bay at the Port of Oakland gantry cranes stood poised over container ships.

"After you invited me to the game, I did some research. The season is winding down and the Giants are on the outside looking in. Everyone is saying today is a must-win game."

"I saw that on the news last night. The newsreader was saying today's game is a sell-out. That the Los Angeles team is two games ahead of the Giants."

"The Los Angeles team, the Dodgers, are San Francisco's biggest rival. It goes back to the 1900's when both teams were in New York. From what I gather the rivalry is not unlike Dublin/Kerry."

"That's Kerry/Dublin. And I find it hard to believe it could be that venomous. Let's head to the stadium we still need to collect our tickets."

Unlike Los Angeles, the San Francisco Giants crowd arrived early. Ticket holders were starting to back up at the gates. They headed to the window marked 'Will Call'; the queue was only twelve deep.

"Good afternoon, name please."

"Sheridan, Bernard Sheridan"

The attendant clicked the keyboard. He frowned. Clicked some more and frowned again.

"Is that with a 't-o-n' or 'd-e-n'?"

"Sheridan, S-h-e-r-i-d-a-n."

The attendant still could not find the tickets to print. Sheridan could feel his blood pressure rise. Normally, Gertrude would have had his tickets on his desk the day of the event. His position had no pull in this town. Was it a harbinger of things to come?

"I was told the tickets would be here waiting for me."

"I'm sorry, sir. Your name is not in the computer. Perhaps you could call the party that was supposed to have left the tickets."

"I would but I don't have Sean's number."

"Did you say Sean?"

"Yes."

"Sean McAuliffe."

"Yes."

"Oh. Why didn't you say so? Sean's an old friend."

The attendant pushed the keyboard away and pulled an envelope from under the desk blotter. He inspected the tickets. His eyebrows hit his hairline.

"Wow. These are amazing seats. Front row behind home plate. You sound Irish. Is this your first time at Oracle Park?"

"Yes. Those seats do not sound like General Admission."

"No. They run around $600 each."

"How much!?!"

"The seats come with concierge service. You do not have to enter through Gate A. If you will stand to the side here, I will have an usher escort you to your seats and take any concession order you may have."

*   *   *   *   *   *   *   *

"My name is Lola. I'm here to help you to your seats. May I see your tickets, please. Have you had the pleasure of seeing the Giants play before? Is that a cane or a club?"

"It's neither. It's a shillelagh."

"Well, clubs are not allowed. I'm going to consider it a cane."

Sheridan informed her that they were Irish and that not only had they not been to a Giants game before in fact this would be their first baseball game.

"¡Dios mío! Your first game and you are front row behind home plate. I grew up watching the three M's – Mays, McCovey, & Marichal. I suffered through the 1970s and the Orange softball jerseys. Came back to life with Will the Thrill and Barry. It all paid off though with the Bochy championships. It has been quite a ride and I have never sat in the front row."

"I heard this is the new ballpark."

"New is a relative term. It opened in 2000."

"Same year Ireland joined the EU."

Lola continued the lesson, "True Giant fans paid their dues at Candlestick Park. Ever since Pac Bell Park, I still call it that, opened it has been a marvel. Home runs hit into McCovey cove. Sights of the Bay Bridge and the East Bay beyond the outfield walls. This park has character, comfort, and cuisine."

She led them up a wide rampway reminiscent of a parking garage. The rampways were designed to allow 45,000 patrons to egress in minutes at the conclusion of the game. As they reached the concourse level their nostrils were attacked with sourdough, garlic fries, spicy Cha-Cha bowls, beef from the grill.

Ginny commented, "Where do I start?"

Lola had no boundaries, "Do you have a date later?"

"…No."

"Then I would start with the garlic fries. They're delicious, but the garlic essence will stay with you for hours. You can stand in line if you want, but you don't have to your seats come with delivery."

"Wow. Service yes but is it the ballpark experience?"

"The concession stands are an experience, but I'd make sure to be in my seat for first pitch. …Back in the day vendors would roam the stands with cases of beer and soda on ice, hot dogs in steamers hawking their fare. That was an experience a hot dog in a wrapper passed down the row, your money headed back to the vendor, and your change returned. Unsanitary by today's standards, but we used to drink from the hose on a hot day."

Sheridan added, "We had a bucket and shared a ladle."

Lola led them to the gate marked sections 112/113. Ginny and Bernard were struck by the verdant baseball field, finely manicured, the outfield cross-hatched with parallelograms. The red infield dirt was brought in from Pennsylvania a specific mix of sand, silt, and clay designed for predictable bounce. The outfield brick wall to the right was closer than that on the left, it was higher and had arches. There was a waterway beyond the fence on the right. On the left, there were stands with benches. A huge electronic scoreboard was beyond the fence in the center of the field.

It was a clear day with a slight breeze that cleared away the haze. Beyond the ballpark walls was the Bay Bridge and the East Bay Hills. From their seats, the San Francisco Skyline was behind them on the left.

Ginny was seated in Section 113, Row A, Seat 9. Bernard had Section 113, Row A, Seat 10. They were just to the left of the catcher and unbeknownst to them they actually had the best seats to observe the pitched ball. Seat 8 was already occupied. Seat 11 on the aisle was empty. He leaned his shillelagh against the empty seat.

Ginny commented, "The view is beautiful. I'd pay just to sit in this seat for an hour."

Bernard retorted, "Yes, but you wouldn't pay €550."

"What are they doing?"

"It looks like they are chalking the pitch."

The gentleman in Seat 8 added, "It's a field, baseball field. We play soccer on the pitch. Not to mention the fact that a baseball is pitched. The grounds crew is chalking the foul lines and batter's boxes. Although they no longer use chalk, the lines are sprayed onto the infield dirt."

"My name is Virginia O'Connor; this is Bernard Sheridan."

"I am Stanley Sullivan."

Bernard exclaimed, "Sullivan! You're Irish."

"Guilty. And from the sounds of it so are the both of you. I lucked into this seat at the last minute. I've been to hundreds of games, but I've never had such good seats. It sounds like you are new to baseball; you should really appreciate the seats."

Bernard agreed, "It does seem as if we are right on top of the action. I'll have to thank our benefactor if our paths cross again."

Ginny pointed to the right field promenade, "What's the view like from out there?"

"If your uncle does not mind and the game allows, I'd be happy to give you a tour around the park. There's surprises and features all over the park."

"She's not my niece. We work together. She's a computer guru."

Ginny's cheeks were flushed, "A girl could have a worse uncle."

The conversation had turned awkward. The umpires

were huddled at the plate and the two managers approached. Bernard would change the subject.

"What's going on there?"

Stanley answered, "Before every game, the team's manager or his representative meets at home plate to exchange lineup cards and go over the ground rules. Each park has specific ground rules as to what is in and out of play, what to do if a fair ball bounces into the stands, gets stuck in fencing, etc. The lineup cards designate the official batting order and starting pitcher. If a team hits out of order, and it has happened, there's a procedure to penalize the offending team."

Ginny asked, "No coin flip?"

Stanley chuckled, "No. The visiting team always bats first, and the dugouts are designated at each park. It's the home team's advantage to bat last. The Giants will take the field and the starting pitcher will take his warm-ups. It looks like the game will start on time, 12:05."

The stands were full, and the fans stood and roared as the Giants sprinted from the third base dugout to their positions. They were an old-school National League team. Their home white uniforms were classic actually a light crème with the nostalgic 'Giants' script logo in black with orange piping. Most of the players wore high black stirrups; the second baseman and starting pitcher had lower stirrups with three orange stripes. Their hats were black with a black bill; the orange intertwined 'SF'.

Stanley stood and cheered. Ginny and Bernard looked at each other. They had that uneasy feeling of being the only ones at a ceremony not to rise for a standing ovation. They stood and applauded unconvincingly. Bernard did not notice the body come down the aisle and slide next to him assuming seat 11.

When Bernard sat down there was already an elbow on the armrest and a beer in his cup holder. He was plotting how he would get the offender's cup removed and he could retain possession of the armrest.

"Hello, Sherry. Is this yours? It's beautiful. How do you like the seats?"

Sean handed the shillelagh to Sherry.

"Sean McAuliffe!?! These are incredible. I was beginning to think you were not going to make it."

"That beer is yours. It's an Anchor Steam, a local microbrew. Pass this one over to your assistant."

"Ginny, this is Sean McAuliffe, the bloke who turned Lady Lavery into $100. Sean, this is Virginia O'Connor, my technical assistant."

"Sean, thank you for the seats. I feel close enough to take a swing at the ball."

"You are welcome. I took the liberty to order some bacon-wrapped hot dogs and garlic fries. They should be here after the top of the first."

Ginny looked at Stanley, "Top of the first?"

He explained, "Each team gets up to nine turns at the plate. When the away team hits it is the top of the inning. When the home team hits it is the bottom of the inning. The object is to advance around the bases and touch home plate, where an at-bat starts without being put out. When a team has three outs their half of the inning is over."

"I see. Thanks."

Sean placed an eye patch over his right eye. Sheridan took note.

"Is that because of the eye damage?"

"Yes. Severe nerve damage. A Stanford butcher tried corrective surgery but made it worse. I see double at times, have lost depth perception, and peripheral vision. I can't track the ball if I don't cover the eye; the input confuses my brain."

"There isn't anything that can be done."

"No. The doctors say the most I can hope for is to stop the rate of degradation. A game like today is more about the ambience. I have to track the action by the motion of the players. If you know the game, you can still enjoy the strategy, the drama."

"If you added a shillelagh to that look you'd really look like an old salt."

The umpire was squeezing the strike zone and the first Dodger walked. After a full count and four foul balls, the second batter bounced into a 4-6-3 double play. Stanley explained how the Giants forced two runners out on the same play with the second baseman flipping to the shortstop at second base and the shortstop gunning down the batter/runner at first.

Sherry was intrigued by Sean, "The will-call attendant pointed out what these tickets cost, and the usher was green with envy. This seems way be on your means. Are you sure I couldn't pay you for them?"

"Wouldn't hear of it. Besides, I was just cashing in some past-due favors owed."

"You are an interesting character."

The crack of the bat echoed through the ballpark louder than the ambient crowd noise. The ball was launched on a line off one of the right-field arches. It caromed to the left where the center fielder corralled it and threw it to the cutoff man. The third batter eased into second with a stand-up double.

Ginny jumped to her feet and began clapping.

Stanley cautioned, "Wrong team."

"Oops. Sorry."

"I'll let it go this time, Rookie."

The Giants starter still struggled to find the strike zone and his pitch count was climbing. It was too late in the playoff race to tolerate a sub-par performance. After another walk, the pitching coach and catcher made a trip to the mound.

Two on and two out the Giants could still get out of the inning unscathed. The starter was pressing; he uncorked a wild pitch that had Ginny ducking out of the way despite the safety net. The runners moved up a base. There were now two runners in scoring position. A base hit could have the Giants down two runs before ever coming to the plate.

Sheridan sensed the moment, "He's choking with the whole season on the line."

Sean's phone received a text. *'Wait 'til next year!'*

"Problem, Sean?"

"No. It's just my brother. Every year when the Giants or 49ers were eliminated our father would say, *'Wait 'til next year.'* Now my brother or I send out the death knell."

"Your father was a fan."

"My father was first generation American. Born in the City. He was a big fan of the local teams. I am a second-generation American. Born in the City. I too am a big fan of the local teams. All of my grandparents came from Ireland in the early 1900s -- Cork, Kerry, and Galway."

"I'm from Kerry."

Thinking the take sign would be on the pitcher grooved a get it over fastball. Crack! The center fielder raced to the wall, leapt, and grabbed nothing but air. It was a three-run homer.

Sherry related it to football, "That's like giving up a

goal in the opening minutes. So far to come back."

"I'm afraid my brother is right. They don't have the pitching or the heart this year. Win or lose they are still my Giants."

"I can respect that. Loyalty survives success and failure."

"Be wary of Johnny-come-latelies and fair-weather fans."

The Giants failed to score in the bottom of the first. The top of the second had the Dodgers with another base runner. It was the bottom of the third when the first Giant reached base being hit by the pitch.

Ginny was confused, "You said he was hit by pitch. Does that mean he got a hit like a single? Or, that the pitched ball struck him?"

Stanley pondered, "No one has ever asked me that before. ...Look at the scoreboard. The hit count does not change. It actually does not count as an at-bat in his personal statistics. ...Struck by pitch would be a better term. You want to take that tour of the ballpark. We can watch the game as we walk."

Ginny nodded and they were off. The Giants lone base runner was stranded.

Sherry stated the obvious, "It doesn't look good for our Giants."

Sean noticed Sherry's allegiance, "Our Giants. You've adopted my team."

"I like your City. You brought me to my first game. I'm a Giants fan now."

"Sherry, if you have to leave for your flight, I understand."

"I don't leave games early."

"McAuliffe's don't leave games early either. No one

wants to be in the parking lot and hear the crowd roar. Now, we might park half a mile away to avoid paying for parking or a quick exit, but we don't leave as long as there is an out left or time on the clock."

"Did you get that from your father?"

"Yes."

"He sounds like a good man."

"He was. I learned a lot from him. I never had an allowance, but he always gave me the opportunity to earn a little money. He would borrow $10 or $20 from me just to pay me interest. To this day I roll my own change and face my bills."

"Sounds like a banker."

"He was for most of his life. He was proud of his profession until the bank was sold to foreign interests and the downsizing started. He was laid off and too old to find another job. I always remember him as a loan officer."

"That's a shame."

"It broke him. He ended up in the bottle. My mother and him split. I was out of the house by then, but my brother had some scarring."

"My God."

"He died a lonely man."

For the next two innings they spoke of athletics, women, and upper middle-aged male frustrations. The seeds Sean had sowed were sprouting.

"You did not follow your father into banking."

"Banking and accounting relied on arithmetic. My mind lent itself more to logic and problem solving. I studied Engineering. We did not have generational wealth. I knew education would be my chance to open doors."

"Did you settle into a career?"

"I don't think settle is the term. I consulted. I worked in a variety of industries in a variety of roles. Wherever I was though, I observed, and I problem solved. All over the country, I was a fix-it man. It was important to be able to communicate with a variety of people from the dock to the board room."

Sherry wanted to hear more, "How did you translate those skills across companies, and industries?"

"It's funny. I learned early that the concepts were always the same. The business and engineering principles were the same the jargon and the scales could differ. Back before there was logistics we had inventory and shipping. We installed the same inventory and shipping systems for Oral-B toothbrushes and Komatsu Tractors. The same concepts held for a million $2 toothbrushes as a hundred $20,000 tractors."

"Being retired, do you miss it?"

"I will always be an observer and a problem solver. A fixer if you will. I just need an outlet."

Sherry was feeling his plight, "I'm not ready to retire. I can't do what I do on the outside. I think I'm feeling like your father must have when his bank was sold."

The Giants picked up a run in the bottom of the seventh on a walk, a fielder's choice, and a single. The score was 3-1 Dodgers as Ginny and Stanley returned. Ginny's face was flush as Stanley had hustled her around left field and down the third base line when he realized how late in the game it was.

Sheridan was in a playful mood, "I'll call off the search party. I thought I might be off to Australia on my own. The local authorities were set to check local hotels to see if you two had gotten a room."

Ginny turned beet red, "Bernard! Stanley was just showing me the Bay. He was a perfect gentleman."

"Too bad. I was hoping you would have a story or two to take home."

"I did promise to take Stanley to a hurling match if he ever made it to Ireland. Show him some real action."

"Is that true, Stanley? Did she promise to show you some real action? At your age that would have me booking a ticket."

Although Patty had gotten used to Sean and Kenny giving him a rough time, Stanley had been concentrating on keeping his cover all day, "Well, if I could get a gig in Ireland, I might be on the next plane. You want to sponsor me?"

Sean smiled. His boy came through.

Bernard had not anticipated Stanley's comeback, "Leave your number with Ginny."

"I already have."

Bernard and Ginny both turned red like boiled potatoes.

The Giants were playing like a team that had lost its will. There was no playoff push. The team was lacking clubhouse leadership and championship talent. When they gave up another run in the top of the ninth the fair weather fans that were left headed for the exit.

Sean was waiting, but there was not much game left. Bernard finally inquired.

"You never mentioned the name of your father's bank. I was just wondering if I knew of it."

Sean removed his eye patch.

"It was known as the Irish Bank. Bank of America was the Italian bank. It was founded in 1859 for the Irish gold miners to have a place to deposit their gold. By 1900 it was the largest bank in California. That's why its demise 80 years later was such a shame."

"Sounds like it ceased just as my career started."

"It was run by the Tobin family from its inception 'til its demise. I recall my dad talking about Tobin this and Tobin that. The bank was Irish to the core even the name. Hibernia Bank."

The color left Sherry's face. He swiveled his head towards Ginny to see if she was paying attention to him or her new friend. His eyes opened wide. He spoke so softly Sean needed to read his lips, "Hibernia?"

Sean confirmed, "Yes, Hibernia."

Sherry swallowed then stammered, "Erin go bragh."

Chapter 22

Shite Show

His custom's declaration was modest: Gifts for his daughter and his assistant Gertrude, a North American cell phone, and a Brisbane by Air coffee book for Margaret. He purchased the coffee book at the airport as an afterthought. Funding her gaming for the past month had burned any desire for him to lavish her.

Once clear of the Revenue Commissioners he thanked Ginny for her help on the trip and said goodbye. Ginny's bestie was waiting to take her home. Bernard scanned for Margaret. Two days ago he had arranged for her to meet him at Arrivals. He had been on the airplane for over 24 hours and there were no messages upon touchdown in Dublin.

She was not inside the terminal. He went to the curb to see if she was parked in the Loading Zone. There was no sign of her BMW. He waited at the curb for fifteen minutes to see if she was circling the airport. No Margaret. Her cell phone went to voicemail. He popped a blood pressure pill and washed it down with the airplane bottle of Jameson he had stowed in his jacket pocket. He was going to have to take a taxi. What a bint!

A beeping metallic green, early-2000's Volkswagen Beetle pulled up. The passenger's arm cranked the window down. It was Ginny.

"Bernie, do you need a ride?"

"Margaret was supposed to pick me up. I don't know where she is. I will take a taxi."

Ginny popped her head back in the beetle and spoke with the driver. Ginny stepped out of the car as the bonnet which on this car was the boot was sprung.

"Nonsense. You live in Ranelagh. It's on our way. We won't take no for an answer."

He was too tired to protest. He stuffed his suitcase and suit bag into the boot. His suits were sure to need a pressing after this ride. Bernie squeezed into the backseat being careful to not impale himself on his shillelagh. He sat sidesaddle behind Ginny; his bald head left an impression on the liner.

*   *   *   *   *   *   *   *

As they pulled up to 14 Westmoreland Park, Sheridan spotted the BMW in the driveway. His head was shaking and he mumbled under his breath as he took his luggage from the boot. He insisted Ginny and her friend take €50; the cost of a taxi plus tip.

He knocked on the door with the shillelagh as his house keys were packed. No answer. He rang the bell. He wrapped the door with enough force that the paint chipped. He heard motion in the house. It sounded like someone stumbling in the dark; it was 2 p.m. Margaret unlocked the door, did not open it, and headed back to the bedroom.

"Margaret! Margaret! Where the divil were you? You knew I was coming in today."

It looked like she had just woke after a rough night. Her hair was out of place, makeup smudged and looked as if she slept in her clothes.

"I've been flying for 24 hours and you look like shite. What happened?"

"I was on an unbelievable streak. I was up €3,000. I couldn't lose. I had more than covered all my advances."

"And…"

"They doubled the stakes. I lost two hands and pushed to get it back. I was so hot I knew I could do it."

"How much did you lose?"

"The €3,000 plus another €750."

Bernard was disgusted, "Go to bed."

He was not due to be at the office for two days to allow himself a day to recover from the trip. His personal phone chimed for a text. It was Gertrude.

'Your new office is finished. You will hate it. They are still working on the north end. …Flood moved the Division meeting up a day to ace you out. She and Dennehy have been running amok. …We have received about IR£ 25,000 for exchange.'

He replied, *'Thank you, Trudy. See you tomorrow.'*

* * * * * * * *

Bernard woke at 7:30 am, his norm for a working day.

"Why are you going in today? They gave you a day to recuperate. You haven't been around here for a month. What about me?" Margaret whined as Bernard dressed for the office.

"Well if you had picked me up yesterday, I could have told you about the goings on at the office while I've been gone. Flood and Dennehy are grasping for power. They are trying to castrate me."

"Who cares? You only have a few months left anyway."

Bernard's fuse was short, "I care. By the way, you can forget about advances for your 'Bridge' game and whatever other gambling you've been doing. I'm cutting you off. We can't afford it."

"It's your fault. What do you expect me to do?"

"You could get help for your problem. Or you could get a job to pay for your vices."

"That's not funny."

"I'm serious. I've left the number of a doctor who could help you by the phone again."

Margaret threatened, "I might not be here when you get back."

"That's fine. Your cards already are restricted. It would be easy enough to cancel them. The car is leased. The company can track it down and repossess it. I don't care about saving face at home anymore."

"You are so mean to me, Bernard. I hate you!"

"I'm off. See you tonight."

Living only six kilometers from the bank, he was easy on the bank vehicle. He would have an option to purchase the Volvo upon his retirement. It was in his contract; Flood and Dennehy could not stop that lest they charge him with malfeasance. The fifteen-minute commute did not give Sheridan time to clear his mind.

"Good Morning, Mac."

"Mr. Sheridan! You're back. Good to see you. They are really shaking things up on the executive floor. I'm afraid it's even impacted me out here. I've worked for you for 15 years. This isn't the way we do business."

"How so?"

"They reassigned all the spaces. I had to re-stencil the entire car park."

Sheridan's blood pressure was rising, "Eejits."

"Exactly. Don't be mad at me."

"Where'd they put me?"

"On the roof."

"With the feckin' seagulls!?!"

"Yeah, Boss."

"Not your fault, Mac. Cheers."

The elevator doors opened and he felt nauseous. Cubicles stretched from one side of the floor to the other. The stately double doors were gone. The thick pile carpet was replaced with industrial-grade carpet tiles. It did not feel like the economic seat of Ireland. It felt like an insurance company. A pile of broken-down boxes blocked the fire exit. Ms. Goodrich, the receptionist, who had been with the Bank for twenty years was not to be found. In her stead was a folding card table with a wire basket containing a ream of paper. The sheets were titled *Revised Floor Plan & Directory.* The floor plan looked like a rat maze. There were open spaces with grids of desks for the most junior of employees.

The directory was on the flip side of the floor plan. He could not believe he had to use a directory and floor plan to find his office. Thanks to an orienteering course in grade school he could read a map. He could only imagine how confused the young fops were with a directory and floor plan. They had taken a floor plan of twenty offices with windows and reduced it to four. Cubicle walls now faced windows. He had left a month ago thinking he was only being attacked on reserve fund issues. He couldn't believe what a shite show they made of the building.

His 'office' smelt sterile. Gone was his leather-top mahogany desk, his 40-year-old executive chair, the couch, all personal touches and the appearance of senior management. His garbage can contained the discarded assembly instructions and Allen keys. He collected the spent blister packs with unused screws and bolts. The furniture was veneer over compressed wood, cheap with a short lifespan.

Gertrude had tears in her eyes, "I'm so sorry, Bernard. There wasn't anything I could do. I packed your desk, files, and personal items when I saw them coming. They are safe. There are a lot of people around here who do not like what is happening."

"I know, Trudy. Thanks for giving me a heads-up. What time is the Division Meeting?"

"10:30 in the River Liffey conference room. It's one of the few rooms they didn't disturb. They don't expect you."

"Well, this won't be the first party I have crashed. Has Roland processed the punt/euro exchanges?"

"He said they are ready to go, but he held onto them just in case you wanted a look. His cubicle is the fourth one on the left. I hate this new layout."

"I'll check with Roland then attend the meeting. I have no calendar today."

"Dennehy has been trying to intimidate Security. They are loyal to you though. There's a network of staffers who are upset."

"Stand down, Trudy. We are not organizing a coup and I don't want anyone to do anything they will regret later."

Before seeing Roland he did a circuit of the floor. Heads were popping up peering out of their cubes to see what the commotion was about. Cube after cube the worker would step out and greet Sheridan. Normally, the returnee would be grilled for a travelogue. Today, Sheridan was the recipient of complaint after complaint. All were lamenting what had occurred during his absence.

"Roland, what's the craic?"

"Bernard! You weren't due back until tomorrow. It's been out of control here."

"How's the stability report?"

"Flood stopped the Dailies. I've still been running them though. Tech is bolstering us. Manufacturing is weak. Ag is suffering from the climate like the rest of the EU. I've got seven foreign requests for the pound/euro exchange for a total of €48,450."

"Did the exchanges come in through the web portal and secure post?"

"They did. Would you like to see them?"

Sheridan nodded his desire. Roland opened the safe. As Currency Manager, he had a safe to store funds and documents for transactions which he was commissioned to conduct. The safe sat on a reinforced portion of the floor. Moving it would have required structural changes to the building therefore it became an anchor in Dennehy's redesign. It was similar to selecting a room's color to match a throw pillow.

Sheridan scanned the three smaller transactions one each from Toronto, Boston, and Melbourne. He inspected the four larger transactions two from San Francisco, one from Seattle, and one from Los Angeles. The larger transactions consisted of 100-pound notes, series A. He rubbed notes between his fingers. He checked for the watermark. He looked for the clarity of proper printing. He sniffed a note. His eyes closed. He exhaled and hmphed from the back of his throat.

He questioned Roland, "All the documentation in order?"

"Yes."

"Are you ready to issue the transfers?"

"Yes. I just thought you'd like to see that we had some action."

"Thanks. It will be good to show some results for the

meeting."

"Good to have you back, Bernard."

"Thanks."

He needed to relieve himself before the Division Meeting. He chose the non-binary bathroom to see what had become of his office. It looked like it was designed by a heterosexual. It contained a toilet with a seat that did not raise, a urinal, a bidet, and a changing table. The convenience vending machine had feminine hygiene products as well as prophylactics. He peed in the toilet hoping splatter would land on the seat.

It was 10:33. Flood was at the end of the table, and Dennehy to her right was speaking into her ear. The other Directors filled the sides of the table. No one had sat directly opposite Flood, his regular seat. The meeting had not been called to order, three or four conversations were ongoing. Sheridan made his entrance. He took a copy of the agenda from the table and plopped into his regular seat. The room fell silent and all eyes were on him.

Sheridan reveled in the moment, "Cheers, everyone!"

Dennehy derided his presence, "You are not supposed to be back until tomorrow. What are you doing here?"

"I felt surprisingly good after the flight and I heard the place had a facelift. I didn't realize there was a Division Meeting today. I haven't prepared any material. I'll just observe and catch up."

While Flood and Dennehy conducted a side conversation, Sheridan scanned the agenda. 'Security – Assignment to Enforcement' caught his eye. He folded the agenda in half and stowed it in his inside jacket pocket. Flood and Dennehy were too self-absorbed to notice.

Flood was not prepared for Sheridan's presence. She had gotten used to railroading her personal agenda.

"I've just been informed that I have an emergency meeting with the Governor at 11:15. Please pass the agendas back to Louis. The formal Division Meeting will be rescheduled to next week. We will go around the table. Just let me know of any issue that needs immediate attention."

Information Technology projects were extended a week and had additional cost overruns due to time lost to construction. Human Resources had exceeded the new hire budget for the year due to the addition of Enforcement personnel. A division-wide freezing hire had been put in effect. Personnel would only be added to backfill separations.

Sheridan thought, 'Finally a Flood meeting my bladder could last through.'

Dennehy spoke of fraud investigations at minor credit institutions in Kerry and Galway. He did not speak of his intentions for Security or his foray into Facilities Management. Sheridan thought, 'He's really not a quick thinker for a J2 man. Must've been why he washed out.'

It was 11:00 and Flood wanted to retreat.

"Bernie, you don't have anything for us do you?"

"Well ma'am, to my surprise we have already seen some pound/euro exchanges. We are also pleased at the web traffic on the exchange portal. …And might I say the speed at which you implemented change on the floor is surprising."

Flood and Dennehy were caught off guard. Flood adjourned the meeting. She and Dennehy walked off confabbing on Sheridan's comment.

The other Directors huddled around Sheridan welcoming him back. Inquiring about his boondoggle and lamenting the new layout. He was assessing who was in Flood's pocket and who still believed in the Central Bank.

Sheridan took another lap around the floor. This time he was estimating the size of the project. As Facilities had been his department for the past 10 years, he had overseen a half dozen major projects. He observed the construction zone; no hardhats, no supervision, scraps strewn about the work zone. The workers were speaking what he believed to be Polish, but it could have been Slovak or Lithuanian. He estimated the project cost between €200,000 and €225,000. Just within Flood's authorization limit. Flood and Dennehy were over their skis; they did not know what they had done.

Chapter 23

The Divil is in the Details

Following the truncated Division Meeting Sheridan retreated to his new office to regroup. He no longer had a closet so he opened the top drawer of the 4-drawer vertical file cabinet to hold the hanger with his jacket. Sheridan got on his knees despite his suit pants. He could be ruining the wool; the crease was certainly lost. The Naugahyde chair in his 'office' had eight levers and knobs for adjustment. Other than the height adjustment, none of the levers or knobs seemed to do a thing.

He leaned back, stretched his arms, and put his hands behind his head. As he closed his eyes he could feel his center of gravity shift from his back under his arse; the wheels of the chair slid forward. The back fell off the chair. The rest occurred in slow motion. His eyes opened to see the ceiling. His arms flailed.

Crash!

The back of his head hit the cheap carpet. He was arse over teakettle.

Gertrude was first on the scene.

"Bernard! Are you alright? What happened?"

Bernard was rubbing the back of his head. He checked for blood, but he only found a lump. His direct reports who had cubicles nearby checked on the commotion.

"The eejit who put this together didn't tighten the screws."

Gertrude offered aid, "Let me see. Do you need the first aid kit? Someone get the ice pack!"

Bernard sat on one of the austere reception chairs in his office and held the ice pack against the ping-pong sized lump. His direct reports had dispersed. Gertrude remained.

"Did you pass out? You could be concussed?"

"I used to knock heads harder than that day in and day out. I'm fine."

"We did not expect you until tomorrow. Your afternoon is open. Would you like me to pull some meetings forward?"

"No. Give the troops all the time they need. I just wanted to take the temperature today."

"Can you drive?"

"I could but after all that travel I'd like to stretch my legs. I'll leave the car to the seagulls."

Bernard grabbed his wool cap and shillelagh.

*   *   *   *   *   *   *   *

He did not cross the Samuel Becket Bridge over the River Liffey and head home instead he meandered west to The Celt for lunch. It had been more than six weeks since he was at The Celt. When Lily spotted him she put the tray of drinks to deliver on the bar and greeted him with a big hug.

"Sherry, it feels like a month of Sundays since we've seen you. Were you locked up?"

"It felt like it. I was traveling for business. The bint and the eejit tried to pull the rug out from under me."

"Glad you're back. Need to see a menu?"

"Let me see the Beer & Ales list if you don't mind."

The Celt was known for whiskey and ale. They had a worldwide selection of both. The beer and ale were organized geographically. He scanned the Americas. He recollected the baseball game.

"Lily, I'd like a fish and chips. Could you ask the cook to chop up some garlic and smother the chips? And, I'll have an Anchor Steam."

"Anchor Steam?"

"Yes. Anchor Steam. I tried one last week. I've taken a liking to it."

"Liam, One and One for Sherry. Make the chips stinky. Give him a Sinker."

His plates were cleared and he was working on his second Anchor Steam. The chef was not as committed to the garlic as they had been at the Ballpark. Sherry scanned the bar for prying eyes. His bank cell phone was on the table. It had been five hours without a message from Margaret. Maybe he got through to her one way or the other.

It was 2:13 pm. He did the math; it was 6:13 am in San Francisco. He pulled the Hibernia phone from his inside breast pocket. An ancillary benefit of the month spent traveling with Ginny was his introduction to emojis and text abbreviations. He had thought an eggplant was an eggplant. There was only one phone number stored in contacts, 'John L'. Sir John Lavery was a portrait artist whose second wife, Hazel, was the model for the Lady Lavery portraits which inspired the Series A banknotes. Sherry opened the emoji menu, selected two symbols, and pressed send.

*　*　*　*　*　*　*　*

Kenny was first to the shop at 8:00 am. There were a half dozen unsolicited realtor cards for agents who wanted to list the building. Kenny walked the floor as he did every morning making sure the machinery and supplies were set for the day's run. It was supposed to be their first full week of production.

Patty was next to arrive while Kenny was still on the floor. He let himself in as Kenny had provided him with a key. He nearly wet his pants when he checked the online accounts. He dialed *11 on Kenny's desk phone for the PA system.

"Kenny to the office. Kenny to the office."

Kenny worked his way back from the intaglio printer.

"My God, Patty, it's not even 8:30 yet. Why the hell did you pull me from the floor?"

"It's the bank accounts. We have $37,240!"

"No shit. Let me see."

"It went in last night. It says pending, but its available."

"That's encouraging, but Sean still may have screwed us with Sheridan. $30,000 doesn't buy me the print shop or you your freedom."

Bing. Bing. Bing. The front door entry alarm chimed. Kenny shot a glance at Patty. He minimized the screen like a clerk looking at porn in the office. Kenny sighed then feigned irritation.

"We've been here over an hour waiting for you. We're set to start production en masse today. We run on a schedule here."

"A thousand apologies. I went by Mom's to check the mail and get these." He held up a manila folder.

"A manila folder. I've got thousands of them."

"Yes, but do you have Hibernia Bank Statements circa 1970 and correspondence from Michael Tobin CEO? My mom does not believe in the 7-year retention rule. She has mortgage stubs that date back to the late 1950s. Her basement is a real archive."

"Ok. But you are on steam only. Don't touch the printers."

"Wouldn't think of it."

"Have you had any contact with Sheridan since the ballgame?"

"No. But I consider that as a no news is good news situation."

Kenny turned to Patty, "Do you think we should tell him?"

"Tell me what?"

Patty replied to Kenny, "Not sure. Do you consider it need to know information?"

"Well, he won't be worth a plug shilling if we don't tell him."

"Tell me what!?!"

Patty maximized the window showing the wire transfers into their accounts.

"I think it's better if I show rather than tell."

He swiveled the monitor so Sean could see.

"Aha! Our exchanges were accepted. We'll need $25,000 for travel, shipping, and lodging expenses. That leaves $12,000. Kenny, will $6,000 help you with back bills here and at home?"

"That would be great, Sean."

"Patty, I'd like you to take $3,000 and pay any back bills or rent you owe, but don't be flashy. Can you do that?"

"All this time around you two has taken all the flash out of this star."

"Patty, did you get a chance to check the Hibernia Phone this morning?"

"No. When I saw the bank accounts, I got sidetracked."

He pulled the Hibernia Phone from the kelly green chrome messenger bag.

"There's a message! It came in around 6 am this morning. I'll put it on the big screen. It's a shamrock and a nose!"

Kenny found it cryptic, "Is that it?"

Patty shrugged, "Afraid so. I think it's a puzzle."

Sean interpreted, "It's not a puzzle. It's a message. He's telling us to do something about the smell of the notes. The shamrock is Hibernia, the banknotes. He said smell wasn't a conclusive factor, but he expected the notes to smell different. It should smell like the City."

"Sean, I know they can add scent at the paint store, but I don't have any means of doing that with these machines."

"I have an idea. It will take me a day to put together. Kenny, can you review the manila folder and see if you could replicate documents that look similar and distressed. I'll give you the content later."

"Sure."

"Patty, could you research money stacks. Mustard straps are used on stacks containing 100 notes of $100. We will use them for 100 notes of IR£100. You and Kenny work on design of the strap and a Hibernia Bank stamp for it."

"Will do."

"Start printing if you finish those tasks before I get back. We will need 500 stacks all told. I put a bill counter at the end of the line by the dryer. Make sure you face the notes before they are counted. That's how the bank would do it. Once the counter spits out 100 notes, run them through again just to make sure. Any questions?"

Kenny and Patty each shook their heads no. Sean

moved to the center of the room.

"Ok. Bring it in."

The three huddled. Sean, rallied the troops.

"Hibernia on three! …One. Two. Three!"

HIBERNIA!

*   *   *   *   *   *   *   *

The fifty-pound sack was sewn shut. He always had trouble opening bulk bags like that. Usually, the string would snag and he would take a utility knife and start cutting loop by loop. When the frustration grew he would take the knife straight to the bag. It was always a mess. Today was different. He pulled the end of the string just right and it unraveled first to the end of the bag then the entire length. He did not spill any product.

He measured 12 ounces of flour on the scale and 2 ounces of sourdough starter. He added lukewarm water and began to knead what would be the first loaf of sourdough. Once it was thoroughly mixed he placed it in the container where it would rise overnight in the basement.

He repeated the process another five times.

Buzz. Buzz.

He pressed the release with an elbow as his hands were covered in dough. When the footsteps on the stair approached he called out.

"Come in! It's open!"

He was already back kneading when the door opened. The pungent aroma of starter and raw sourdough was so strong she could taste it.

"I'm in the kitchen."

"No shite. What's the craic, Sean?"

"It's a pleasure to see you too, Francess." She was wearing Levi's that made her legs look so long and a yellow top that clung to her shape. It was a very California look.

"Sorry, A ghrá." She leaned over and gave him a kiss on the cheek taking care to not come out flour-dusted.

"What are you doing?"

"I'm getting ready to bake 50 loaves of bread.'

"Fifty loaves!?!"

"I could use your help. I broke my starter into five portions last night and fed each so that I'd have plenty for the batch. I've started to make individual loaves. I have plastic containers for each loaf and my basement is cool enough where I can let them rise overnight."

"So, I'm just an extra pair of hands to you."

"There's nothing extra about your hands. And you've become very special to me. I was going to wait until later, but why don't you open the envelope over here now."

"What is it?"

"I've just come into some money and I want to share it with you."

"Sean, I couldn't"

"Just consider it a three-year tip advance."

"There's $1,500 here! It's too much."

"Francess, I want you to have it."

"Oh, Sean." She dropped the money on the counter and pulled Sean away from the loaf he was kneading. She draped her arms from his shoulders and drew him close. Her leg slipped up between his thighs. The kiss was passionate. When they broke she was covered in flour from head to toe.

They spent the afternoon breaking off starter, measuring flour, adding lukewarm water, and kneading.

They tossed flour at each other. They laughed and talked of Ireland, Hawaii, and Grenada. She bounced up and down the stairs carrying four loaves at a time to the basement. He would carry four loaves but extended his elbows to feel the rails taking care to not miss a step as he had trouble assessing the distance. His knees ached as he climbed the stairs pulling at each rail to shift weight off his legs to his arms.

"Francess, thanks for helping me today. I couldn't have finished without you."

"It was fun. You know my daughter would love to run a bakery. It's her passion. Working with the dough reminded me of being in the kitchen with her."

"You don't have to work tonight do you?"

"No. When you asked me to come over this afternoon, I traded shifts for Friday. Better tips anyway."

"I should have told you to bring a change of clothes, but I was afraid that would have scared you away."

"You could wash them for me."

"I can do that. You can take a shower if you want. Either way, I have a robe you can wear. It's hanging on the back of the bathroom door."

Francess exited to the bedroom as he finished sweeping the floor and wiping the counter. She inspected his laundry basket. He changed his underwear and shirts daily. There were two pairs of jeans in the wash and three bath towels. She put her flour-infused jeans and shirt in his laundry basket; she also added her black, lacy bra and panties. She closed and locked the bathroom door.

Sean came to get her clothes and saw they were on top of his laundry basket. The shower was running. He took the whole thing down to the basement using the back stairs. They were narrow and the treads were shorter than the code. Carrying a load of laundry he had to take it one step at a time lest he lose balance. After emptying the basket into the machine, he topped the load off with the clothes he had been wearing.

Running naked to get to the shower before Francess finished he stubbed his toe trying to take the stairs two at a time. He hopped in pain to the bedroom. Aaggh. She locked the bathroom door. He took a nail file and bobby pin from his dresser. The old lock was not hard to pick.

Francess was facing the wall letting the water cascade down her back. He slipped in under the stream and started to scrub her back.

"Oh, Sean."

Chapter 24

Crossing I's and Dotting T's

Sean's Cougar was at the loading dock. He had loaded totes in the trunk, backseat, and passenger seat. The totes contained the risen loaves of sourdough. He was emptying the employee refrigerator in the break room. He dumped the expired milk. He put the two six-packs of Harp on the table along with the butter and the bowl of mustard and ketchup packets. He removed all the racks. Patty rolled in a utility cart with three totes. He was block stowing the containers in the refrigerator. Kenny followed five minutes later with the other two totes. Sean left the loaves from one tote out.

Sean was surprised and pleased with the progress, "So, you are telling me that you increased the batches to 70 sheets from 60 and reduced the steam to serial time to 30 minutes from 40. That's incredible. That will cut the production run to 60 hours."

"We put in 12 hours yesterday. Once we hit our groove we didn't want to stop. We produced a million pounds worth of notes. Frankly, I'd rather you don't mess with the process. Another four or five days and we will complete the entire run."

"Did you randomize them with the dryer on tumble?"

"Yep."

"Did you strap them?"

"Yep. 100 stacks of 100-100's."

"Where are they?"

Kenny pointed behind Sean. There was a table against the wall with a St. Patrick's Day tablecloth. Kenny stepped over and tugged at his sleeves like Bullwinkle J.

Moose.

"Nuttin' up my sleeve. Presto!"

He pulled the tablecloth off with flair and panache exposing an even layer of Hibernia stacks. Sean took a stack and fanned the end. The serial numbers were not sequential. There was no bleeding of ink or dull lines. The notes were near perfect. The stack smelt fresh.

"Sean, do you really think this will work?"

"The notes should smell like they have been stored in the City for 50 years. There's nothing more San Francisco than sourdough bread. Sheridan's message was to do something about the smell. I believe the sourdough will mask the fresh scent and by the time of the exchange in Dublin the smell will be indistinguishable."

"What's the recipe?"

"We can do the first batch now. Make sure the dough is removed from the fridge and allowed to come to room temperature."

Sean had brought a large chopping block and a large bucket of flour. He spread a handful of flour on the block and removed the dough from one of the containers. He kneaded it looking for a spring back in the loaf. He shaped it and cut three slits along the top.

"I have 10 loaves to bake with each million. 475° for 45 minutes."

Having worked with the senior members for months, Patty was a burgeoning curmudgeon, "That's a lot of bread. What are we going to do with it?"

"Eat it. Give it to friends and family. I will take a batch to Flanahan's. You can take a batch to Java Beach Café."

The smell of sourdough competed with the permanent Murphy Printing ink aroma. The buzzer sounded; the loaves and banknotes were done. The bread had to cool, the banknotes did too. The sourdough would take 2 hours to cool before they could slice it. The stacks of notes were spread on a series of racks in the breakroom. After 90 minutes the stacks were handleable. They each took a stack and a good sniff.

Patty fanned his stack under his nose and inhaled.

"It's not ink or sourdough. It's something in between."

Kenny agreed.

"I can't describe it, but it doesn't make you think anything."

They stowed the notes in a tote.

*　*　*　*　*　*　*　*

Kenny and Patty could not wait to get back on the print floor to produce more banknotes. They believed in the product. They believed in Hibernia. They believed in Sean.

Sean had moved to Kenny's office. Although considered sacrilege by most, he took a warm Harp from the breakroom and made himself a bucket. A beer and a bucket was an order he had learned in Hawaii; the bucket was a large tumbler of ice to thwart poor refrigeration and humidity.

He reflected on how far they had come. How he guided Patty to infiltrate birth records, Social Security, the State Department, and DMV. How Kenny dissected the real banknote. How he helped solve the watermark problem and the scent issue. How they bugged Flanahan's and handled the Sheridan curve ball. He could not have admitted it to the others, or himself for that matter, but had he been asked before Hibernia started he would have given them a 80/20 chance that the project would have fallen apart or they would be in jail.

He thought of Francess and how she had kept him going. How she had helped Hibernia without ever asking for an explanation or a cut. He could depend on her.

There was not much left to do in San Francisco. They needed to forge fifty year old Hibernia Bank statements and correspondence from the Chairman of the day Michael de Young Tobin. After that it would be time to contact the Central Bank and arrange travel.

He felt light-headed. His heart was racing. He could not catch his breath. It was noon and the beer seemed to be hitting him hard. He had doubts about Sheridan. He had fears that he could not fool the Central Bank of an entire country. He was sensing panic. He slowed his breathing and cleared his mind. He reminded himself he had little to lose, but his cohorts were desperate for the opportunities Hibernia would afford.

Once he was collected he entered a message on the Hibernia phone. It contained four icons: a nose, a checkmark, an airplane, and an outline of Ireland.

It was 8 pm in Dublin. Margaret was in a snit from her scolding in the morning. Even though he had only been home less than 48 hours she was giving Bernard the silent treatment. He was fine with that.

... Mush-a ring dumb-a do dumb-a da
Wack fall the daddy-o, wack fall the daddy-o
There's whiskey in the jar...

Bernard's sock drawer was ringing. She heard it from the living room. He heard it from the kitchen.

She broke her silence, "What's that?"

... Mush-a ring dumb-a do dumb-a da
Wack fall the daddy-o, wack fall the daddy-o
There's whiskey in the jar ...

"That was my Australia alarm. I forgot to shut it off. Sorry."

He raced to the bedroom and caught it before the next *Whiskey in the Jar*. He took the phone in the bathroom and read the message. Sean would be coming to town. He was more and more impressed with Sean's talents, gumption; he believed Sean was a problem solver. He wanted Sean to know the construction project had not been put to bid and was using scab labor. His reply contained an image of a worker, red strikethru circle over the word bid, and a bandaid.

*   *   *   *   *   *   *   *

Sean yelled into the phone, "Hello, Gene! It's your nephew Sean!"

"You don't have to yell. I got new aides. How'd you like the seats?"

"They were great. The Giants sucked. They're done. I'm moving on to the Niners."

"Everyone is."

"Gene, I'm going to be out of town for a few weeks. Could you give my mom a few calls? Check in on her?"

"Sure. Where are you going?"

"Dublin."

"That's hardly out of town, Sean. It's only 40 miles away. Though I understand your aversion to crossing the Bay Bridge."

"Not that Dublin, Gene."

Gene was surprised, "You mean Ireland!?!"

Sean uttered, "Uh-hmm."

"Just Dublin? I'd go visit the counties where Mom and Pop were from."

"I'm taking some meetings. I can't afford to spend a month touring."

"Bring me back a whiskey. Something expensive that I've never had."

"Will do. Gene, I need to find a union bigwig in Dublin. I know you worked with a lot of expatriates in the trades. Were any connected back in Ireland?"

"What are you up to, Sean? ...No. No. Don't tell me. I don't want to know. Sounds like you need to meet the Nolans. Seamus and Dickie settled here in the City. They are about your age. Dickie worked electrical with me. Seamus is in general construction. Last I heard their brother Brian is an officer with CONNECT a super union there."

"Could you give me a number for Seamus or Dickie?"

"No. Best if I introduce you in person. A cold call isn't likely to work."

"The Niners play Monday night. Do you think you could get the Nolans out to Flanahan's?"

"My God, Sean, don't you ever go anywhere else? They should charge you rent."

"I go to Java Beach Café in the morning."

"I'll make the call and let you know. Now, get off the line."

"Ok, Gene. You have a nice day too."

* * * * * * * *

Gene was holding court. It wasn't often that he got out for anything but a medical appointment. The Nolans came to the City in the mid-90s. Dickie worked at AT&T with Gene for 15 years. Seamus and Gene worked side jobs for 20 years. The Nolans and Sean had respect for Gene like former athletes visiting a favorite coach.

Francess brought the potato skins, bacon-wrapped shrimp, and nachos that Sean had ordered. It would be a beer night. The Nolans were drinking Guinness, Gene had a long-neck Budweiser, and Sean his Harp.

The Niners were playing their arch-rival, the Cowboys. The Nolans spoke of the Steve Young years and knew the legend of Joe Montana. They thought Aikman was the greatest quarterback in Cowboy history. Gene shook his head; he spoke of John Brodie and two NFC Championship losses to the Cowboys in the early 70's. He talked of never being scheduled for Monday Night Football, of never making the halftime highlights. He talked of paying dues and always being loyal.

Dickie spoke of how in 15 years he never saw Gene go under a house or crawl through an attic. Seamus added he never saw Gene float cement or move a wheelbarrow.

Gene noted, "It takes some longer than others to learn how to work smarter rather than harder."

The Niners' halftime adjustments had turned a 9-point halftime lead to a 23-point lead at the end of the third quarter. Francess cleared the dinner plates. It was time for Sean to make his pitch.

"I understand your brother is an officer at CONNECT."

Dickie replied, "That he is. Brian is the Assistant General Secretary."

"I have a friend in Dublin. He's in management but has worked with the trades for years. He understands the value of quality work. He's getting screwed and forces out of his control circumvented corporate policy and authorized a rogue project."

Seamus was nonplussed, "What do you want us to do about it?"

"Give me a private email or phone number for your brother. Something untraceable. A way he can be contacted anonymously with the specifics."

Dickie and Seamus conferred behind the security of a napkin.

Dickie began the interrogation.

"What's in it for you?"

"I'm tired of seeing men our age get the shaft. Being forced out by less experienced, less knowledgeable people for the sake of politics and appearance."

"Why this bloke?"

"He crossed my path. We shared some pints. We swapped tales. He's going through the same shite I went through."

"Have you ever even been to Ireland?"

"No, I haven't yet. I do know Dublin's climate is a lot like the City's. I do know Hurling is the world's fastest sport on turf. My eyes are just good enough that I can stream Gaelic Football most evenings."

Seamus continued the inquisition.

"Why should we trust an American?"

"First, you've lived in the City for over 25 years. You know I'm not your average American. Second, I feel more allegiance to Ireland than I do most of the US and it's backward politics. And, third, what if I were to tell you an American was honored as the face of Ireland for years."

"Bollocks!"

"Francess, can you bring me the frame from behind

the register? You know the one."

Francess had been keeping a pulse on the conversation. She nodded and gave Sean a wink. She handed the frame to Sean face side down. He took up the offensive.

"You moved here before Ireland went on the euro. Right?"

"Yes."

"Do you remember Irish currency?"

"They were beautiful banknotes. It's a shame they had to go away."

"Would you say they represented the essence of Ireland?"

Seamus' and Dickie's eyes met. They shared an almost imperceptible shrug. Seamus conceded.

"Alright."

"The back of the notes represented different Irish rivers based on the denomination. And, on the front…"

"On the front was Lady Lavery, an Irish beauty. A representation of all that is good about Ireland."

Sean handed the frame with the Hibernia note to Seamus. Seamus passed it to Dickie.

"What would you say if I told you she was an American from Chicago?"

"Don't bullshite a bullshiter, Sean"

"I'm not. Go ahead and check me?"

"Stephen! Stephen, can you come over here for a minute?"

Stephen extricated himself from the bar. Francess came along. The commotion was enough to get the patrons at the bar to shift their focus from the mirrored wall of bottles 180° to the Nolan brothers.

Dickie started. "Stephen, you're a Dublin man, aren't

you?"

"I am."

"This bloke is trying to tell me that Lady Lavery was an American. That the essence of Irish beauty was born in Chicago."

Stephen confirmed, "Sorry, mate. He's right."

The Nolans were as red as boiled potatoes. Francess tried to contain her smile. Stephen laughed.

Seamus and Dickie shook their heads in disbelief and resignation. They were out Blarneyed by an American. Dickie took a cocktail napkin.

"Does anyone have a pen?"

Francess and Stephen each produced a pen. Dickie wrote his brother Brian's personal email address.

The Nolans paid their respects to Gene. Sean settled the tab and returned the frame to Stephen. He nodded for Francess to meet him in the office.

"Sean McAuliffe, I don't have time for slap & tickle in the office right now."

"That's not why I asked you off the floor. I have something for you."

"Do you now?"

He handed her a small white box with a green ribbon. The kind of box that would hold a bracelet. It was a brass Irish knot key ring.

She asked, "What's this?"

"It's a key ring for my house key." He handed her a freshly cut door key. "I thought you might prefer one roommate in a bigger space with no rent."

"Oh, Sean."

She embraced him. They kissed. She slid her leg between his. The way she knew drove him crazy.

Chapter 25

Meet Dan Reilly

The flight attendant shook Sean McAuliffe's shoulder to wake him. He was sitting in seat 6A, business class, port-side window. Aer Lingus flight EI60 was nearly full and would arrive fifteen minutes late.

"Mr. Reilly. Mr. Reilly. Please fasten your security belt and raise your seat."

Sean McAuliffe woke a tad startled and confused. He raised his seat and fastened the belt.

"How soon will we be arriving?"

"You can see the city out the port window now. The lead attendant should make the final announcement directly."

"As we make our final approach to Dublin please fasten your security belt, raise your seat forward and stow your service tray. Aer Lingus would like to thank you for your patronage from San Francisco today. If Dublin is your final destination, welcome home. If you are here for a visit may the sun shine warm upon your face, the rains fall soft upon your fields, and, until we meet again, may God hold you in the palm of His hand. Dublin shares Greenwich Mean Time, it is 11:50 am."

He reviewed his passport one last time. 'Daniel Reilly' looked just like Sean McAuliffe. They shared birthdates, and mother's maiden names. He squirmed to remove the billfold from his back pocket. The California Driver's License also read Daniel Reilly with a photograph of Sean McAuliffe. But not the same photo used on the passport just in case an official reviewed both documents. The Visa, Macy's and San Francisco Library Card were also in Reilly's name. He had €500 in cash and another €1,500 in traveler's cheques.

Sean had practised. He would soon compartmentalize his past. One last time though he thought of his father a Vice President of Hibernia Bank, but really nothing more than a loan officer; his childhood Hibernia coin bank, the one that had no hole for emptying. How the layoff broke his father's spirit. He hoped Sheridan would not face the same fate at the Central Bank. Sean used self-hypnosis to reinforce that Dan Reilly's story would flow naturally.

The Dan Reilly story had to flow from Sean's mouth without thought or hesitation. Sean was not playing Dan Reilly; he was Dan Reilly. Addresses, girlfriends, education, job history – he had the answer. Reilly, thanks to Patty, had used the same mobile phone carrier for the past three years. His phone was full of contacts and text history. He had a social media presence, active but not addictive.

Sean had faith. He had to. The flawless work of his compatriots held his fate. To date it had been successful at opening bank accounts, establishing credit, passing through airport screening. The identifying documentation and electronic footprint had so far passed all authentications with ease. The big tests lay ahead though. Dan Reilly was about to step off the Airbus A330.

Flying business class negated the need to queue for customs clearance. Reilly wished to control the process.

"Officer Wyse, is it? I am Mr. Reilly, San Francisco, California. My declaration has already been filed. Principal Officer McBride is expecting me. Would you ring him please?"

Without looking up she stated, "Passport, please. Do you have a carry-on bag?"

"Here is my passport and carry-on. The purpose of my trip is personal business, and I will be staying for no more than two weeks."

"Yes, Sir. Thank you. Your passport appears in order. I will contact the Principal Officer directly."

Wyse's radio microphone was connected to her epaulette. She pulled it closer to her face and wrenched her neck in that direction. She called for the Principal Officer then put a finger to her earpiece not wanting to miss an instruction from her superior. Next came a series of head nodding and a 'Yes, Sir'. All the while, Dan Reilly waited patiently choosing to not be agitated or bothered. Reilly used the controlled breathing technique from the self-hypnosis course to calm himself and control his blood pressure. He exuded confidence and respectability.

Officer Wyse looked to the end of the counter. Reilly noticed as she gave the high sign to a well-dressed man who had been monitoring the security radio. He left the terminal for a waiting vehicle. Wyse returned her gaze to Reilly.

"Sir, the Principal Officer has directed me to escort you to the Aer Lingus Cargo operation at Terminal 1. It is only a five-minute drive in my vehicle."

Her vehicle was a glorified golf cart with the customs 'Revenue' logo on the bonnet, black and white checkered shrink wrap on the sides and a blue flashing light on top. Wyse had other officers collect Reilly's luggage and stow it in the back of the 'vehicle'. Reilly hopped into the passenger side of the front bench and hit his knee on the steering wheel. It was Ireland even the security (golf) carts are right-hand drive.

"Slide over mate and hang on!" Wyse directed as she

toggled the power switch and stepped on the accelerator. She weaved amongst the travelers, blue lights blinking like a K-mart special. The cart even had the distinctive Eeee-Aaah European siren. It was set to startling rather than ear-piercing. Reilly, unable to find a handle to grab, wedged himself in place with his left hand pressed against the roof and his right foot planted under the dashboard. Reilly had not anticipated his demise could be the driving of Officer Wyse before he even left the airport.

They had cleared the passenger terminals; the cargo bays were a mile down the frontage road. Reilly took a deep breath. It was 50^0 Fahrenheit, overcast. He could sense the marine influence. It felt just like San Francisco, home. Wyse, however, took this as an opportunity to redline the golf cart. Reilly was hanging on for dear life.

"Wyse! I'm not escorting a heart for transplant. Let's get there in one piece."

"Sorry. Don't like to keep the Principal Officer waiting."

Wyse cut the turn into Aer Lingus Cargo at full speed. Reilly swore the cart was on two wheels through the turn. She locked the wheels and the cart skidded to a stop two meters short of the Principal Officer. Reilly had experienced zero gravity in a golf cart. His suitcase separated from the cart. It bounced just wide of the Principal Officer.

"Wyse!" barked McBride.

"Sorry, Sir. Must not have been stowed properly. I'll collect it."

McBride turned his attention to Reilly.

"Mr. Reilly, on behalf of the Irish Revenue Commissioners we are sorry for your loss. Principal

Officer McBride at your service. The paperwork for your shipment cleared before your arrival. The shipping crate is on the tarmac and en route to the inspection bay. After a brief review, you may take possession for transport."

"Thank you, McBride. We need to make the Central Bank before 3:00 pm to store the vault until processing."

"Wyse let's move inside the inspection hanger, get the canines ready."

"Both sets, sir?"

"Aye."

The wooden shipping crate was 5' long by 3' wide and 3' tall. After hearing the Principal Officer's comment she thought it might contain a coffin but there was an unmarked armored 2020 BMW 750i wagon waiting to transport. She directed the handler with the drug-sniffing dog to proceed. Lucky circled the crate a half dozen times but found no trace of narcotics. She directed Lucky to be removed before Shamrock would have her turn. Shamrock was trained to indicate stashes of currency which had not been declared. Shamrock did not complete a single lap around the crate before indicating as she had never indicated before. Wyse turned to McBride.

"Sir, we are getting a strong indication of currency from Shamrock. Shall we proceed to open the crate?"

Reilly noticed the well-dressed man from the counter was observing from a distance. Reilly was clandestinely observing the observer.

"Mr. Reilly had declared the import of a significant quantity of Irish Pounds."

"Irish Pounds, Sir? They were removed from circulation 20 years ago when Ireland joined the EU."

"Thank you for the history lesson, Wyse. For your information, the Central Bank continues to exchange punts for euros. Mr. Reilly, may I have a moment of your time."

"Certainly."

McBride and Reilly strode to the far side of the hanger. McBride signaled for the mystery observer to join them.

McBride made the introductions.

"Mr. Reilly, this is Mr. Louis Dennehy, Chief Enforcement Officer for the Central Bank. Mr. Dennehy, this is Mr. Daniel Reilly of San Francisco, United States."

Reilly had not expected to be received by the Central Bank at the airport.

"Mr. Dennehy, I wasn't expecting a representative of the Central Bank to meet me at the airport."

"Just making sure everything is on the up and up."

Reilly probed, "I had been in contact with Mr. Roland O'Connor and his superior Director Sheridan. Do you work with them?"

"In a manner of speaking."

McBride stepped in to move things along.

"Reilly, I do not know how familiar you are with our ways here in Ireland. The Office of the Revenue Commissioners or Revenue, my department, oversees customs and taxes. The Central Bank is in charge of currency, but we work closely with them to protect the integrity of the system. We have not seen a shipment of your magnitude. It is something of a grey area process-wise."

Reilly concurred. "Yes. The circumstances are quite extraordinary. I realize everyone has a job to do. The armored vehicle is unmarked. Are you sure it will get to the Central Bank safely?"

McBride continued. "We are using Dublin's finest,

Synergy Security Solutions. That being said the lads downtown have asked me to assign you an officer as liaison. You may consider her your personal escort, driver, and concierge for the duration."

"Her?" Reilly queried.

"Yes. As you have already established some rapport with Officer Wyse, she will serve as your liaison during your stay. She will be issued a Revenue staff vehicle for your convenience. She is committed and energetic. Surprisingly, she has not posted any traffic accidents."

"Yet." Reilly emphasized.

"Where are you staying? We will get Wyse a room there."

"The Dylan."

"Damn, man! We don't have that kind of budget. I'll have to instruct her to not use room service. We do need to check that the case is carrying Irish Pounds and not some other valid currency?"

"Certainly."

McBride and Reilly returned to the shipping crate.

"Officer Wyse, a word please," McBride commanded.

"Aye, Sir."

Wyse, McBride and Dennehy huddled. McBride gave her a quick briefing and the assignment. Wyse listened and nodded. Dennehy, who could not speak without waving his hands, appeared to give directions also.

When they broke, Wyse used her radio to contact the airport office; she ordered a car to replace the security cart. She pulled a pry bar and hammer from the stash of tools Revenue kept on hand for inspections.

"Shall I go ahead, Sir?" Wyse addressed Reilly now.

"Allow me." Reilly countered as he took the pry bar.

Reilly forgot how thorough they had been closing the

wooden sarcophagus in San Francisco. There must have been 50 nails affixing the top of the crate. Despite the 50° temperature he was starting to break a sweat. At five minutes, McBride had seen enough.

"Mind if we break out a few more pry bars?"

Reilly conceded, "It seems a bit over the top now. That sounds like a good idea."

Wyse took back the pry bar from Reilly. The two armored car attendants also joined the battle. The three made quick work of the prying. As they lifted the top back, Wyse gasped. Dennehy and McBride leaned in for a view.

The transport vault was suspended in place by airbags on all six sides. A treasure chest of stainless steel and Kevlar protected by an electronic lock requiring a six-digit key, one million combinations. There were tamper-proof storage seals on each side of the lock intact. The vault, a long stout trunk, fit snugly within the crate. There were handles along the sides of the vault. The armored car attendants and the dog handlers lifted the vault from the crate.

Reilly entered the code, and McBride broke the seals. Everyone but Reilly gasped at the site of 500 stacks of IR£ 100s. The vault was closed and McBride used Revenue seals for security.

They carried the vault-like pall bearers to the armored vehicle a good 50 yards.

Reilly signed for delivery with Revenue and Aer Lingus. The armored car company provided a receipt for the transport which was about to take place. Reilly turned to Wyse.

"Could we follow the armored car?"

"I was thinking police escort, Sir. We will be taking

two motorways. We can avoid tolls and any undue delays. The trip should be no more than 20 minutes. You ready, lads?"

Lights ablaze and the Eeee-Aaah siren blaring at 120 decibels Wyse drove like she was trying to lose a tail rather than escorting an armored vehicle. Reilly kept looking back for the armored car. Once again Wyse locked the wheels to stop. This time at the doorstep of the Central Bank between a half-dozen pickups and construction vehicles. The 20-minute trip took 12. It was 2:30 in the afternoon.

"I'm glad we made it here in time, but we are going to have to talk about your driving. I don't want to get a heart attack while I'm here."

"Sir?"

"It's alright. Would you stay here with the armored car attendants while I find Director Sheridan."

The receptionist paged for the Director. He called directly. She notified the Director that Mr. Reilly was on hand with an armored delivery. He would be down shortly to inspect the transport vault. Dennehy was lurking in the wings again.

"Reilly? I'm Director Sheridan, Currency Exchange. I understand you have an appointment with us day after tomorrow at 10:00. This is Roland O'Connor the processor for exchanges."

Reilly acted as would any customer dropping of IR£ 5 million. Clandestinely, though, he observed every detail.

"Yes, Sir. I just arrived, Aer Lingus from San Francisco. I'm delivering it so that you may store and process before the formal exchange."

"May we have a look at her before we take possession."

"Certainly."

The Director waved his arm and two porters emerged to collect the vault. He reviewed the Revenue security seals and observed the electronic lock. He knocked on the sides and top of the vault like a magician.

"O'Connor!" he called.

O'Connor listened to the vault through a stethoscope.

"Shhh."

Not hearing a peep from the vault O'Connor removed the stethoscope from his ears. He waved his hand one more time.

"Bring on Fido."

Fido was the Central Bank's canine trained to identify explosives and explosive residue. Fido took his turn circling and sniffing the vault. No danger was indicated.

Sheridan was satisfied.

"Alright, Mr. Reilly. We are prepared to accept your vault. Do you have any questions for us?"

"May I see the vault where my banknotes will be stored?"

"It is not standard procedure to tour the vault, but given the circumstances, I understand your request. Roland, escort Reilly's vault to the vault. Mr. Reilly please follow me."

Sheridan led Reilly to the inner chambers of the vault floor located in the sub-basement of the building. They passed the security desk and were buzzed through two checkpoints. The safe was manufactured by Fichet Bauche, a French company with over 200 years of history. The round safe door, two meters in diameter, was open. Reilly took note of the time lock and combination mechanism.

Sheridan asked, "Can you unlock your case so that the

notes may be processed. Let me prepare you a receipt."

Reilly found it ironic that the Central Bank of Ireland would write a receipt from a book you could pick up at Irish Office Depot. When he pulled the receipt from the book thereby releasing it from the carbon copy, Sheridan scribbled a brief note:

Don't trust Dennehy.

Reilly cast a line in the water, "Seems like you have some construction going on?"

Sheridan bit, "Yes. Always dealing with change. Sometimes planned. Sometimes impromptu. Let me know if I can be of any help during your stay, cheers."

"Cheers."

Reilly and Wyse took their leave for the day. The Revenue vehicle although equipped with lights and sirens was unmarked. The late model Volvo sedan was an Irish statement of EU unity shunning British options. Wyse opened the rear door for Reilly. He shook his head, shut the door, and chose the front passenger seat instead.

"Wyse, if we are going to make this work for the next few days, I'd like to drop all the formalities. You can stay proper in front of McBride, but in the car and about town I'm just Dan. What's your name?"

"Really, Sir. Must we."

"We must. Give."

With a touch of sarcasm, she starts, "Alright, Daniel. ...It's Penelope."

"Penelope? Oh, my. Penelope Wyse. .... Penny Wyse."

"Yes, yes. And pound foolish. I've heard it all my life. I like to think that the idiom is more ironic than applicable in my case. Shall I take you to the Dylan now or are there other stops you need to make?"

"Well, Penny, unless you sleep in that uniform,

perhaps we should stop by your abode so that you could collect a few things. Unless you Revenue agents always travel with a packed bag."

"The Principal Officer said I could charge any incidentals to the Governor. Perhaps we could stop by my car in the employee lot. I can let them know it will be there in a few days and I can get my gym bag. Later I will retrieve additional uniforms and casual clothes. I live thirty minutes from downtown."

"To the Dylan it is. I do need to stop at a drugstore along the way. I need a shave."

Wyse was confused, "Drug Store? ...Do you mean Pharmacy?"

Wyse pulled up to Hickey's Pharmacy along the River Liffey and O'Connell Bridge. The age and beauty of Dublin were striking. He conducted his business.

"Get everything you need, Dan?"

"I think so. Shaving – check, nails – check, teeth – check."

*   *   *   *   *   *   *   *

"Welcome to the Dylan. Valet, ma'am? ...err Officer?". The valet wore a gold waistcoat over a finely pressed white cotton shirt, black trousers, kelly green bow tie.

"No. I cannot release the keys. Send a bellhop for Mr. Reilly's luggage."

"Yes, Sir. ...I mean ma'am, officer". The valet turned and piped a high pitch whistle that sent bellhops, green waistcoats and black bow ties, scurrying.

The Dylan, housed within a Victorian building erected in 1901, is a relatively young boutique hotel banking its reputation on five-star plus service featuring seventy-two luxurious rooms on three floors. The sturdy wooden entry doors with large panes of glass swing under an arch of masonry and 48 window panes.

The doorman sported an overcoat too heavy for the weather replete with faux military accoutrements and top hat.

"Welcome to the Dylan, Sir – Ma'am. Dining or Staying with us?"

"Staying, Jeeves," Wyse replied, beginning to enjoy her assignment.

"Wonderful. The front desk is directly ahead through the lobby."

The lobby was appointed with crystal chandeliers, thick pile carpet, hardwood floors and sturdy furniture. The front desk was intentionally unmanned begging for the bell on the mahogany counter to be rung. It was larger than the standard bell nearly five inches in diameter. Brass with Victorian filigree the chime was deeper and held the note longer than the norm. It called the front desk clerk to make his appearance. Again, they would be welcomed to the Dylan.

He spoke with a British affectation that most found off-putting.

"Mr. Reilly, we have you guesting in suite 312 as requested. Your credit card is on record. Do you have a document, passport or driver's license, to complete your registration?"

"Both, dealer's choice." Reilly placed his passport and driver's license on the counter.

"Officer Wyse, we received your late room request via the exchequer earlier. We performed some manipulations and have a room for you on the second floor, 218."

"Thank you."

The clerk was full of attitude toward the officer, "We would appreciate more notice in the future."

"So would I."

"Luggage?"

"Not yet."

"The exchequer provided an account for the room stay but did not leave a charge card for incidentals. May I register a card for you?"

Wyse scrambled, "I'm afraid Officers do not carry wallets on duty. May I provide one later?"

"That is a problem. Could you ring your office?"

Reilly had had enough of the phony Brit.

"Use my card. Just notify me if she caters a blowout in her room."

"Very well, sir." He also had a whistle that made bellhops jump in Pavlovian response.

As they were led to the elevator bank Officer Wyse tried to keep it all business, but she was grateful to Reilly.

"Dan, would you like me to make dinner arrangements?"

"No. Not at this time. Let me get settled. I'll call you in a bit to let you know if I feel like going out or whether I will just eat in. The restaurant and room service both have good reviews."

Wyse's tone softened, "You didn't have to you know."

"Didn't have to what?"

"Let them use your credit card for my incidentals. We're breaking Revenue rules."

"First, you have not charged anything yet. Second, if a friend can't cover another friend's incidentals, what is this world coming to."

The bellhop must have been new as he struggled with the timing between inserting the key card and turning the door handle. After a half dozen tries, Reilly took the card, inserted it in the slot, paused and pulled the knob up rather than down. Locks whether they be mechanical, electric, or biometric were an interest of Reilly's.

The bellhop thanked Reilly and gave the tour. The suite featured two bedrooms with king-size beds so tall they had stepstools, a sitting room that could easily sit eight, a fully stocked wet bar rather than a mini-fridge with a menu, the master bathroom was fit for royalty – multi-head shower, soaking claw foot tub, bidet. Room 312 was at the end of the floor providing views to the North and East. It adjoined Room 310 each room featuring a pass-thru door with a locking knob and deadbolt.

Reilly tipped the bellhop five euros and unpacked. He called room service to press the two suits he had brought as well as the five dress shirts. They promised the order would be completed within four hours. He felt sandblasted after the shower heads had attacked from every angle. Reilly's five o'clock shadow felt more like 8:15 so he took advantage of the Dylan's old school shaving mug, brush & lather soap. Presently, he sported a moustache and goatee. The degree of beard varied over time, but his upper lip had not seen the light of day for 40 years. He snickered internally recalling his mother making him shave it off for his high school senior portrait.

Hygiene addressed, Reilly slipped into some casual slacks and a cashmere V-neck sweater. He perused the selection at the wet bar. His poison of choice in San Francisco was a few fingers of Jameson on ice. On the flight over, he had read a piece on the Irish whiskeys of the mother country. Killbeggan, distilled in Dublin, had received high marks. He thought it worthy of a try. The ice bucket was full of ice, no traipsing the hallways looking for the ice machine. It was like a scene from the Thin Man. He took the sturdy crystal tumbler from the shelf, used tongs to place two oversized ice cubes and generously poured the Killbeggan.

He uttered, "Ahhh. Smooth."

He called Penny to let her know he would not be leaving the Dylan that evening. She could run to her place or go shopping on the Governor. He suggested they meet for breakfast at 8 am. He hung the 'Do Not Disturb' card on the door knob to room 312. He looked down the hallway and saw the same card next door. In the bathroom, he removed the nail files from the manicure kit and the probes from the dental kit. He opened his side of the pass-through to Room 310. He turned the handle, locked. He shook his head.

"Damn." He smiled.

He took the small file and a dental pick with a medium crook. He used the file to put tension on the cylinder; the pick would find the pins. He began to work the deadbolt, eyes closed so he could feel the tumbler pins set – one, two, three, four, five, six. Pop! He turned his attention to the door handle. He switched to a pick with a smaller crook. Again, he used the file, eyes closed – one, two, three, four, five. Pop. He pulled the handle up and swung the door open.

"Sean! You made it."

"Reilly. Dan Reilly. Don't forget it."

Chapter 26

Penultimate Day

He had not given himself enough leeway to adjust to the time difference from California. The whiskey the night before helped him to sleep, but the 7:30 am wake-up call felt like the middle of the night. He had 90 minutes until Officer Wyse would escort him about town. The shower was refreshing; unlike showering with a water-saving head in drought ridden California. The local oat soap exfoliated his epidermis in a manner which put his Irish Spring to shame. He missed having Francess do his back.

Reilly picked the locks on the pass door again. He improved his pick time by 45 seconds. Room 310 was provisioned as well as room 312. It was unusual to find a hotel with a desk and chair that were functional. Stanley Sullivan's laptop was connected to a large display monitor. It made it easier to manage all the hooks he had into the Central Bank's infrastructure.

"Rise and shine, Girls. The day's a wasting."

Ollie grumbled, "Really, Dan. We've been up for hours."

Dan Reilly wanted a status update but not before admonishing his mates.

"I'm only going to say this once. It is mission-critical. Dan, Stan, and Ollie are in Dublin. As far as the world is concerned Sean, Patty, and Kenny are in San Francisco. If we were overheard using those names or flinch at your aliases, we're cooked."

"Penny, Officer Wyse, is going to escort me to breakfast and a tour of Croke Park this morning. I want to get out of the hotel and give you two the freedom to do your business. I'm sure she is under instruction to report my activities to Dennehy."

Ollie had the jitters, "Sean, he worries me. Are we in trouble? Do we need to bail? It's not too late."

"DAN! It's DAN. And, we are not bailing. You can monitor my progress from here. If it goes south, you have your return tickets. Just go straight to the airport. Take any evidence from here and put it in my room. Just do me a favor. I need your help for one last day. If it goes squirrely it won't be until tomorrow."

"Sorry, Dan."

"Focus and confidence. Look at all we have achieved. Ollie your craft work, and Stanley your systems mastery have brought us halfway around the world, to the brink of success. We've fooled cities, states, and countries. We even have an inside man."

Ollie was giving Dan more concern than Stanley.

"Can you trust him?"

"I have to. Remember, he's never met you. The two of you are insulated from exposure. Tell me you were successful this week. That you took care of business."

Stan reported first.

"Hacking the email system was a breeze, but email is practically snail mail today. The Bank prohibits cell phones due to security; it's full of jammers. I was able to tap the PBX system though and I am monitoring the key players and their admins."

"Nice. Ollie, how about you?"

"Signs are printed. I am Kumbaya with a local printer. The ID you asked for was no problem. And, I was able to modify the machine per your specifications. I delivered it to The Mayson. It's only a block from the Central Bank."

"Good. What about the signs?"

"Killian of Dublin Print will be dropping them off at the respective halls this afternoon."

"Stan, it's time to release the dogs. Email Brian Nolan's personal account. People pay more attention to their own account. He's a CONNECT officer and I've never met a union officer who wasn't a whore for the camera. Here's the message."

Central Bank using electrical, construction scabs. Wildcat strike tomorrow 9:00, BATU and CONNECT invited. RTÉ and Virgin Media on notice.

A Friend to the Cause

Stan sent it as fast as he read it, "Done."

"Did you make the calls to the tip lines for the two unions and the news outlets?"

"Yep."

"Excellent. I need to send one last text message to Sheridan. Break out the Hibernia phone."

The final message contained an image of picketers and the image of a television cameraman.

Reilly slipped back into 312 seconds before Penny knocked on the door. In honor of The Dubs he was wearing a sky blue golf sweater, khakis, and hiking shoes. Officer Wyse wore her fall uniform a navy sweater over her short sleeve blue shirt and bulletproof vest. She was armed with mace and a taser.

Rather sardonically Dan inquired "Are those to protect me or to keep me in line?"

Wyse replied, "Yes."

"I see. Do you have a suggestion for breakfast?"

"Keogh's Café. They have a great Irish Fry. Then to Croker. The Dubs should be training today. My uniform should get us in the park."

As Penny pulled up to Keogh's, Dan could see the

outline of a man sauntering away. He recognized the exaggerated use of the shillelagh; it was Sheridan. Dan ate baked eggs, potatoes, tomato, bacon – double order, and sourdough toast. He eschewed the white pudding and baked beans. Penny had granola, yogurt and tomato juice. If Dan ate like that every day he'd be as big as Ollie.

At Croke Park, they toured the GAA Museum and the Hall of Fame. He took photos with the original Sam Maguire and Liam McCarthy Cups. He tried the interactive Hurling and Football skills, but his lack of depth perception showed him as a rank amateur. He lamented not playing Gaelic sports as a young man. In his mind, he thought the games lent themselves to the skills he had.

Even with his poor eyesight, the pitch was massive, longer and wider than an American football field. Croke Park, Croker, opened in 1884. Croker was three-tiered and open to the North. Following an update in 1984, the largest stadium in Ireland seated over 69,000 and the bleachers on Hill 16 held another 13,000. He recognized the smell. There was only one other place that had the same scent, Candlestick Park. Eau de Stadium -- stale beer, cigarette smoke, and peanut shells.

"Dan, will you be staying for the All-Ireland Final this Saturday? It's against Kerry, a classic match."

"Not sure. Guess I'll know tomorrow whether or not I can afford a ticket. Are you for the Dubs or the Green and Gold?"

Penny cared for the sport but not the teams, "I'm from Donegal. I don't have a dog in the hunt. You?"

"If I don't have an interest, I generally root for the underdog. There's no underdog here."

Penny did not know the plans or what to report, "Do

you have any engagements for this afternoon or evening?"

"Nothing tonight. I'm still adjusting to the time. I might go sculling on the River Liffey this afternoon."

"You'd be on your own there. I don't swim."

"I guess it's a good thing you are in Revenue rather than the Navy."

*   *   *   *   *   *   *

Sheridan had woken up alone again. The two weeks at home felt different than the four weeks traveling, not bad just different. He had not heard from Margaret since his first morning back in Dublin. Maybe he had finally gotten through to her that the well was dry. Perhaps he would consult a solicitor. He had not considered filing a missing person report.

His shillelagh waggling had become quite pronounced. The morning and evening constitutionals and full nights of sleep were doing wonders for his health. And, the thought of seagull guano damaging the finish on the Bank's Volvo helped his disposition.

The Dylan was between his home and the Bank; he did not want to cross paths with Reilly. He assumed that Dennehy was running surveillance. He had become a regular at Keogh's Café in the morning. Irish Fry – eggs, bacon, white pudding, potatoes, beans, sourdough toast, and a milky to wash it down.

... Mush-a ring dumb-a do dumb-a da
Wack fall the daddy-o, wack fall the daddy-o
There's whiskey in the jar...

Bernard chuckled as he read the text. Flood and Dennehy had no idea what was heading their way.

Sheridan pushed aside the empty construction boxes with his shillelagh. There was no professionalism in this construction project. Gertrude had been at her desk for 45 minutes.

She spoke softly, "Bernard, there's scuttlebutt about the floor."

Gertrude kept him apprised of the pulse of the staff more thoroughly and accurately than any of Dennehy's surveillance techniques.

Bernard bit, "About?"

"You! Dennehy is out to get you. Deputy Governor Flood sees you as a thorn in her desires for a Commission seat."

He feigned surprise, "Really?"

"Dennehy put the screws on Roland. Checking his authentication of the notes and documents."

"I see. Ask O'Connor to come see me. Have him bring some sample notes and the documentation."

Roland O'Connor, 32, had been with Central Bank for six years. Being just 12 years old when Ireland joined the EU, he had not seen a series A 100-pound banknote before he was assigned to exchange. He verified the notes using the Central Bank Currency Certification Guide. A guide which was authored by Bernard Sheridan.

"Roland, we have not had an exchange this size since I had your job. What have you found?"

"The banknotes are authentic: the feel, weight, clarity of print, colour, watermark. See."

Roland produced six banknotes. Sheridan held one to the light and observed the watermark, snapped it, and inspected it with the aid of a loupe. The note had a faint scent. It wasn't fresh print. He closed his eyes. Sourdough. San Francisco.

"What were the print dates?"

"There were four dates in 1970, 1972, 1973, and 1975."

"That is correct. What about the documentation?"

"Reilly's uncle passed away. He provided a copy of the death certificate and funeral notice from Sullivan's and Duggan's Funeral Home."

"That sounds Irish."

"The paper trail is from a defunct San Francisco bank, Hibernia Bank. The funds to purchase the pounds were deposited just a month before they were acquired in March of 1976. I am unfamiliar with the printer used for the correspondence."

"That was a bank that was founded by Irish immigrants during the gold rush for Irish miners to deposit their riches. It was the largest bank in California at the turn of the 20th Century."

Sheridan had researched Hibernia Bank on his flight en route to Australia.

"How did you know that?"

"We're bankers Roland. There is much to be learned by studying banking history."

"Yes, Sir."

Sheridan took an educational moment with O'Connor, "What did you make of the purchase funds not being deposited until just before Reilly senior made his exchange?"

"I wasn't sure."

"Well, in those days American deposits were insured to only $15,000. There was little incentive and even less assurance to hold large deposits in savings. May I see the documentation?"

Sheridan was impressed with the attention to detail. Unlike current statements, the paper had the perforated edges from paper which had been tractor fed through a printer. The back of the stock carried the worksheet for balancing a checkbook. The letter signed by Michael de Young Tobin, grandson of the founder and Chairman of the Board, was printed on column textured paper. Stanley had won the contest to forge Tobin's signature.

"What's with the print on the letter?'

"It's from an IBM Selectric typewriter. They were all the rage last century. They used a ball full of letters to strike a carbon ribbon. It was the be-all and end-all of office technology before the advent of word processors."

Roland was lost, "You're talking a foreign language."

Sheridan wanted the decision to be Roland's, "What's your recommendation?"

"The notes are good. Considering the age, the documentation is more than sufficient. This is the largest transaction I've handled, but I see no reason not to approve it."

"Nor do I. How does Reilly want to complete the transaction?"

"Euros. €6.25 million."

"What have you arranged for the banknotes?"

"I've contacted Synergy Security Solutions to take them for incineration."

"Prepare the draft against the Irish Pound Exchange account. This is your show; you run the meeting tomorrow."

*　　*　　*　　*　　*　　*　　*　　*

Marcella Flood's new office, the only corner office on the floor, had mid-Century wood and leather furniture. Her desk was teak; the guest chairs were stylish and uncomfortable. The white carpet was impractical. Dennehy was shifting to find a tolerable position. He spent more time in her office than his own.

"Louis, you said the office project would last four weeks. It's week seven and I'm still walking around construction tape. What's the problem?"

"The contractor has supply and labor issues. The Chinese furniture and cubicles are held up at Revenue. Their labor is unreliable. It's a shite show."

"This is making us look like bumbling eejits. I'm hearing grumblings from the other Deputy Governors that this sort of thing never happened on a Sheridan project. I don't need that. I'm losing respect. I'll never be put on the Commission this way."

"Cella, I need more control if we are going to get anything done around here. I want Security. I will turn them into my eyes and ears within the building. Transform them from aged door openers into agents. We need to shake this place up. Show them who is in charge."

"It's not that easy. I can't swap departments and shuffle the org chart without a proposal to the Governor. Even then it has to be approved by the Commission. The climate is not good now. What's the story with this punt exchange? I thought the Sheridan trip would be a big flop."

"Apparently, this bloke's uncle bought millions of punts, two to a dollar, back in the 1970s. Our economy was failing at the time. Americans poured dollars into Ireland to support the economy and the IRA. Anyway, the old coot was sitting on them for years. He died and Daniel Reilly appeared at our door."

"Is it plausible?"

"Roland O'Connor says he submitted the death certificate as well as bank letters and statements to back the story. It's Sheridan's game but I don't trust him or Reilly. Revenue assigned Reilly an officer as an escort. She's keeping me informed of his activities. He went straight to the Dylan from dropping off his vault yesterday. After breakfast at Keogh's this morning he is touring Croker."

Flood cautioned Dennehy, "Formally, you don't have a role in the exchange process."

"If I can bust or foil Reilly, we can get rid of Sheridan for dereliction of duty. That would send shivers through the organization, solidify your power."

"Risky."

Dennehy shared the latest intel, "His escort just texted me that he is thinking of taking a row on the River Liffey this afternoon. I could arrange an accident."

"No. It's better if we could discredit him and embarrass Sheridan."

"I have ways to make him talk."

"This isn't J2. You can't beat it out of him or use truth serum. ...Yet."

Chapter 27

Theoretical Chaos

"Central Bank!"
   "Scab for me!"
   "Shite on me!"

"Central Bank!"
"Do it Right!"
"Or, You're in for a Fight!"

Amplified megaphones led the chants. CONNECT and BATU, the largest service and trade unions respectively, had emptied their hiring halls. The picketers filled the sidewalk in front of the main entrance to the Central Bank. Executives with parking, like Flood and Dennehy, did not have to cross the picket line.

Brian Nolan, the Union Leader, was preparing to be interviewed by Pat Kelley, RTÉ correspondent when Bernard Sheridan and his shillelagh strolled along. Nolan and Sheridan had worked on a number of union/management agreements in the past.

"Excuse me, Pat. I need to have a word with Sheridan."

Nolan and Sheridan crossed the street. They sat on a bench overlooking the River Liffey. From the roof, Dennehy observed the conversation with binoculars. He lamented not taking a parabolic surveillance microphone from J2.

Nolan began, "Bernard, what happened here?"

"I was out of the country and the new wingnuts broke all protocol."

"Can you make this right?"

Sheridan assured, "I can make it right, but it's not my shite show to fix. I'd like to leave the perpetrators hanging in the wind."

"How can I help?"

"Squeeze them publicly and through Leinster House. If they are gone and I have anything to say about it, I will make things right by you and your people. The Bank is being run by a BREXIT-obsessed Brit, an Insurance Agent, and a hitman. It needs to be returned to an Irish banker."

Privately Nolan understood, "Amen. I'm going to ream the Bank right now, but I'll make a phone call for you too."

"Fair enough."

"Is your leg bothering you?"

Sheridan twirled his shillelagh, "Oh, this. I just like the look of it."

"Never know when you might need a cudgel. ...Well, Bernard, I have some hell to raise. Don't be a stranger."

"I won't."

They shook hands. Nolan headed to Kelley and the television camera. Sheridan passed the picket line and took the elevator up to the executive floor.

"Central Bank!"
"Scab for me!"
"Shite on me!"

"Central Bank!"
"Do it Right!"
"Or, You're in for a Fight!"

As Sheridan exited the elevator he was met by Dennehy, "What were you doing down there?"

"Once a snoop always a snoop, Louis?"

"Who were you talking to?"

"Were you on the roof? You really don't know the players. Do you?"

"Can't you give me a straight answer?"

"Why don't you watch RTÉ 2. Good day."

"Can you tell me why the Garda is in your office?"

"No. I can't." For the first time, Sheridan gave Dennehy a straight answer.

*   *   *   *   *   *   *   *

Gertrude intercepted Sheridan as he approached his office.

"The Garda is waiting for you. They wouldn't tell me why? Are you alright?"

"As far as I know. We shall see."

His mind raced through the scenarios. Somehow they were on to Dan Reilly's real identity, Sean McAuliffe. Perhaps their text messages had been intercepted. Maybe a banknote had gotten out. He could get in front of the questioning. Admit his knowledge. Say he was letting the scheme play out before snaring the culprit. No. What would Sean do? Wait and field the questions as they come. Calm down.

"I'm Chief O'Hara and this is Detective McGrath. Are you Bernard Sheridan?"

Sheridan answered without elaboration, "Yes."

"Is your address 14 Westmoreland Park, Ranelagh?"

"Yes."

"Are you married?"

"Yes. Is this about Margaret?"

"Do you know the whereabouts of your wife?"

"We had a row the morning after I returned from a four week trip abroad. I have not heard from her for a fortnight."

"Aren't you concerned about her wellbeing?"

"I was fed up with her gambling and told her so. I told her to get help. I figured she was getting help or plunging into the deep end. I am done funding her addiction."

"She was arrested for vehicle theft. She tried to sell the BMW."

Sheridan did not expect that, "It's leased!"

"So this was done without your knowledge or consent?"

"Yes, I did not know or consent to her selling a leased vehicle."

"She's going to need legal representation. Can you come over to the Irishtown Station? She is in a holding cell there."

"No, but I will make a call to a solicitor. Is there anything else?"

"Will you be making that call soon? She is due for arraignment in the morning and will be transferred to Dóchas Centre if bail is not arranged."

"I will make the call directly."

"Thank you, sir. Slán."

"Slán, Chief O'Hara."

Sheridan called Gertrude into his office.

"Gertrude, Margaret surfaced and she's in trouble. Get me Donall Johnston of Johnston Solicitors on the line. Don't let the receptionist put you off. I need to monitor the Reilly meeting. And there's a tsunami coming for Flood and Dennehy."

"Yes, Sir."

Gertrude used her executive assistant to executive

assistant charm and got Johnston on the line.

"Bernard, Johnston on line 2."

"Thanks, Trudy. You're the best."

He punched the button for line 2.

"Donall, Bernard Sheridan. Margaret is in trouble again."

...

"She tried to sell the BMW. ...That's right. It's leased. ...Vehicular theft."

...

"I need you to go see her. I want you to make her this offer: bail and defense for divorce. ...Yes. All or nothing. ...No. If she contests the divorce, she can sit and rot at Dóchas."

...

"Thanks, Donall. You'll let me know how it goes. I've got to run; there's evil to thwart."

*   *   *   *   *   *   *   *

The pickets had traffic stopped on N. Wall Quay. Officer Wyse could only go north or west off the Samuel Beckett Bridge.

"I've never seen traffic backed up on the Wall before. Maybe I could drop you around back."

"It's only four blocks from here. Just pull up on Guild Street. We are early enough, I won't be late."

"Central Bank!"

"Scab for me!"

"Shite on me!"

"Central Bank!"

"Do it Right!"

"Or, You're in for a Fight!"

Reilly was impressed with the racket he had orchestrated. He made sure to not be caught in the background of the television cameras lest someone who knew Sean McAuliffe stream the news report. Roland greeted Reilly at the main reception desk with a firm handshake.

"Mr. Reilly I am Roland O'Connor. We were not formally introduced the other day. I was charged with reviewing your submission for euro exchange."

"Pleased to meet you. May I call you Roland? Or, do you prefer Mr. O'Connor?"

"I already feel like I know you. Please call me Roland."

"Roland, pardon me if this is out of place, but I noticed a smudge on your hand. If I'm not mistaken its cordovan Kiwi shoe polish."

Roland looked at his hand and started to rub at the smudge with his other thumb.

"I'm an eejit."

"Rollie, I only pointed it out as I spent years polishing my own shoes and pressing my own shirts."

"I do my own shirts too. Do you have a trick for the crease?"

"Do the sleeves first. You have to work around the board for each arm. Pinch the end of the shoulder and pull it taut at the cuff.. Smooth it out. Hit the crease hard. Steam it. Light starch if that's your preference. Flip the shirt over. Smooth the back side. Hit it with the iron, but respect the crease you just made."

Roland escorted Reilly past the construction to the Liffey Conference Room. There was a sign on the door:

O'Connor 10:00-11:30. The conference room, unaltered by the construction project, overlooked the River Liffey. The building was six kilometers east of the rowing club near Dublin Bay and the Irish Sea. Reilly took a moment to observe the view.

"I don't know how you could get any work done here."

"Oh, yes. I suppose it is scenic."

"I was talking about the pickets."

"We've never had that before. From what I can gather it's related to the construction project."

Roland was carrying a cordovan leather folder emblazoned with the Central Bank's logo. It matched his shoes. He did not know where to sit. Although he had attended many meetings there, this was the first time he had called the meeting and reserved the conference room. He deferred.

"Sit anywhere you like."

The room, like the river, ran west to east. The conference table had fourteen seats. Reilly determined that the meetings were run from the west end. He sat at the head of the table.

Roland had not expected that. He chose the third seat down on the River Liffey side. Sheridan entered just before 9:00. He shook Roland's hand and spoke a few words to him privately. Reilly stood to meet Sheridan.

"Pleasure to see you this morning, Mr. Reilly."

"Please, call me Dan."

As the gentlemen sat down, Sheridan to Roland's left, Gertrude rolled in a cart with a teapot and scones.

"Mr. Reilly, good day. I'm Gertrude O'Shea, Mr. O'Connor's and Mr. Sheridan's assistant. They told me of your meeting and I insisted we serve you a proper cup."

"I'm honored Ms. O'Shea, but I have to admit I'm a novice. May I leave it to you to prepare?"

"Certainly. Let's try two lumps and milk. Here you go. Plus a scone."

"Thank you."

As Gertrude was preparing cups for Roland and Bernard the door opened. In strode Marcella Flood and Louis Dennehy. Flood stared daggers as Reilly was in her chair.

She scowled, "You are in my seat."

Reilly retorted, "I did not realize it was reserved."

Roland interjected, "My apologies, I did not know you were planning on attending today."

She addressed Sheridan, "Bernie, you don't mind if we observe. Do you?"

Roland looked for direction. Sheridan nodded slightly and gave a barely perceptible eyebrow raise.

"You are always welcome, Governor. Mr. Reilly, this is Deputy Governor Marcella Flood, our Chief Operating Officer. And Mr. Louis Dennehy, Chief Enforcement & Anti-Money Laundering Officer. This is Mr. Dan Reilly of San Francisco, California. His uncle passed away earlier this year; the Irish banknotes were part of the estate."

"How do you do, Governor? Mr. Dennehy, we met briefly at the airport. I also saw you in the lobby when my vault was delivered."

Always prepared, Gertrude brought service for eight.

"Ma'am may I prepare a cup for you?"

"We've contracted with Compass for meeting catering. What are you doing?"

"Well, ma'am cardboard cups and a trip from downtown may suffice for coffees and sodas. I just believe a proper tea for business needs to be steeped just before serving and delivered in a porcelain cup. Besides, Compass charges €6; this is a better cup and costs less than 50 cents. I believe you are milk, no sugar. Mr. Dennehy?"

As Gertrude completed the orders, Sheridan smirked. With Flood and Dennehy at the other end of the table, they could not catch the wink he threw at Reilly with his left eye.

Reilly couldn't resist, "Ms. O'Shea, this is delightful. Thank you."

"Oh, please. Call me Gertrude."

"Thank you, Gertrude."

It looked like a high school cafeteria standoff: O'Connor, Sheridan, and Reilly at the west end; Flood and Dennehy at the east end. The chasm was much wider than the eight chairs. Flood and Dennehy were huddled in hushed conversation as Roland proceeded with the formalities.

"Mr. Reilly, let me begin by offering my and the Central Bank's condolences at the loss of your uncle."

"Thank you."

"I'd also like to commend you on the thoroughness of your Application for Pound/Euro Exchange per the year 2000 provisions of Ireland's entrance to the European Union. You have presented us with five million Irish pounds. The banknotes have been authenticated per Central Bank guidelines."

Dennehy interrupted, "Where did you get the guidelines?"

"They were developed when the Central Bank adopted ISO20022 in 2004. It standardized the process for verifying all former Irish currency outstanding."

"How do you know this?"

O'Connor sounded like Sheridan, "It's my job to know the history of the processes for which I am responsible."

Sheridan wanted to give Roland an 'attaboy' right there, but refrained.

Dennehy challenged, "Shouldn't it have been updated since then?"

"Well seeing as it documented currency, which was no longer printed after 2000, no."

"How do you know it wasn't written by some junior hack?"

O'Connor held his own, "It had to be authoritative to be adopted as ISO 20022. But why don't you ask the hack yourself?"

"What?"

Sheridan leaned back, "I wrote it."

"Oh."

Roland was prepared to complete the transaction, "I was going to review the documentation, but we have already approved it. Mr. Reilly, do you have any questions before we proceed with the disbursement instructions?"

"Not so fast." Flood interrupted the proceedings.

Sheridan took up the defense, "The notes are authentic. The documentation is indisputable. I object to this breach of authority, protocol."

Flood flexed her authority, "Overruled. Proceed Louis."

Dennehy went to the door and motioned down the hallway like a manager calling for a relief pitcher. Moments later a cart entered through the door with a computer and some machinery. It was pushed by a tall woman, 1.75 meters – in heels 1.8 meters. Her hair was pulled in a business-like bun. Her deep brown eyes were masked by glasses with large lenses and a tortoiseshell frame.

Roland was first to identify the machinery, "It's a lie detector!"

Dennehy corrected, "Ms. Fiona Richards is a polygraph examiner. I have contracted her services to clarify our suspicions as to the veracity of the claim."

Although Flood outranked Sheridan, Roland's respect and allegiance lie with his direct supervisor.

"Polygraph examinations are not included in the approval process."

Sheridan added, "Our clients are not criminals and should not be treated as such."

Reilly consented, "I have nothing to hide. The ask is definitely offensive. You are definitely impacting your 'easy to do business with' score on the customer satisfaction survey. Strap me up."

Without emoting any body language Sheridan used his eyebrows to communicate to Reilly that he would have fought to keep from allowing the polygraph to proceed. His concern was as much for his own well-being as Reilly's.

Richards attached leads to the middle and index fingers of his left hand, a blood pressure cuff to his right arm, and a respirator strap around his chest. She instructed him that the examination would consist of questions which only require a 'yes' or 'no' answer. Any elaboration would muddle the results.

"I am Fiona Richards, licensed polygraph examiner. The examination will consist of a series of yes/no or true/false questions. Please do not elaborate or engage in any conversation. Do you understand?"

"Yes. But will I have a chance to explain?"

"'Do you understand?' is a yes or no question. Do you understand?"

"Yes."

Gone were the days when the examiner would mark a log tape with a felt tip pen. The monitor results were stored on digital media. Fiona clicked the mouse with each query.

"Is your name Dan Reilly?"

"Yes."

"Do you live in Dublin?"

"No."

"Today is Thursday."

"False."

"Today is Friday."

"True."

"Did your uncle die earlier this year?"

"Yes."

"Did your uncle b Irish pounds in the 1980s?"

"No."

"Did your uncle accumulate Irish pounds through the Hibernia Bank?"

"Yes."

The voice. Sheridan recognized the voice. It was the waitress from Flanahan's in San Francisco! She had saved his shillelagh. He searched for her name. Catherine. Mary. Elizabeth. Francess! That was it. It was Francess. His back shot straight in his chair. He stifled his elation.

"The Irish pounds you submitted are counterfeit."

"False."

"You are part of a conspiracy to defraud the Central Bank."

"False."

Flood appeared agitated at Reilly's calm demeanour. Dennehy could not sit still; flop sweat formed on his forehead.

"You are not an agent for a third party."

"True."

"Had you met anyone from the Central Bank before this week?"

"Does seeing Director Sheridan on television count?"

"Yes or No!"

"No."

"That concludes your examination. Thank you for not elaborating much. Let me release you from the monitors."

"Well? Was he lying?" demanded Dennehy.

The door flew open. It was Gertrude. She went to the conference room control console and lowered the bookcase to reveal a large, flat-screen television monitor.

"Excuse the interruption, ma'am. Governor Makhlouf is on the line for you. He has instructed me to interrupt your meeting and put him on the speaker phone. He also wanted me to put RTÉ 2 on the Telly."

Governor Makhlouf was in Brussels attending board meetings regarding BREXIT impacts within the EU. Gertrude patched him into the speaker assembly on the conference table and muted the television.

"Sir, this is Ms. O'Shea. You can now be heard in the conference room with Deputy Governor Flood, Misters Sheridan, Dennehy, O'Connor of the Central Bank, and Mr. Daniel Reilly of America. And, excuse me, who are you?"

"I am Fiona Richards, polygraph examiner."

Makhlouf was riled, "Thank you, Ms. O'Shea. ...Marcella what the divil is going on out there? I'm catching flak from the other EU Governors and Higgins' office wants answers. So do I. Are you watching what I am? Are you aware that you are being picketed? Why do you need a polygraph expert?"

"The pickets appeared this morning without warning. We have RTÉ on the big screen now."

"This is Pat Kelley reporting for RTÉ2 live from the North Wall Quay at the main entrance to the Central Bank. CONNECT and BATU have formed protest lines. Joining me today is the Assistant General Secretary of CONNECT, Brian Nolan. G'day Brian."

"Were it only, Pat? Were it only?"

Dennehy exclaimed to Flood, "That's the bloke Sheridan was talking to!"

"Brian, what is happening here today?"

"For some reason, the Central Bank has abandoned our agreement and its own charter and undertaken facilities work with non-union labor on a project which was never put out to bid to proper contracting firms."

"Why would they do that?"

"It's not clear to me why they would undertake such a blatant affront to fair play. Labor and the Bank are two components of a strong Irish economy. One could only conjecture that the Bank has lost focus on where their responsibilities start."

"Brian, what needs to be done about this?"

"The Bank needs to explain this breech or face greater repercussions. There are union office workers and security guards who might be asked to honor the line crippling the Bank's day-to-day activities."

"It's a real fiasco."

"It's a shite show."

"Thank you, Brian."

"No, Pat. Thank you for bringing this injustice to the eyes of the Irish populous."

Now livid Makhlouf fumed, "Flood, are you out of your feckin' mind? Is that true? Who is the head of facilities?"

She would try to throw Sheridan under the bus, "Bernard Sheridan is Director Currency, Facilities & Security."

"What happened, Sheridan?"

"Sir, while I was out of the country on a currency project requested and authorized by Deputy Governor Flood, Mr. Dennehy, Chief Enforcement Officer, and Flood undertook a major redesign of offices at the Central Bank. Apparently, they were unaware of Bank policy regarding requirements for union labor and competitive bidding."

"Fix this now, Flood. Or, I will. Higgins is ordering me back to Ireland. I had been planning two weeks on The Continent. My wife is not pleased. I've been called to the President's House day after tomorrow."

Click.

Flood uttered, "I hate this feckin' place."

O'Connor looked to Sheridan with raised eyebrows and palms turned to the air. Dennehy and Flood were in shock. Richards remained in character.

Sheridan took charge, "Ms. Richards please send your invoice to Mr. Dennehy. I'm sure he has a slush fund for your charges. By the way, what were your findings?"

"I found Mr. Reilly to be completely honest during the examination."

Sheridan directed, "Roland, let's proceed."

Roland pulled the draft receipt from his folder.

"You presented the Central Bank with IR£5,000,000.

The statute exchange rate is €1.25 to IR£ 1. Therefore, you will receive €6,250,000. There are no bank fees or Irish taxes due. You can see that I have already signed as to the authenticity of the notes presented. And, Director Sheridan has countersigned as head of currency regulation."

Reilly had practised his signature, "Where's the dotted line?"

"At the X."

"Do you have a pen?"

Roland fumbled through his pockets, checked his folder, and then checked the drawers in the conference room. Sheridan snickered.

"Roland, when I was a 13-year-old bagboy at the SuperValu, I learned I would go far if I started every day with two pens and a box cutter. I cannot count how many times I have been asked, 'Do you have a pen?' or 'Do you have a box cutter?' To this day I carry two pens, but I have upgraded to a Swiss Army Knife. Some days I end up with three pens. Some days none. Here you go, Mr. Reilly."

Reilly took the pen and pulled his readers from his shirt pocket. He signed the document as though he had written his name ten thousand times.

Roland wanted to leave the conference room as soon as possible, "Mr. Reilly, allow me to escort you to the vault so that we may complete your transaction."

Reilly felt he was moments away from success, "Certainly. Thank you for your service, Ms. Richards. That was the first time I have had my blarney checked."

She nodded stifling a smirk.

Flood and Dennehy had not noticed that Roland and Reilly had left the conference room. Sheridan moved to the window.

"Central Bank!"

"Scab for me!"

"Shite on me!"

"Central Bank!"

"Do it Right!"

"Or, You're in for a Fight!"

Sheridan had salt for the wound, "I have seen them picket for weeks sometimes months at a time. They have no shortage of members to walk. The problem is when they ask the union labor at the employer to respect the line. President Higgins came from Labour. He was known to join a picket line in his younger days."

Flood was feeling queasy. Dennehy was seeing red; the rage was beginning to boil in his veins. Although the personnel records were confidential, Sheridan knew that it was rage that had washed him out of J2.

Dennehy needed direction, "You are not helping, Bernard. Cella, what do you want to do?"

"Stop calling me Cella. Get down there and do something about that."

"What about Reilly and the six million euro?"

"I don't know. You fecked that up as well. What a shite show. See if you can get something under control."

Flood turned to Sheridan.

"Bernard, I don't suppose you want to help me?"

"That is correct. I do not want to help you, Cella."

She swallowed her pride and appealed to his honor, "The Bank needs you."

Sheridan enjoyed the upper hand, "The Bank will prosper with or without you or me. The only question is which one of us will last longer and whether or not either of us survive without disgrace. I'm sure my wife the gambler would put my money on me."

"I don't even know who to call."

"That sounds like a problem. I'd suggest the phone book, but they don't make those anymore."

Flood growled as she fumed away.

Gertrude straightened the conference room to ready status. She approached her boss.

"Bernard, I have never witnessed anything like that. Are you alright?"

"They were asking for it. It's been quite the day. Can't wait to see what the rest of the week brings. Trudy, why don't you take the afternoon off? Let Flood and the eejit dial their own phones."

"Yes, Sir."

Sheridan and Richards were left.

He turned to her, "Do you need any help packing up your equipment?"

"No. I've got it. Thank you."

"By the way, I never thanked you properly."

"For what?"

"I nearly left my shillelagh in San Francisco."

Fiona winked, "Whatever do you mean?"

Chapter 28

Applied Chaos

Excepting the two security guards at the vault, the entire Central Bank security force had assembled in the main lobby. They were huddled around their sergeant and Dennehy. The picketers continued to march on the sidewalk; their chants reverberated between the arched ceiling and marble floor. O'Connor was in the vault preparing the euros. Reilly, whose bladder still needed frequent emptying, stepped out of the elevator as Sheridan entered from the stairwell. Sheridan waved Reilly down. Dennehy was animated as he barked commands at the security guards.

Sheridan leaned into Reilly, "He's an eejit. He has no idea what he is doing?"

"They won't follow him?"

"Not a chance. First, they report to me and are sticklers for chain of authority. Second, they are private guards, not governmental garda. Third, they have no authority outside the building. And fourth, they are union. They are members of CONNECT."

Reilly needed to make sure the maelstrom he created was not about to backfire on Hibernia, "What happens if they walk off the job?"

"It's never happened. If it did though, the Bank would have to close. We cannot have the vault open with no security on the premises."

Reilly's sense of urgency was heightened, "The shite is about to hit the fan. And, he's turning it too high rather than off. I think I better get to Roland in the vault."

"The elevator to the basement vault is through the

door behind us. I am going to observe the chaos a bit longer. Roland should have your shipment just about ready. I will stop by and make sure you are alright."

Dennehy adjusted the battery pack around his waist. It powered a megaphone twice as loud as that of the picket captains. He used it for his rally-busting orders.

"Men! Follow me. Let's go bust some heads!"

Dennehy turned from the security guards and ran towards the front door. He burst through the door, alone, and shouted into the microphone. Kelley directed his camera operator to roll tape.

"Cease and desist! I order you to disburse or face the full penalties of the law! ...Men, start taking them into custody."

The security sergeant and his officers had not moved an inch.

"Men, men! Get out here now! I will not tolerate this insubordination."

Brian Nolan approached Dennehy.

"Put that thing down. This isn't an illegal action. We are on public property, nor are we threatening anyone. I suggest you rethink your position."

"I am Louis Dennehy, Chief Enforcement & Anti-Money Laundering Officer. And I say break this up now!"

"Well, I am Brian Nolan, Assistant General Secretary of CONNECT, and you are about to lose your security staff."

Nolan stuck each index finger in his mouth. The shrill of his finger-whistle pierced the air. He held a hand high and circled a finger in the air. The security staff walked.

Dennehy pleaded into the megaphone, "Stop! Stop! You cannot leave your posts."

Nolan snickered, "You've never read the contract have you?"

*　　*　　*　　*　　*　　*　　*　　*

Roland and Reilly were at a workstation about 15 meters into the vault. The Central Bank vault unlike commercial banks had no safe deposit boxes. It was an incredibly secure warehouse of gold bullion and pallets of shrink-wrapped euros. A small reach lift had been assembled within the vault to pick orders. A handful of Bank employees had been certified to operate the lift.

Reilly had to know, "Do your people operate the lift in their suits & ties or do they put on coveralls?"

"We have coveralls, but most just undo a button and tuck their tie inside their shirt. Dan, I have arranged to complete the exchange with €500 notes for convenience. You indicated that you would like the €6.25 million packed in the same vault you used to carry your banknotes. I understand you are using Synergy Security for transport. We are using the same firm to take your banknotes for incineration. Of course those will be in a pine box."

"Could you put €500,000 of that in my briefcase? Before that fiasco upstairs I had been thinking about buying some property here."

The Synergy security guards were waiting with flat carts to take the two shipments. The portly one spoke.

"I have a wagon. I'm showing two shipments. One from Central Bank for incineration, the other from a Mr. Dan Reilly for Dublin Airport."

The 2020 BMW 5-series wagon rented from Sixt that morning was parked at the loading dock behind the

Central Bank. There were no signs of picketers at the back entrance. The plate holders identifying the car as a rental had been removed.

The other guard, younger and thinner, had receipts for Roland O'Connor and Dan Reilly.

Roland asked who would be signing for possession of the banknotes.

The portly guard replied, "I will. I am lead agent on transport, Oliver McGee. Stanley Sullivan here is my driver."

"Dan, it has been quite the day. I'm glad I was able to help you."

"Thank you, Rollie. May I have a word with the Synergy guards."

Reilly huddled with the security guards. The carts were between them and Roland.

Softly, Dan acknowledged his cohorts, "Great job boys. Ollie, are you set?"

"Yes. The facility is about an hour into the country. The town's name is Trim. Then we'll head back to the hotel."

"Stan, remember to keep left. And, no speeding!"

Sheridan passed the security guards and their flat carts as he went to check on Reilly and Roland.

"Did those Synergy men have both shipments?"

Roland confirmed, "Yes."

"Good thing. The eejit mucked it up so bad the security force has walked off. We will have to close the vault soon and close the Bank for the day. It will take some magic to be able to open on Monday."

Roland could not believe what he was hearing, "Close the Bank? That's never happened before."

Dennehy's failure with the pickets and security force

had him at wit's end. He could not face Flood. Not being able to return to the executive floor he retreated to the basement. He knew it was moments before the two vault guards would be called off the job.

"Men, I'm Louis Dennehy, Chief Enforcement Officer. I understand you are under orders to leave the facility. Are Misters O'Connor and Reilly still in the vault?"

The guard at the desk responded, "Yes. And Director Sheridan is with them also."

"I see. With Director Sheridan and myself on hand, I am officially relieving you of your duties. You may join your brothers upstairs."

The security guards vacated the floor. Dennehy moved to the west wall so that he could not be observed from inside the vault; the position also allowed his approach to the open door. He wanted to trap Sheridan and Reilly. He did not know what he would do with them, but he needed to give Flood some leverage. Dennehy was not authorized to open or close the vault. He positioned himself low for leverage; he wanted to move quickly. With all his weight he leaned into the door. He slipped though as the door's hinges were balanced to minimize resistance.

As it swung shut Dennehy yelled, "You won't make a fool out of me anymore!"

He spun the five-armed handle clockwise to engage the time lock. The lights went out like a refrigerator.

Chapter 29

Break Out!

The vault was completely dark and silent. There was no emergency lighting, no blue light emanating from cell phone screens, no green, red, or amber LED light from electronic devices. Even the chanting of the picketers could not be heard through the thick walls. They were in a three-person sensory deprivation tank with billions of gold bullion and millions of euros.

Panic struck Roland, "What happened? Did he lock us in here? It's Friday. The vault won't open until Monday. We'll die!"

Reilly asked, "Sherry, have you been locked in here before?"

"No. This is a first."

"HELP! HELP! HELP!" Roland screamed.

Sheridan focused Roland, "O'Connor, listen. Do you hear the picketers?"

"No."

"Well then, stop screaming. If we can't hear that racket out there, no one can hear you scream in here. You will just lose your voice."

"Yes, Sir."

"Think of your training. What is the first thing you are supposed to do?"

"Turn on the lights. The switch is to the left of the door. It's too dark. I can't see."

Roland's breathing was deep and rapid. He was hyperventilating.

Reilly offered, "I'll get the lights. Sherry, see if you can talk Rollie off the ledge."

Reilly extended his elbows as he had done at the print shop using them as antennae to keep from stumbling. His hands were forward reaching for the wall. It took thirty seconds to navigate the fifteen meters. He landed at the hinges on the right side of the vault door.

"I'm at the wall. I feel hinges."

Sheridan informed, "The switch should be at chest level about 30 centimeters in from the other side of the vault door."

Reilly groped like a teenager at the drive-in searching for a bra strap. Click! They had light, but Roland's symptoms persisted. He was on the verge of a panic attack.

Reilly reasoned with him, "Rollie, what is the vault supposed to do?"

Rollie answered, "Keep criminals from breaking in."

"Exactly. We are already in. It's not designed to keep us from breaking out."

*   *   *   *   *   *   *   *

"You did what!?!" Flood was flabbergasted.

Dennehy reported as though he was still with J2, "I locked Director Sheridan, the Currency Manager O'Connor, and Mr. Dan Reilly in the vault. I engaged the time lock. The vault cannot be opened until Monday morning."

"Why? Do you have a plan?"

"No. But I'm building a story. Security walks out. The vault has to be shut. The Bank closes and the picketers go away."

Flood leaned back, closed her eyes, and exhaled.

"I see. Trapping Sheridan and Reilly puts them on

pause for the moment. Isn't there a phone in the vault?"

"I disabled the line from the guard's desk outside the vault. They can't call for help."

Flood took the handset of her phone like a microphone and dialed *44 to access the Public Address system.

"This is Deputy Governor Flood. The Central Bank is closed for the remainder of the day. Please leave the building within the next 20 minutes. Please check the Employee Portal or call the Employee Information Line to see if the Bank will be open Monday. Once again, this is Deputy Governor Flood and the Central Bank is closed."

From the window, Flood observed the employees and picketers flee the scene like fans trying to beat the traffic at Croker after a loss.

"Louis, I may be able to make this work, but I need to know if you are all in. I mean, will you do whatever I ask without question?"

"Cella, I don't mind getting my hands dirty."

"Meet me at the Celt in 2 hours."

"Yes, Sir."

*　*　*　*　*　*　*　*

Sheridan was disgusted that he had allowed himself to be locked in the vault. Reilly's thoughts were with Stan, Ollie, and the money. He was concerned about letting his guard down in front of Rollie. Sheridan was practically an accomplice, but Roland was an innocent. There was no telling how he would react to the truth.

Sheridan spoke directly to Reilly.

"That bint. I can't believe the damage the Bank has taken these past few months. Agreements discarded,

273

unscheduled closure, trapped in the vault. …We have a procedure though should someone be locked in the vault."

Reilly was not surprised, "Did you write that procedure too?"

"I did. It was just before Ireland joined the EU. ISO Certification required standardizing and documenting just about every procedure you could imagine."

"Taking a shite?"

"No. But I could see it now. Twelve squares allowed: 2x6, 3x4, 4x3, or 1x12."

"What's next?"

"Turn on the ventilation system so we have air to breathe. …O'Connor, initiate the ventilation system."

With a task at hand Roland could focus for a moment. The ventilator face plate was 15cm long by 30cm high. He unscrewed the locking pin lever and flipped the on/off switch. The small fan moved less air than a blower on the overhead in the last row of a Jet Blue flight. Below the fan was a cylinder 6cm in diameter which could be pushed through the wall. Roland pulled the cotter pin and used the lever to push it out. Unfortunately, there was no one on the other side with whom to speak, The opening would only allow for a screwdriver or small wrench to be passed. As for food, it seemed only a foot-long hot dog could be delivered.

Reilly's confidence in Sheridan's ability to release them from the vault was rising.

"What's next, Bernie?"

"We open the glass panel door on our side so that I can advance the time lock mechanism. Once it reaches Monday morning, I can unlock the vault and we can open the door."

"That's encouraging. You know we have a case for False Imprisonment against Dennehy."

"He's just the symptom. Flood is the cancer. …O'Connor, the key please."

Roland turned white as a ghost. He patted his pants pockets. His voice broke as he reported.

"My keys are upstairs in my desk. I couldn't imagine getting locked in during the middle of the day while Security is on hand."

Reilly queried, "Don't you have an access key hanging in here?"

Sheridan explained, "If we just left the key hanging in here, we wouldn't need a lock on it. The idea is that the person uses the house phone to alert security that they are trapped. The key would be pushed through the access portal with instructions."

"Let's get on the horn then."

"We can try, but I'm afraid everyone has left the building."

Sheridan picked up the receiver. There was no dial tone. He pressed the hook switch a half dozen times like a private eye from a black & white film.

"The line is dead."

Roland's hysteria returned, "My God, we're dead."

He cupped his hands to the cylinder opening and wailed for help.

Reilly commented to Sheridan, "He's not very calm under pressure."

Sheridan concurred, "A banker's forte is procedure and accuracy. I won't hold this against him come review time."

"You sound confident that there will be a review time."

"One thing I've learned these past few months is to not underestimate you or myself. I believe we will make it out of here no worse for the wear."

Reilly queried, "If I can get you inside the glass panel, you can get the vault open. Right?"

"Indeed."

"I think I can do that, but we need to do something about Roland first."

Sheridan wanted no harm to come Roland's way.

"I'd rather not hurt or drug him."

"I took a Master Class in hypnosis. I've used self-hypnosis to help with concentration. If I can put him under, I can try to crack the lock on the glass panel without exposing my secret identity."

"You sound like a damn superhero."

"What's the premier men's store in Dublin?"

"Louis Copeland and Sons. Custom suits and footwear. They cater to the top 1%."

Reilly called Roland away from the pass-through cylinder and had him sit in the faux leather executive chair.

"Roland, we need you to calm down so that we can use all our resources to get out of here. Would you mind if I guide you through an exercise that might help?"

"No. Go ahead."

Sheridan positioned himself behind Roland so that he could observe without interfering. Roland loosened his tie and undid the top button of his shirt. Reilly cleared the desktop in front of Roland and began.

"I am going to give you a task to perform. I want you to follow my directions very carefully. You will need to use your imagination for this task."

Reilly took Sheridan's shillelagh, he waggled the

handle back and forth. Slowing the pace with each wag.

"Focus on the knob. As the knob slows so does your breathing. Your eyes are feeling heavy. ...Watch the knob. You can barely keep your eyes open. ...Your mind is clear.

Close your eyes.

You have just been hired at Louis Copeland and Sons. Mr. Copeland has made you the Senior Shoe Shine Specialist. It is your job to final polish the shoes before delivery. There are 30 pairs of shoes: 10 black, 10 brown, 10 cordovan. On the desk are large tins of shoe polish, cloths for the polish, and brushes for buffing.

If you see the shoes, without opening your eyes nod your head."

Roland's head slowly, deliberately nodded up and down.

"When I ask you to begin you will take a pair of the black shoes and position them in front of you, toes pointing towards you. You will begin with the right shoe. You will cover the entire shoe with a coat of black polish. You begin buffing at the heel and work up the outside of the shoe then down the inside of the shoe returning to the heel. You repeat the buffing process three times for a high polish before shining the left shoe.

Once you have completed a black pair of shoes, you will shine a brown pair of shoes followed by a cordovan pair of shoes. After three pairs of shoes are polished, you begin with another black pair of shoes. You will continue to polish shoes until all 30 pairs of shoes are polished or I snap my fingers to end the task.

While you are shining the shoes you will be oblivious to anything I say or anything that is going on about you. Your subconscious mind will react to any instruction I give.

If you understand these instructions, again please nod your head without opening your eyes. "

Roland's head slowly, deliberately nodded up and down.

"You may begin shining Mr. Copeland's shoes paying careful attention to the instructions you have been given. "

Roland's eyes remained closed as his hands began to shine phantom shoes. He was deliberate in following the instructions he had been given. Reilly observed as he completed his first pair of shoes. Reilly shook his head in astonishment as Roland switched from the imaginary black tin of polish to the imaginary brown tin. Reilly motioned Sheridan to the vault door.

"That is phenomenal. I'm going to have to start taking those Master Classes. How do you plan to get beyond the glass door?"

"I'm going to pick the lock. I will need your Swiss Army Knife."

Sheridan handed it to him. Reilly opened up the nail file. It was appropriate for tensioning the lock. Reilly still needed a probe to set the tumbler pins.

"I'm going to need a stiff wire-like piece of metal, like a dental probe, to set the tumbler pins. See what you can find."

Sheridan searched about the vault. For all the gold and euros on hand, there were no tools. There wasn't even a ballpoint pen to take apart. He did, however, find the Vault Operating Procedures an 80-page manual bound with a 41mm green binder clip.

"It doesn't look good, Dan. I couldn't find anything probe-like. I found the Procedures Manual. I'm going to review it to see if I have overlooked anything."

The words were in and out of Reilly's ears. His eyes were on the manual.

"Is that a binder clip?"

"Yes. Can you use it?"

"Maybe."

Reilly took the spring wire handles off the binder clip. He straightened the big bends with his hands. He got on his hands and knees among the pallets of gold to pound out the small bends between two gold bars on the floor. The wires were not perfectly straight, but he likely could use the remaining imperfections to his advantage in setting the pins. He bumped his forehead against the stack of gold bars as he rose. He winced but refused to rub it like a ballplayer not wanting to show weakness.

"Are you alright, Dan?"

"It happens all the time. Damn peripheral vision. Luckily picking a lock requires touch and listening rather than vision."

Reilly tensioned the lock with the file and reached for the first pin with his improvised probe. The lock was better machined than the previous locks he had been picking. The tighter tolerances required a defter touch and greater concentration to hear the pins pop. Perspiration formed on Reilly's forehead as his hands started to seize with arthritis. At five minutes the last tumbler pin fell into place. The glass panel drawer swung open.

Sheridan stepped up to advance the time lock. Reilly held up his hand to interrupt and spoke softly.

"The panel door won't lock without a key. Let's bring Roland back out and have him find the door unlocked. Then the two of you will get us out. You can send Roland home with orders to not discuss the incident with anyone.

Then you and I can discuss what to do about Flood and Dennehy."

"They're my problem."

"I think I could help you with them."

Reilly shut the panel door and positioned himself across the desk from Roland. Sheridan moved behind Roland who was still polishing imaginary shoes. Reilly placed his middle finger on his thumb. He pressed down hard and slid his thumb toward his index finger.

SNAP

"You may stop polishing the shoes. At the count of three, you will open your eyes and you will not remember anything that was said or done during this session. You will be relaxed and have a sense of control.

One....Two....Three."

Roland's eyes opened. His heart rate was normal and his respiration was calm. He was unaware of the past fifteen minutes.

"I'm ready. Let's get started."

Sheridan took the point, "Reilly already took you on a little meditation. I know you are concerned about the key, but did you try the glass panel door?"

"Why, no. I didn't."

Roland went to the door and the panel door swung open. A huge grin came across his face.

"I don't believe it. The panel door was unlocked. We can get out. What a relief."

Sheridan came forward. He supervised Roland in advancing the time lock to 09:00 Monday morning. The spinning of gears could be heard as the time lock was released. Roland entered the combination on the internal dial and as he was inside the vault spun the handle clockwise to free the bolt.

They were out.

Sheridan directed, "Roland, we have been through quite the trauma today. I intend to hold Flood and Dennehy responsible for the mayhem they have caused. To that end, I ask that you not discuss this incident with anyone until further notice.

"Yes, Sir."

"Furthermore, I'd like you to take Monday off, paid of course. Hopefully, I will have things settled before Tuesday, but you can check with me Monday afternoon."

"Yes, Sir."

That left Dan Reilly, Bernard Sheridan and an open vault.

Chapter 30

Confessions

Stanley drew no undue attention from authorities behind the wheel. He kept left and observed his kilometers per hour. They had listened to Pat Kelley's news reports on the radio; they knew the Bank had shut early. Stan and Ollie stopped once along the way to change from their Synergy uniforms to street clothes.

They were met by a meticulously styled man who spoke softly, and empathetically.

"Mr. McGee, Mr. Sullivan, I'm sorry for your loss. We here at Pawprints Cremation take the greatest care with your loved one. If there's anything I can do for you do not hesitate to ask."

Oliver spoke, "Our beloved Hibernia is in the pine box in the boot of our vehicle. Do you have someone who can retrieve him?"

"Of course. The ceremony is scheduled in twenty minutes. Would you like to be alone with him in the chambers?"

"That would be fine."

It was the longest twenty minutes of Stan and Ollie's lives. They acted respectfully. Five minutes before the appointed time, the oven began to rumble as the gas was raised the temperature exceeded 1000° Celsius.

The box rode the belt to the oven. As the door closed, the fire roared. A tear rolled down Ollie's cheek; his finest work was up in flames.

* * * * * * * *

Even though Flood was the Chief Operating Officer and Dennehy head of enforcement neither had ever been the last employee out of the building. They had neglected to set the alarm on the front door or turn on the motion detector sensors.

Sheridan informed Reilly, "Those fools didn't even turn on the alarms. We can move about freely."

Reilly assessed their circumstances, "They don't know we are out. We can use that to our advantage. We have options."

"Such as?"

"Go to the authorities and expose them now. Wait until Monday and expose them when the vault opens. Leak their deeds to the Press. Or, gather the evidence and blackmail them. We could leave the vault wide open or stage it so that they think we are still trapped. We definitely want to take control of the security video tapes before they have a chance to scrub them."

Sheridan nodded in concurrence, "I see your point. We are in the catbird seat. Don't tell me you are an expert in security systems also."

It was time for Sheridan to receive full disclosure on Hibernia's players. Reilly began with a disclaimer.

"I'm not, but I know someone who is. Bernard, I have not been working alone all this time. We need their help now. You have to promise me though that should any of this blow back on us my people will never be mentioned. I only wish that I be at risk."

"Am I included in your people?"

"You are as far as I am concerned. Do you have the Hibernia phone?"

"Hibernia phone?"

"Oh, you don't know. That's what we call the phone I

slipped you at Flanahan's."

Sheridan retrieved it from his office and returned to the ground floor. Reilly called from the riverfront outside of the Bank's cell phone blockers. Stan and Ollie were driving back from the pet crematorium; they had Reilly on speakerphone.

"That's right. We were locked in the vault, but we got out."

"How?" asked Stan.

"I'll tell you about it later. I need you guys to get back to the Dylan and download the security footage of Dennehy locking us in the vault before they can destroy it."

Stanley continued, *"What do you want us to do with it? Burn it to a thumb drive, blast it on Twitter, or send it to that reporter, Kelley?"*

"We're not sure yet. Sheridan and I will meet you at your room in 90 minutes."

Ollie piped in, *"Sheridan!?!"*

"Yes. Nothing like being locked in a safe to drop all pretenses. Get word to Fiona at The Mayson. She should be checking out soon. We may need all hands on deck."

Ollie confirmed, *"On it, Sean. I mean Dan."*

Sheridan and Reilly returned to the Bank to reset the scene and discuss strategy. The Bank did not employ overnight cleaners so no one was scheduled to return to the building until Monday.

Sheridan wondered, "Would you come back to the scene of the crime?"

Reilly postulated, "I'd have to. There is no way I would let you stew in there for three days then release you with no control over the message. Do they even have a key to the front door?"

Nonchalantly Sheridan replied, "Would not having a key stop you?"

"Good point."

Sheridan took the key to the internal glass door from the guard's desk and locked it. They left the phone disconnected.

"Bernie, if we replace the cylinder and pin, we can control the communication when they return. Can a phone call be initiated from the guard's desk into the vault?"

"I don't know. Let's try."

Sheridan released the vault line from the phone at the guard's desk. He then selected the guard's line and dialed the extension for the vault. The ring of a phone could be heard from the vault.

Reilly noted, "That answers that question. There must be security cameras inside the vault?"

"There are."

"We can deal with that. My systems guy can control the security monitoring console should they try and get eyes inside. Also, he could transfer the vault line anywhere we want."

Sheridan rebounded the manual with a binder clip from the guard's desk. They left the vault as they had found it. He closed the vault door and spun the handle to initiate the time lock. Now, it would remain shut until Monday morning. As difficult as it was for Sheridan, they did not set the alarm for the building or lock the deadbolt.

Sheridan asked Reilly, "How did you get here?"

"The Revenue driver brought me. I released her though. I think she was reporting my movements to Dennehy."

"I've been walking since I got back. My car is on the

roof under a ton of bird shite. The Dylan is about a half-hour walk."

"Probably best that we leave your car and avoid any type of paid carriage. I walk Ocean Beach daily. I can hoof it."

*   *   *   *   *   *   *   *

Lily brought soda bread, butter, and menus to the booth occupied by Flood and Dennehy.

"Welcome to The Celt. I'm Lily. I'll be your server…"

Flood interrupted Lily's introduction, "We won't be eating today. Bring me a double Jameson neat. He'll have a pint of gat. No tab, we won't be here long. Bring it directly, don't dilly about taking a slew of orders."

"Yes, ma'am."

Lily went directly to the bar. Under her breath almost inaudibly she uttered, "What a bint."

Flood's eye twitched as she downed her double like a shot. Dennehy sipped at his Guinness. She had no problem crushing careers or disregarding fiscal law for her personal gain, but imprisonment, extortion, and potentially murder were descending her to another level of malfeasance.

"Is the €6.25 million still in the vault?"

Dennehy replied, "I don't know. I was at the front door trying to rally Security to quell the pickets. When they walked off the job, I went to the vault and realized I could trap Sheridan and Reilly. It was the only thing that went right today."

"What about the pissant manager?"

"O'Connor? Collateral damage. Acceptable consequence."

Flood shivered as she succumbed to a chill. Dennehy leaned in as she spoke softly, deliberately. "I want the euros."

"What about the Bank?"

"Screw the Bank. It's too old and set in its ways. I can't operate here. I want to extract a payout and move on."

"What about me?"

"You'll get your cut."

"When?"

"Clearly not until the mess is cleaned up and I get mine. Now meet me across from the Bank on the riverfront at 10pm tonight. The North Wall should be deserted by then. Pay the bill and get out of here. I don't want you soused tonight."

*　　*　　*　　*　　*　　*　　*　　*

Although he was Irish American, Reilly's family conventions were similar to Sheridan's. Conversations often centered around trivialities like sports and weather. Serious matters were rarely discussed with the notion that ignoring them would let them go away.

"This weather reminds me of San Francisco. It's comfortable for walking. It must be about 55°."

"13°. We use Celsius."

"That sounds colder."

They crossed the River Liffey at the Samuel Beckett Bridge and headed south. Macken Street was experiencing gentrification similar to that around Muphy Printing on Bryant Street in San Francisco.

"Sherry, is that whole block a WhatsApp campus?"

"It is. What do you know about WhatsApp?"

"My systems guy introduced it to me."

Sherry laughed, "Ginny had to introduce it to me too."

Reilly's tone turned a bit sheepish, "I have to apologize to you."

Sheridan absolved, "You didn't lock me in the safe. And your trick with the protestors was effective. You could not control their idiotic response."

"No. I was talking about the football final tomorrow. I don't see how you can go if you are supposed to be locked in the vault."

"You're right. You owe me one. There's always next year."

They were walking alongside the Grand Canal which connected Dublin with the River Shannon in the West.

"You know, Sean, you have an amazing skillset."

"I've been trying to use Dan exclusively here in Dublin. Thank you. I really see myself as an observer, a researcher, and a problem solver."

"Were you looking for a bank to rob?"

"No. I was disgruntled with my lot in life."

Sherry empathized, "I know that feeling. Why did you choose the Central Bank?"

Dan smiled wryly, "You are not going to believe me."

Sheridan gestured to get on with it.

Dan continued, "I had picked up a copy of the Irish Times one morning. I had brought it to lunch at Flanahan's. Hurling matches were streaming on the big screen. There was an article below the fold that caught my eye."

Sherry interrupted, "'Ireland 20 Years of EU a Review' complete with a quotation from Bernard Sheridan, Director of Currency."

"Exactly. As that money had been sitting there so long

it didn't feel so larcenous. I looked at it as an intellectual and operational exercise."

"How did you know I would come to San Francisco?"

"I didn't. There was some serendipity there. When you had Stephen reach out to me cause of the Lady Lavery trick the jig could have been up."

Sheridan confided, "The few days in the City were the best I had in quite some time. Stephen and I took it to the louts. And, you were a breath of fresh air – purple bollocks, bad eyes, inextinguishable spirit."

Reilly confessed, "From the moment I read that article one thought has guided me: *300 million 20-year-old Irish pounds worth 375 million euros are out there. How can I get a piece of that action?*"

Sheridan twirled his shillelagh and tapped his forehead, "Amen, Brother."

Chapter 31

Et Tu Brute

Reilly led Sheridan to a side entrance of the Dylan so that they would avoid the crowded lobby. Reilly's heart rate topped 100 beats per minute as he navigated the six flights of stairs to the third floor.

Sheridan commented, "Are you alright, Dan? Those stairs seemed a bit of a challenge."

"My eyes have cost me more than my vision. I can't bicycle, golf, or play soccer; I have no cardio. My balance and depth perception are shite as well."

At his room, Dan manually picked the lock rather than use his key card and have the entry recorded on the computer. It was Sheridan's first time at the Dylan; the opulence was obvious. He was seconds from an accident as his bladder had been on lock down since the vault closed.

"Where's the jack?"

"The guest one is through the door next to the wet bar."

The subway tile floor reminded him of the former Men's Lavatory at the Bank. The fixtures were heavy, chromed. The hot water was instant. His stream was strong, satisfying. It was a bonus that the struggle to fasten his pants was minimal.

Sheridan commented, "This place is five-star."

"I was collecting €6 million. You wouldn't expect me to stay at the Travelodge. I'm going to get out of this suit. Would you like to borrow a change of clothes? You are not a giant like Stephen. My togs should fit."

Sheridan realized he was still buttoned down tight. He

loosened his dark blue tie and rolled his sleeves to three-quarters.

Reilly raised his voice from the bedroom, "Help yourself to a whiskey. The bar is well stocked. I'll take a Kilbeggan on ice if you don't mind."

Sheridan poured two Kilbeggans one on the rocks, one neat.

"What now, Dan?"

"One more lock to pick."

*   *   *   *   *   *   *   *

Reilly had expected some fanfare as they had liberated millions of euros from the Bank and escaped a locked vault. Instead, they were greeted by Stan and Ollie's backs huddled over Fiona at the computer. The three were in deep discussion.

"Ahem!" he called to catch their attention.

Three heads swiveled around. Stanley reached back and used the boss key to hide what Fiona had on the screen. Their expressions were reminiscent of the three wise monkeys – see no evil, hear no evil, speak no evil. Sheridan broke the awkward silence.

"Fiona, always a pleasure to see you. And, you; we met at the baseball game. Your name is …wait, don't tell me. …Sullivan."

Stanley looked to Dan who gave him the go-ahead nod.

"That's right. Stanley Sullivan."

"As I recall you and Ginny hit it off. Did she take you to that hurling match?"

"Not yet. But I have been pretty busy this trip."

"And you, sir. I am Bernard Sheridan, Director of

Currency Central Bank of Ireland. I am also in charge of facilities and security."

Oliver shook Sheridan's hand.

"Oliver McGee, master printer and chief fix-it man. If it is comprised of screws, gears, or wires, I can fix it."

"Well Mr. McGee, that was the finest example of printing I have ever come across."

Ollie acknowledged the team, "Stanley aided in breaking the note down. And, believe it or not, Dan figured out the mystery of the watermark."

Sheridan took a moment to observe the team: a geeky string bean, a portly printer, and an enchanting waitress. He marveled at Sean's vision, planning and execution. Stanley and Oliver; Stan and Ollie. It could not have been a coincidence.

Bernard winked at Dan, "This is another nice mess you've gotten me into."

*   *   *   *   *   *   *   *

Stanley had control of the security and communication systems at the Bank. There was a live feed of the exterior of the vault. He had edited together a 45-second time-lapse clip showing O'Connor then Reilly entering the vault, Sheridan joining them later, and Dennehy dismissing the guard and shutting the vault.

Sheridan slammed his shillelagh on the desk, "That arse! I'd like to be locked in the vault with him for 10 minutes."

Stanley had prepackaged the footage, "I've prepared the video for posting to the internet or broadcasting on the news."

"Look! Look!" cried Ollie as he pointed at the live

monitor.

Flood and Dennehy were in the building at the security monitoring station near the vault. Dennehy carried a sledgehammer he had "borrowed" from the construction zone. Flood pointed at the vault wall and Dennehy began striking it with all the force he could muster.

"What's he doing?" asked Fiona.

Sheridan replied, "He's disabling the emergency ventilation system. Basically, signing death warrants for anyone trapped in the vault. He's off my Christmas card list."

Dennehy succeeded in disabling the small ventilation fan and hammered shut the vent openings to cut off the natural exchange of air. He took his sledge game to the computer tower at the security station.

"What a dumb-ass." added Stanley, "He's not disabling any cameras. He's just ruining that station. I'm still capturing everything."

Buzz. Buzz.

Stanley exclaimed, "It's the vault phone!"

Sheridan put on the headset. He held a finger to his mouth indicating for the others to be quiet.

"What were you thinking? Locking us in here eight hours ago was a bonehead play."

Flood drawing on her background, "There's a theory in the insurance world. If a trucker runs over a pedestrian, it's better to kill than to maim. There's not enough air in there for three people to survive the weekend."

Sheridan remained composed, "You've already committed false imprisonment. Tampering with the fan is attempted murder. How would you explain three bodies come Monday morning?"

"We've destroyed the security footage. I'll blame the pickets and your security guards. I may call Kelley and RTÉ 2 in for the vault opening Monday."

"What about Reilly and O'Connor?"

"I think Reilly is as phony as a three-pound note. O'Connor is just collateral damage."

Sheridan wondered, "Why are you even talking to me?"

Flood spoke low, deliberately, "I want the money. Reilly gives up the money, I save your lives."

"You're insane. What makes you think I can make him agree to that anyway?"

Flood demanded, "Put him on the line."

Sheridan passed the headset to Reilly.

"This is Dan Reilly. When I get out of here I'm going straight to the American Embassy and file a formal complaint."

Flood's tone turned devious, "You mean 'if' rather than 'when'. There's not enough air in there for the three of you to survive the weekend. I can help you for a price."

"Not interested. My family's legacy is not going for ransom. I've lived a full life and the money will go where I want. No deal."

Reilly turned to Stanley and made the cutthroat sign to end the call.

Flood was stunned. Reilly had hung up on her. She dialed the vault again. Reilly handed the headset to Sheridan but held up his hands to Stanley indicating he should let the phone ring. At eight rings Sheridan answered.

"Yes?"

"No one hangs up on Marcella Flood." She liked using

the third person. "Who does he think he is?"

"Sean Reilly. Irish American caught in your crossfire."

The team members gasped. They held their tongues but gesticulated at Sheridan. He nodded realizing his gaffe. Flood was not sure what she heard.

"What did you say?"

"I said. He thinks he's just a man who from the moment he set foot in the Bank has been treated with disdain and suspicion. I don't blame him for not wanting to deal with you."

The team members nodded in concurrence as if Sheridan had just saved a penalty shot.

"Let's see how he feels after a night of heavy breathing in there. You have 12 hours to change his mind. If he doesn't, I suggest you find some writing material to complete your wills and testaments."

Chapter 32

Double Double Agent

As Fiona had checked out of The Mayson, Francess spent the night with Sean in suite 312. She rooted through his closet and found his periwinkle button-down shirt; he had packed it for just such an occasion. For the first time in months, he let his guard down and enjoyed the moment. She looked stunning with her long legs making the shirttails dance. She only had two buttons done around her waist.

She led him to the shower where she began to wash his back like she did in San Francisco. No one before Francess had ever washed him like that before. She was thorough. It was relaxing, invigorating, and erotic all at the same time. He returned the favor although she was so much better in the shower. Sean, however, would sate her after the shower. He considered it his responsibility and pleasure.

"Sean, this whole adventure has been fantastic. What are you going to do with all the money?"

"First, Kenny and Patty will get their shares. Over and above that, I want to help Kenny purchase Murphy Printing, and I will get a lawyer to clear up Patty's probation."

"You're loyal."

Sean continued, "Bernie has been good to us. I want to make sure the Bank does right by him."

"What about you?"

Sean rolled over and looked Francess in the eyes, "Well, I've been thinking more about us than me. I'd like to build a villa in Grenada on a hill with a view of the ocean. It would have a wonderful veranda where we would watch the sunset."

"Oh, Sean." She whispered, low. Slowly.

*   *   *   *   *   *   *   *

Flood was startled. She had been in the flat almost nine months and the doorbell had never been rung. Could it be the Garda? She suddenly realized the flat had no other egress. The bell rang again. She could not ignore it. She approached the peephole. All she saw was a deep brown eye. She stepped back and then took a second look. Why was she only getting a deep brown eye? She couldn't perform a retina scan.

Flood eased the door open. It was the woman who had performed the polygraph examination. Flood was confused.

"What are you doing here? How do you know where I live?"

Fiona had slipped out of the hotel before Sean awoke. She had exited though through room 310 where Stanley and Ollie were up and monitoring the Bank's security cameras. Lansdowne Place was a 10-minute walk east towards Dublin Bay from the Dylan. The luxury apartments and penthouses were million-euro listings.

Fiona spoke confidently, "Marcella, you don't mind if I call you Marcella, you can call me Fiona. I'm here today because I find the men in power are shortsighted and egotistical. I have goals and vision. I think you do also."

"What are you talking about?"

"Reilly wasn't very ambitious. He left a lot of food on the bone."

297

"Why are you telling me this?"

"You're ambitious. Any woman who is put in charge of a Central Bank coming from outside the industry is a driver."

Flood had motioned Fiona into the apartment. The kitchen appliances looked as though they had never been used. There was a slew of takeout and delivery containers overflowing the trash bin. Flood offered her a zero-calorie Fanta, the twelve-pack was the only thing in the fridge.

Flood was nibbling at the bait, "Are you saying that the banknotes exchanged were phony?"

"That's exactly what I am saying. Phony but flawless."

"I knew it!" Flood felt vindicated and nauseous simultaneously. The fact that she had Sheridan, Reilly, and the other guy locked in the vault compromised any advantage she could have gained.

"But why have you come to me now?"

"You are in power now, but that shite show yesterday does not bode well for you. I need someone on the inside to push through an exchange."

"How much?"

"I contracted the fat man and the skinny man to produce another IR£16 million."

Flood wasn't familiar with Ollie and Stan, "The fat man and the skinny man?"

"His technical accomplices. ...That's €20 million."

"And Reilly doesn't know about this?"

"He was so caught up in his scheme he couldn't see the forest for the trees."

"What's to keep me from reporting you all as frauds?"

"You and your staff approved the transaction. You could report us and look like an incompetent. How much is your severance agreement worth – a year's salary if there was no malfeasance? I'd be happy with €10 million. What about you?"

"What about Fat and Skinny?"

"I'll take care of them. You take care of whoever you need."

Flood's mind turned to mechanics, "Where, when, and how can I get the banknotes?"

"The banknotes are already in the country. I can have them delivered to the Bank, or you can send a truck for pickup. Sooner rather than later. Monday or Tuesday at the latest."

"How can I get a hold of you?"

"I've got your number."

Flood's respect for her was growing, "Of course you do. I have some cleanup to do from yesterday. Could we meet late this afternoon?"

Fiona suggested, "Tea, 4 pm at The Merrion."

"Bring a sample."

*　　*　　*　　*　　*　　*　　*　　*

It had been ten hours since Flood and Sheridan had spoken. She called Dennehy.

"Circumstances are changing. We may want them to survive. Get a pry bar, a tank of oxygen, and some hose."

Dennehy was confused. "What's changed?"

"Don't worry about that. Just get the pry bar and oxygen. Pick me up in 90 minutes. Understand?"

"Yes, Sir."

Thank God, Irish Hospital Supplies was open. Oxygen in hand he picked up Flood with time to spare. It was only a 15-minute drive across the River Liffey to get from Lansdowne Place to the Central Bank. Dennehy was too intimidated to ask what had changed.

Flood and Dennehy returned to the vault guard security station and dialed the extension for the vault. It rang twelve times until a recorded message played.

"The user at extension 7515 has not established a voice mailbox. Goodbye." Click.

She dialed the vault again and received the same result. She was confused and concerned.

"They should not have run out of air yet. You're sure they were locked in there."

Dennehy reminded her, "You talked to them yesterday. They were there."

Quietly, Sheridan and Reilly entered the vault room from the staircase rather than the elevator.

Flood surmised, "Maybe they turned on each other."

Sheridan slammed his shillelagh on the table behind Flood and Dennehy. They flinched and then ducked as if they were under fire. Flood peeked over her shoulder and spotted Sheridan and Reilly. Flood was sick to her stomach.

Dennehy uttered, "What the feck?"

"How?" was all Flood could muster.

Sheridan enjoyed watching her squirm, "You see, Marcella. You assume that adversity brings out the worst in people. The fact is it can galvanize strangers united for a goal."

"But the vault was locked, I spoke to you yesterday."

"Cella, Cella, Cella, when will you learn I have forgotten more about the Central Bank than you will ever know."

Reilly snapped his fingers and said, "Check your phone."

The video of Dennehy locking them in the vault and the subsequent sledgehammer incident played.

Reilly continued, "Is that too small for you to see?"

He snapped his fingers twice and the video played on the information monitors posted throughout the Bank.

Flood screamed, "Stop! Stop it!"

Reilly gave the cutoff sign running his fingers across his neck under his chin. The video stopped playing.

Sheridan informed, "For all the damage you did with that sledge hammer you didn't actually disable the cameras. The feed continued and we captured it. Louis, the damage will be coming out of your final paycheck."

"Final paycheck?" parroted Dennehy.

"Shut up, Louis." Flood had lost the upper hand. "What do you want?"

Sheridan handed her a letter and his 25th Anniversary jewel-encrusted Cross pen.

"This is your resignation letter. You acknowledge your errors: authorizing a non-bid construction project, and failure to comply with the union contract. You further endorse me as your replacement citing my knowledge of Bank procedure and union relations as being the only person that can restore order."

"Uh-huh." She was reduced to grunting.

"Further, when you tender this to Makhlouf, you will convince him that I need to be your replacement. For if you do not, the tape goes to the authorities and the media. I will see that you are prosecuted and never work in the EU again. Understood?"

"Understood. Where do I sign?"

"Here and here. There are two originals. One for you to take to Makhlouf. One for me to hold."

"Anything else?"

"Yes. As you have been with the Bank for less than a year, your previous position affords you a three-month severance package. It does not say that you retain all your perks. I will take the keys to Lansdowne Place. I will have your personal belongings boxed and brought to your cubicle by the elevator. You will vacate the COO office. Finally, I will take the keys to the Bank's Mercedes Benz. You may use the Volvo."

He tossed her the keys to the Volvo, "You will find it on the roof under all the bird shite. Please get it washed."

"Yes, Sir." Flood was in shock.

*   *   *   *   *   *   *   *

Fiona arrived directly at 4 pm and went to The Garden Room at The Merrion expecting to meet Flood for tea. The hostess informed her that Flood was waiting for her at The Cellar Bar.

Flood and Dennehy were at a table. Each was nursing a whiskey.

Fiona sat down, "I thought we were meeting for tea."

Flood answered, "It's been a whiskey kind of day."

"I see. What's he doing here?"

The waitress came over and Fiona ordered an Irish Coffee. Flood and Dennehy asked for another round.

"You remember Louis from last Friday. He's my aide. You have the fat man and the skinny man. I have Louis."

"I see. Are you interested in proceeding?"

"Definitely. Can I see the sample?"

Fiona handed an IR£ 100 note to each of them. The Cellar Bar was well-lit for a bar, but not well-lit for inspecting currency. Neither knew how to inspect a banknote. It felt like money. Each turned their cell phone flashlight on the note. It looked like money.

Fiona had no intention of watching Flood and Dennehy get soused. "How do they look?"

Flood looked at Dennehy. His expression was noncommittal.

"We like them."

Fiona pushed, "When and where do you want the notes? Can you handle the entire IR£16 million?

"I want it all. Tuesday 8 am, Croke Park Car Park."

Fiona had her own conditions, "Take the euros in cash as I do not want an audit trail between us. I've recorded our conversations to keep you honest. Double cross me and I will have the Garda on you like stink on a pig."

"You don't trust me?"

"No."

"Fair enough."

"And one last thing." Fiona snapped her fingers. From the other side of the bar, the thin man, Stanley, shone a laser pen beam on Flood's chest. It emulated a rifle site.

"We have eyes on you."

Chapter 33

Fibernia

Flood tendered her resignation directly to the Governor Sunday afternoon. He expressed his annoyance at her for having been called back from The Continent. She made him look bad. He dismissed her and called the Bank's chief solicitor to prepare a contract for Sheridan.

Monday morning Makhlouf summoned Sheridan.

"Bernard, as you may or may not know Flood is out. She had tendered her resignation in the wake of last week's fiasco. My job is in Brussels. Your job is here, Dublin, running the Central Bank. You are Irish. I am not. This is your birthright. Can I trust you to right the ship?"

"Sir, it is my honor to set the Bank straight. We lost our way this past year, but I have the people, the connections, and the knowledge to return the Bank to its rightful place in the community."

"Bernard, I am offering you the post of Deputy Governor and Chief Operating Officer of the Central Bank of Ireland. The position will be 'Acting' until approved by the Commission. I had the Solicitor prepare an agreement with all the benefits of the previous office holder and a 20% increase in salary acknowledging your tenure and the storm you are entering. Is this acceptable?"

"Yes, Sir." Sheridan, in timeless fashion, removed the Cross pen from his starched breast pocket and signed the agreement. "Now if you will excuse me, I have work to do."

"Of course. I am headed back to Brussels. I do not expect to see you again until the Commission meeting next month. Your presence will be required going forward."

*   *   *   *   *   *   *   *

Director's Row was the moniker given to the cluster of cubes which housed five of the Bank's directors. The other three cubicles were not assigned. Gertrude's workstation stood watch over them like an attendant at the insane asylum. Roland, whom Sheridan called on Sunday, was waiting with Gertrude.

Sheridan arrived with pace.

"Greetings. Greetings. Excepting yourself, Gertrude, who is the best Executive Assistant at the Bank?"

"Why, Mary Rahilly of course. She's smart, dedicated, and young. I like her spunk."

He picked up the receiver from Gertrude's phone and upside down he dialed *44. Throughout the company his page was heard.

"Ms. Rahilly to Deputy Governor Flood's office. Ms. Mary Rahilly to Deputy Governor Flood's office."

Gertrude and Roland looked at each other with confusion. Sheridan's energy was dynamic and contagious.

"You two come with me." As Sheridan led them to the river side of the floor he took a roll of black duct tape from a construction cart. He stopped in the quiet Deputy Governor Hallway. It was quiet as most employees were too intimidated to step foot there. He took a 24-inch strip of duct tape and covered the top half of the gold leaf letters. A second strip covered the bottom half; he had covered Marcella Flood. He handed a white paint marking pen to Gertrude.

"Your writing is much more legible than mine. Would

you do the honors?"

Gertrude's eyes opened wide and a tear formed. Her voice trembled, "Bernard?"

He smiled and winked, "I was thinking Bernard Sheridan."

Sheridan sat behind the teak desk, he adjusted the height of the chair. At Sheridan's behest, Roland and Gertrude sat in the uncomfortable chairs. Their heads were spinning with conjecture.

"Saturday afternoon Marcella Flood resigned. This morning I signed an agreement with Governor Makhlouf to become Acting Deputy Governor and Chief Operating Officer."

"Yes! Bernie, yes!" Gertrude could not hide her elation.

"Congratulations, Sir." O'Connor sensed the Bank was returning to normalcy.

"I will need help to put the Bank right. There will be changes. Some things need to be undone. Some things need to move forward. I am dividing up the responsibilities of my former position. Roland, I am offering you the position of Assistant Director Currency Operations effective immediately."

O'Connor was caught off guard. He sat up straight. "Thrilled, Sir."

Mary Rahilly knocked and entered.

"I was asked to report here."

"Ms. Rahilly, I am Director ...check that. I am Deputy Governor Sheridan. We have not met but Ms. O'Shea informs me that you are the best Executive Assistant in the Bank next to her."

"Thank you, Sir."

"Ms. O'Shea's position as Executive Assistant to the

Operations Division Directors needs to be filled and I'd like you to take it. Your pay grade of course will reflect the senior nature of the position."

"Sir, I am shocked. There are a number of Assistants with more tenure."

"Time is good, but we need talent and dedication."

"I am honored. When do I start?"

"Ms. O'Shea will contact you later this morning. Congratulations. Please keep this to yourself until a communique is published."

She nodded and left. Gertrude could not sit still.

"Bernard, am I coming with you?"

"In a manner of speaking, yes. The other position I am creating is Assistant Director of Facilities & Security. Gertrude, this is your opportunity to formally run all the things you have been taking care of from behind the scenes. Your compensation and retirement will more than double."

"But, Bernard I'm not management."

"You are now. I do not have time to train anyone. You know the policies. You know the labor agreements. We won't let you fail. Right, Roland?"

Roland jumped in, "We're Team Sheridan we watch out for each other. You can always come to me if you have trouble navigating the politics."

"Well then, I know my first task as Assistant Director Facilities: Order the painters to change the name on this door."

$$* \quad * \quad * \quad * \quad * \quad * \quad * \quad *$$

Croke Car Park was deserted save a lone black rented cargo van parked far from the road. Dennehy kept checking his phone for the time. Flood was impatient also.

She scolded him, "Stop looking at your phone. It won't make them get here any faster. They are not late anyway."

They sat in silence for six minutes.

"Thank God." Dennehy's pucker on the seat released when a white cargo van sped across the car park. It circled Dennehy and Flood three times then backed within two meters of the rear of the black van. The cargo doors of the white van opened and the fat man and skinny man popped out. Dennehy opened the doors of the black van. The banknotes were transferred in under five minutes.

Fiona wanted to know Flood's plan, "When are you turning the notes in for exchange?"

"I will tender them this afternoon for exchange Wednesday at 11 am. I should be able to meet up with you late Wednesday or early Thursday."

Fiona set the time, "This is good, isolated. Let's do Thursday morning at 8 am, here. €10 million. Remember we have eyes on you."

The white cargo van sped away. Dennehy looked at Flood; he did not know where to go.

"Louis, your share is worth a million euros. You can exchange it any time after Wednesday. If you don't have the bollocks for it, find someone who does. Now take me to your vehicle. You can take IR£ 800,000. Leave the rest and the van with me."

*   *   *   *   *   *   *   *

Marcella was using her indignance like a coat of armor as she had to be escorted into the offices at the Central Bank. She had requested to see Roland O'Connor the Currency Manager. He received her in the River Liffey Conference Room.

"Marcella, I am now the Assistant Director, Currency Operations. You wish to present pre-EU currency for euro exchange."

"Yes. Your security guards are watching it at the loading dock."

"One moment." He picked up the phone.

"Gertrude. This is Roland. …Are your guards monitoring a van at the loading dock? …They are. Good. …Marcella Flood is tendering Irish banknotes for exchange. …That's right. Flood. …Prepare her a receipt of shipment and keep it sequestered in the vault. …The repairs to the vault are complete, aren't they? …Good. …Cheers."

Flood's indignation had turned to disbelief, "Is that bint running Security?"

"That bint is now the Assistant Director, Facilities & Security. Is your application for exchange complete?"

Her indignation returned, "We both know all that information is just administrative bullshite. I'll let the notes speak for themselves."

"We'll need 24 hours to process your tender. I can see you tomorrow at 11 am."

Gertrude's first office and his new office were side by side. He poked his head into her office.

"How's the setup going?"

"Just trying to get the job done. Unruffle security's feathers. Get the bid packs out to restore the floor."

"Could you have a sample of five notes drawn from

the shipment Flood tendered and have them brought to my office for authentication?"

* * * * * * * *

"Testing 1-2-3. Testing 1-2-3." Roland was sitting at the head of the conference table waiting for Flood and Dennehy to be escorted upstairs.

Roland did not bother rising as they took subordinate seats with their backs to the window.

"Well, here we are again." Roland set the tone.

Mary Rahilly rolled in a cart with tea service. She was followed by Sheridan and Gertrude.

Sheridan parodied Flood, "Cella, you don't mind if we observe. Do you?" He and Gertrude sat at the opposite end of the table.

Rahilly served Gertrude, Sheridan, and Roland. Dennehy was about to take a tea until Flood shook her head and he declined.

"Thank you, Mary. We'll call you if we need anything else." Roland had settled into the role as host.

"Can we get on with this?" Flood's indignance was only matched by her impatience.

Roland had a newfound confidence, "Cella, I'm surprised you haven't asked what it was like being locked in the vault. It was an experience I wish on no one. To be locked in a room with no means of escape, to be robbed of one's freedom it does make one reflect and appreciate the opportunities of life."

Sheridan leaned over to Gertrude and whispered, "He's grown a lot. This is priceless."

Roland set the stage,

"For the record, what are you doing here today?"

Flood replied, "I am tendering pre-EU Irish banknotes for euro exchange."

"Are you acting as an agent for another party?"

"No."

"So, the notes tendered are yours and yours alone?"

"Yes."

"You wish to exchange these at 1.25 euros to 1.00 Irish pound?"

"Yes."

Roland winked at Dennehy and Gertrude.

"Cella, I have reviewed your so-called banknotes. The paper feels good. The print quality is excellent."

Flood was impatient, "Yes. Yes. Come on."

"Here is one of your notes. And, here is an authentic note taken from our Archive. Inspect them."

Roland handed her the two notes and a magnifying glass. She began to inspect them. She looked at her note. She looked at the authentic note. The dates were good. The signature was the same. She inspected the back of the notes, each depicting the River Erne.

"They are identical. Please can we conclude this?"

"Yes. We will conclude this momentarily. Deputy Governor, would you be so kind as to inspect the notes."

Flood passed the notes to Sheridan. He rubbed them between his fingers. Popped them to check the paper. He held them up to the light. He looked at Roland and smiled. He took them over to the window; it was a bright day. He put the notes to the window.

Roland asked, "Do you see it?"

Sheridan shook his head, "Plain as day. Erin is looking left rather than right. The watermark is reversed. These are phony."

Flood's indignation was replaced with shock, "But.

But. …Let me see. I don't understand."

Sheridan laughed.

Roland spoke at the phone, "Chief O'Hara, Principle Officer McBride will you join us now."

O'Hara and McBride entered the conference room with two of the Bank's security guards.

Chief O'Hara spoke, "Marcella Flood, you are under arrest for attempting to fraud the Central Bank of Ireland in the amount of €19 million. You are not obliged to say anything unless you wish to do so, but whatever you say will be taken down in writing and may be given in evidence."

Click. Click. The sound of handcuffs was surprisingly loud. Sheridan looked out the window and saw that Pat Kelley was on the sidewalk to report the perp walk live on RTÉ 2.

On the riverfront he spotted a couple watching the Bank rather than the river, it was Fiona and Dan. Or, was it Francess and Sean? It did not matter he offered a tip of his hat.

I must acknowledge Celeste Davidson and Adam Simon, co-founders of Bardsy. How two published, former university professors could mold this sarcastic engineer into a novelist is beyond comprehension.

313

About The Author

David Devine is a second-generation Irish American. Today, the lilt of an Irish brogue touches his heart. A native of San Francisco he was raised across the Golden Gate Bridge in Marin County. He earned a Bachelor of Science Degree in Industrial Engineering & Operations Research from the University of California, Berkeley.

He worked in Ocean Transportation holding roles in Engineering, Marine Terminal Management, and Sales. He also provided Management Consulting services in Silicon Valley. Having not suffered enough anguish from the corporate world he owned and operated a bicycle store.

A prolific technical writer, David began creative writing on a whim with short stories. Having anthology success with *Murray, The Disgruntled Reindeer*, he went on to write a novella and a radio play script. *Hibernia* is his debut novel.

He has two daughters. David currently resides near the mist of Niagara Falls with his Grenadian (he swears she sounds Irish) wife.

He takes inspiration from Julia Child, Lee Trevino, and W.C. Fields. He is an avid chef. Do not ask for his guacamole recipe! There is none; it's guacamole.

Made in the USA
Middletown, DE
05 September 2024